Stella Duffy

Lullaby Beach

virago

VIRAGO

First published in Great Britain in 2021 by Virago Press
This paperback edition published in 2022 by Virago Press

1 3 5 7 9 10 8 6 4 2

A CIP catalogue record for this book
is available from the British Library.

ISBN 978-0-349-01238-4

Typeset in Bembo by M Rules
Printed and bound in Great Britain by
Clays Ltd, Elcograf S.p.A.

Papers used by Virago are from well-managed forests
and other responsible sources.

Virago Press
An imprint of
Little, Brown Book Group
Carmelite House
50 Victoria Embankment
London EC4Y 0DZ

An Hachette UK Company
www.hachette.co.uk

www.virago.co.uk

For all my nieces and nephews
with all my love.

Acknowledgements

My thanks to my agent Stephanie Cabot, who supports all of my dreams – not just the writing ones. Huge thanks to the tag-team of two great editors, Sarah Savitt and Rose Tomaszewska, who, along with Zoë Gullen and Jane Selley, have helped me make a book I am proud to share. To all at Virago, especially Zoë Hood and Emily Moran, my deep gratitude for the sharing.

My love to the Fun Palaces HQ team for always understanding I have many roles, and to my wife Shelley Silas who has to live alongside these many roles.

And to the people who do the constant work of supporting those of us affected by domestic violence, by sexual violence, by curtailed choices for our own bodies, to those who hold a space for justice and for healing, and to those who speak out when so many are unable to do so – thank you.

One

Westmere, May

She has made plans for today, has been working towards this moment for decades. She had not understood this before. She knows it now.

Tomorrow will dawn bright and fine. Late spring mornings are beautiful to her these days. There was a time, many years ago, when she thought she could not face another dawn; she had wrapped herself in silence and the chorus that threatened to unravel the tight-knit quiet felt as if it might break her. There was a light seeping through closed curtains, demanding access from the other side of a locked door, pulling at sticky eyelids – it was a light she agreed to, eventually allowed in. She was stoic and strong and proud of it.

She is stoic and strong in this choice too. Everything is in order; there are a few clues and fewer answers. She gave up explaining herself a long time ago. It won't be easy for them, but she has done what she can.

She will light three candles, and when they are burned out, then.

The candles were used as a sign, a long time ago, needed and valuable. Perhaps they stand for more now, for the layers of secrets, for three generations of recurring stories. She feels this repetition keenly, would end it if she could.

She hopes this might end it.

The tide was very low earlier this evening, the water far out and wanting, so much exposed at the moment of the turn, that brief pause and then gone again. A ritual drowning of secrets twice a day.

No more days, no more times, no more tides.

No more secrets.

Two

Westmere, May

In another part of town, in another old home, this one empty and rotting, they work quietly. They are practised, will be in and out in less than thirty minutes. They do not speak as they work, methodically ticking off a list that is memorised and perfected – damp items to the centre, dryer and more flammable objects against the walls; if there are nylon net curtains, so much the better. If no windows are smashed, open one or two to create a through-draught. If there are no windows, remember to wedge the exit open as they leave. No smashing, no breaking, no noise. Firelighters are placed at strategic points around the main room. This has been a learning of trial and error. At first they used too few and the result was a brief flicker, too much smoke for safety and an appalling waste of their fear and excitement. The next time, overcompensating, they were lucky to get away with sore throats from the sudden and shocking plume of smoke, luckier still to run from the site without being seen. Now they are skilled at the task.

They are two streets away before the fire fully takes hold, down on the shore well before a neighbour is alerted by the smell of smoke or a strange orange light where usually there is darkness. Far from the pier and the street lights along the front they wash their hands in the incoming tide, ripples of sea foam delineating the water's edge, feet braced against the heavy stones as they look at each other, eyes wide with the thrill of getting away with it, relief at ticking another one off the list.

A flame of sheet lightning flares far out at sea. It is very late, very early. Time to go home, back to bed. These interrupted nights are hard, and there is always the fear that someone will have noticed them gone, the empty bed, the room too quiet. They part, as they met, with no words. It will be done soon.

Three

Westmere, May

Lucy ran along the front, heading away from the pier and the tired old town threatening to slide down the hill and into the water. Behind her, hidden by a bank of dark purple cloud, the morning sun sent out an odd, tinted light. A fourth-generation child of Westmere, she knew the rain would be onshore within a quarter of an hour, perhaps sooner given the look of the choppy waves slamming themselves against the shingle. She shivered and picked up her pace. It was all very well her school coach telling the team they needed to run five days a week, rain or shine; their coach was white, she would never have to deal with brown girl's hair. She might just make it to Kitty's place before the storm hit.

Her mother's great-aunt Kitty lived at the end of the second bay, where the front receded first into a wasteland of brambles, ferns and grasses and half a mile later into marshes. Lucy thought she heard someone behind her, panting breath, pounding feet, and turned to look over her shoulder, running all the while. No one was there, she was alone on the front, and she turned back, set her face to the far distance. She'd feel safer with Kitty. She grimaced; she hadn't felt safe all year.

5

Just round the corner of this bigger bay and into the small one and she'd be within striking distance of Kitty's home. Her great-aunt was no children's book granny, knitting and smiling with boiled sweets in her pocket. At this time of day and with a spring tide, she was more likely to be drinking whisky in her tea and leaning on the railing of her deck, smoking and swearing into the wind about the bloody Westmere council and the bastard developers and how the only thing protecting her was the swathe of marshland to the west.

'Don't know about this "natural interest" bollocks, Lucy,' she'd said, 'but if you and your mates kicking off about all that climate business stops them building down this end of the bay, you have my blessing. Not that God exists, you know.'

Lucy picked up her pace, the wind behind her urging her on. She counted her footfalls as they landed, wondering if this was the morning she'd have the courage to talk to Kitty, ask for her help. She hoped she might. As she rounded the curve that dipped into the smaller bay, she expected to see Kitty out on the deck, or maybe walking the shoreline collecting rubbish and cursing the day-trippers along the coast who left their bottles and cans on the beach, the tide depositing them days later for Kitty to deal with. She was an easy figure to spot, one shoulder higher than the other, her gait slightly twisted and, recently, a stick to balance her bad hip, although she professed to use it to frighten off seagulls more than anything else.

Kitty had never walked straight as far as Lucy knew, but she was strong and tough and her feet were as sure as her words. She wasn't soft or gentle or even particularly welcoming, but she was always there. She was the person Lucy had run to whenever she was upset, at school or at home. Her little sister Etta was doing the same now, just as her mother and aunt had done in the past. Kitty was their constant. They knew she'd tell them off if they'd been stupid, but she'd also listen, holding shame and blame at bay and just listen to the story, the one in their words and the one they couldn't bring themselves to say. Lucy wanted to tell Kitty her story.

Kitty wasn't on the beach and she wasn't on the deck. Her boots were in the corner of the deck as they always were when she was inside. The door was closed. Kitty must be out already, unless there was actual hail coming directly off the sea, the door would be wedged open with a big stone from the shore. Lucy rubbed her gritty eyes and checked her watch. It was just after eight thirty. It wasn't unusual for Kitty to be out walking or fishing in the morning, but something felt odd.

Lucy wasn't sure why she tried the door, but she reached out and turned the handle. When the door swung open, catching in the wind, she knew for sure that something was wrong. Her father was always saying how Kitty was going to have a fall one of these days. He'd suggested she move in with them, but Kitty told him he was being an idiot and he could make his own plans; she had hers.

Lucy called out. There was no reply. She took the half-dozen steps across the main room to Kitty's bedroom at the back of the hut. Later, she thought she had already known what she'd see when she opened the door; that she had known Kitty was dead before she saw her lying on the bed, took in the empty pill packets and bottles laid out beside her; had known Kitty would be dead before she saw her eyes closed, her skin grey and cold.

She heard the sound coming up from her chest, a keening she hadn't known was in her, then her knees buckled and it was all she could do to put out her hand and stop herself toppling into Kitty's dressing table. She knelt down, breathing slowly. She'd had panic attacks at the start of last term and Kitty had shown her the breathing techniques. She was

7

remembering now. In for four, out for four. Slowly, paying attention to the breath as it moved through her body, noticing little details in her immediate line of focus, nothing big, nothing too much. As she counted, she looked down at the strands of summer grasses and the tiny pebbles from the shore that lay between the floorboards. They could have been there for decades. Kitty swept her rooms once a week and said that was more than enough; she lived in a hut after all, not a palace.

When Lucy felt her heart racing a little less, her skin less clammy, she slowly stood up. She walked closer to Kitty, looked at the packets and pill bottles on the bed, the whisky bottle beside her. She was glad Kitty's eyes were closed. She hoped it had been easy, falling asleep. This was the first dead body she had ever seen, and while part of her wanted to run from the hut, another part, stronger, was drawn closer.

Kitty's body was there but she was clearly gone. Her stuff was all around her; she was laid out on the bed. Kitty and not Kitty. Lucy got as close as she could without touching anything, then leaned in and carefully kissed her on the forehead. Her lips met skin that was too cool; it felt waxy, unreal. She stepped back shuddering, sorry that she felt repulsed and repulsed anyway.

A little while later, Lucy was on the deck, the doors to Kitty's bedroom and to the hut itself firmly closed behind her. She took out her phone and wondered who to call. Her mother and her aunt were both very close to Kitty. It would be horrible to tell either of them that she was dead, and she couldn't face her mother's questions right now: why was she up so early on a Sunday, hadn't she already done loads of training this week? She didn't trust herself to give the right answers. She called Sara.

Four

Westmere, 1956

Kitty Barker sidled into the dining room to take the break-fast orders. It was the first day of a new week and she liked to get a good look at the guests first thing. These days she preferred to have a glance over them before they saw her. She'd changed a lot in the past year; she was taller for a start, and her bust had filled out. She knew her figure looked good and was fine with it being noticed by the fellows she fancied herself, but a few of the dads this season had made a point of insisting on a cuddle or a kiss to welcome them back. It was getting embarrassing and their wives looked daggers at her too. As if it was her fault their old man couldn't keep his eyes or his hands to himself.

She stood by the sideboard listening to the new guests, their excited exclamations filled with a week's worth of hope.

'Those seagulls don't half make a racket.'

'The music from the merry-go-round on the pier is lovely, isn't it? I was just dozing off and caught a bit of it on the wind.'

'Ooh, the sea breezes were strong last night.'

'I do like a proper seaside, all the bustle.'

'It's how you know you're on holiday, isn't it?'

'That and the kids screaming blue murder for another stick of rock.'

And they would laugh and dip a triangle of bread and marge into a runny yolk, crunch a crisp rind of bacon, pour another cup of milky tea and plan days of pebbles and sand and candyfloss, slow afternoons and long nights, and Kitty would wish herself anywhere but Westmere. Preferably London. Uptown, downtown. She knew all about Soho: frothy coffee and cocktails with sweet cherries, smart lads on scooters with girls who jumped on the back and rode off with good-looking boys, hair flying out behind, cheek nestled into the back of his neck, aftershave and Brylcreem and change.

Danny Nelson was change on a stick. He was a bit flash for a start; his people were a step or two up from the Barkers and their Westmere Views guest house. Danny's mum had been Emma Sutcliffe; her family were the closest Eastmere had to gentry, with a couple of dirty great farms stretching right across the coastal tip of the county. His dad was Charlie Nelson, a builder and big man on the council. The Nelson family business had come into its own after the war, rebuilding the damage and laying foundations for the hope they'd been promised during those long, dark years.

Danny, born in 1932 and bright enough to get into the grammar, had surprised his mates when he left school at sixteen and went to work for his dad, studying for his draughtsman's, plumbing and electrical papers at the Mechanics Institute in the evenings. On his twenty-first birthday, Charlie Nelson handed him the key of the door – to the works office. Danny was running two teams of men within a year and the whole of the Westmere side by the time he was twenty-four. Even that was not enough; he had bigger dreams and needed extra cash for his plans, which was why

10

he took on the Lullaby Beach job when his dad made the hush-hush deal with Mr Barker, letting the Barkers buy the land outright courtesy of a useful legal loophole and a large backhander.

For the whole summer of 1956, when Pat Boone and Doris Day were vying for the attention of all clean-cut kids, Danny Nelson spent his Sundays remodelling the old hut right at the end of the bay. A grubby, nicotine-stained room papered with pin-ups brittle with age, next to an old toilet with a urine-soaked floor and cracked washbasin, slowly but surely became a perfect holiday cabin with a kitchenette in the front room, a small comfortable bedroom in the back and a lovely little bathroom with a modern boxed-in bath. Westmere Views guest house would offer Lullaby Beach as the perfect getaway for honeymooning couples and anyone for whom the noise of the pier and the front was just too much.

Kitty was drawn by Danny's dirty-blond hair and his knowing smile. She was drawn by how it felt to have him look at her. Kitty knew she looked good; those annoying guest-house dads made it only too obvious. She was tall, with fine, shapely legs, dark-haired, her eyes ringed with long dark lashes. Jane Russell to Marilyn Monroe. As it turned out, Danny Nelson preferred brunettes.

'Sweet sixteen and ...?' he said, half questioning, half expecting, when she brought him a thermos of hot sweet tea and a slice of her brother's birthday cake, a slice she'd refused to eat herself, cinching in the narrow belt on her deep blue dress one more notch.

'I'm seventeen, actually, and never you mind,' Kitty replied, leaning back against the big rock wall that separated Lullaby Beach from the wild field and the marshes beyond. She was well aware of her stance, with one foot up behind, one firmly on the ground, her neck held long, head tipped back, nipped waist and everything else just right; she knew how good she looked.

'Seventeen going on twenty-five,' Kitty's mother had said, her mouth pursed, coral-pink lipstick cracking into the lines above her upper lip, vertical etching to match the horizontal grooves on her forehead. All her mother did when she spoke like that was make Kitty even happier that she was young and smooth and her Rimmel Ravishing Red stayed exactly where she wanted.

'Seventeen and not too old to go over my knee, young lady,' her father added, shaking his head, leaving his wife and daughter to it, out of his league with this stuff, women's matters.

'Seventeen and old enough to know better than knocking about with a bloke like Danny Nelson. It'll get you a reputation, and me,' her brother Geoff complained, happy in Westmere, happy with his lot, no idea why she was not happy with hers.

Nothing they said deterred Kitty. Westmere was just noise. The same noise, day after day, year after year, seagulls and the waltzer and the merry-go-round and crying children, laughing visitors, endless smashing waves. Danny Nelson was a very different sound.

Kitty left school as soon as she could and took a job in Woolworths six days a week. She did an extra shift in the Sea Shore Café on Wednesday afternoons when the shops were closed and every second Saturday evening, making sure to keep the alternate Saturday nights free for Danny. She would rush in from work, race up the stairs and be back down again in the time it took to throw off her work clothes and pull on a blouse and skirt – both far too tight in her parents' opinion. She'd tease up her hair and put on her lipstick in the front-room mirror and be off. She was earning her keep, paying her own way, so there wasn't much either of her parents could say, but they looked at each other as the front door slammed and they heard her laugh ring out along the street. They were not happy.

Kitty was very happy. Danny made her happy. He was tall for a start. Kitty was tall herself, and getting boys to dance with her had been the bane of her life, dozy Westmere lads at school who were as short-sighted about their ambitions as they were about her height. Not Danny; he was big enough to stand right up to, in heels, and he was man enough to hold her tight and make her feel good being held. He had big dreams too.

Like most of the middle-aged men, her dad had been in the war and he'd seen Berlin, Cologne, Dresden, seen the mess of them right at the end when they came through on their way home. He came back and all he had to say about those years of fighting was what a waste it had been and how the damn Yanks could have the glory if that was what they wanted. All he was after was a quiet life and some peace.

Danny, however, had loved his National Service, told Kitty it had opened his eyes, not just to the problems of the world but to the possibilities. Basic training wasn't much fun, kowtowing to the bosses wasn't his usual style, but he bit the bullet and got through it, did damn well in drill and physical training too. He loved the long runs, even with a heavy pack of gear on his back and the odd lazy comrade to chivvy along; he came into his own in the physical side of things. It was true they'd had a tricky time in Malaya, but then he and his mates were sent to Germany, change of pace, change of scene and all the more welcome for it. After they were demobbed Danny reckoned he had a taste for new places. He went back to the continent, to Paris,

Rome, even spent a bit of time in Spain. When he came home for good, it was with the intention of making a go of it in his father's building firm, but not in Westmere if he could help it.

They had been seeing each other for almost four months when Danny first mentioned London. 'I reckon you'd like it, Kit, Soho. I think you'd fit right in.'

Kitty loved that he called her Kit; it made her feel impossibly sophisticated and just the right amount of wild, like Audrey Hepburn in *Roman Holiday*.

She cocked her head to one side and blew out her cigarette smoke slowly, the way Danny had taught her. 'Why d'you say that?'

'Ah, Soho's great. Loads of girls like you.'

She play-frowned and looked at him from beneath her lashes. 'You mean I'm not special?'

'One in a million,' he said, leaning his arm round her shoulder and kissing her on the forehead. 'I mean they're girls with verve, style. Soho's full of young lasses from all over England. They've come down from factories in Manchester and farms in Northumberland and they're keen on a good time.'

'They must have jobs. It can't all be a good time?'

'Damn sight more choice than there is round here, I can tell you that. Office work, clerking, typists are in huge demand. Mate of mine, his girl is what they call a mannequin.'

'Like a dummy in the tailor's window?'

'Yeah, but live. My mate said they're daft as a brush, the posh bints, and the fashion houses know it, so they get a girl like you, tall, nice figure ... ' He broke off to hold Kitty at arm's length, looking her up and down.

'What's that for?' she asked.

'Very nice figure,' he said, adding a whistle for good

measure as he put his heavy arm across her shoulder again and pulled her closer.

Kitty loved the weight of his arm around her, loved how it made her feel wanted, welcome at his side.

'D'you think I could get a job like that?' she asked.

'You're wasted down here, girl. We all are.'

They were in a coffee house on the front. Westmere was popular, but not in the off season. It was just shy of six o'clock and they were the last people in the room; the waitress had been looking daggers at them for the past half-hour. They'd go on to the pub soon and see people they both knew, drink the same drinks they had every time they went out, go to the pictures and see something they'd seen last week because the cinema manager said there was no point in changing the films more than once a fortnight in winter.

Something about tonight was different, though. Kitty had felt it since Danny first grabbed her in the high street and kissed her, smack bang in the middle of the market stallholders closing up. Danny didn't sound as if he was talking about maybes and possibilities; it sounded as if he was making a proposition.

She found her words were coming slowly, worried she was being presumptuous, worried she had him wrong. 'Are you asking ... I mean ...'

'I'd like to take you up to London, Kit. I want you as my girl, in the city.'

'Come to London? With you?'

He smiled, a grin as wide as his face. 'I've got plans and I'm going to need a clever girl with me. You're smart as a whip and bloody gorgeous – you'll do me. What do you say?'

He wasn't offering the engagement ring that might make going to London bearable in her parents' eyes, and Kitty well knew that her mates thought she was daft getting in with Danny Nelson, but she had plans of her own. If Danny could help her get out of Westmere, then he'd do, engagement ring or no.

'All right, Danny. I'll come up to London with you.'

Five

Westmere, May

'It's Kitty.' Lucy's voice was calm, ordinary, but Sara heard something in it, a kind of catch. Her niece sounded much younger than usual. She sounded her age.

Sara spoke carefully. 'Lucy, are you with her? Is Kitty there?'

'Yes. No. I'm on the deck.'

'Is she sick? Is she breathing?'

Lucy suddenly sounded very far off. 'She's been sick. There's vomit, beside her. On her face. It's dry. She's on the bed. She's cold. It's cold, Sara.'

Sara felt a twist low in her belly. 'Lucy,' she said slowly, 'is Kitty dead?'

'Yes, I think. I mean ... I don't know. Yes.'

Sara pictured her seventeen-year-old niece seeing Kitty, feeling her cold. 'I'll be there in an hour and a half, two at the most. Is your mum there? What did she say?'

'I didn't call her yet. I wanted ... I wanted to tell you.'

Sara's heart sank. This was no time for her to have to deal with Beth's jealousy, yet again, that Lucy had turned to her instead of her mother.

'Call your mum, tell her I'm on my way.'

'They've gone to see Mary, Dad's sister. They're coming back this afternoon. Etta's with them.'

'OK, I'll call her. And I'll probably get there before she does anyway. Then we can sort it out.'

'Sara ... ' Lucy's tone was small again, scared.

'Yes?'

'There's a load of stuff – pill packets and bottles, on her bedside table and on the bed. They're all empty. And a whisky bottle too. The glass – it's still in her hand.'

'Sweetheart,' Sara said, understanding, her heart breaking for her niece, anger with Kitty already flaring. 'I'm so sorry you saw that. I'll be there soon. Promise. Leave it all as it is, lock up and go home.'

'Shouldn't we call someone? The police or an ambulance?'

'Shit, yes, we should. I'll do it, you go home, OK?'

'Do I just ... do I just leave her?'

'I think so. I mean, I don't know, but ... ' Sara thought for a moment. 'Lucy, I'm sorry, I think you might have to stay there so they can get in. And they'll probably have questions for you, about finding her. I'm sorry. If you felt OK to go inside, you could make some sweet tea?'

Lucy smiled and then managed to say, 'I think they only do that in films, Sara. And anyway, if it's not laced with whisky, I'm not having it.'

It was Kitty's phrase about every cup of tea she was ever offered, and they both half laughed, half sobbed.

'If she were in our place,' Sara said before hanging up, 'I doubt she'd have bothered with the tea.'

Sara called Beth as she made her way down to her car, leaving a clumsy message and assuring her sister she would get there soon to make sure Lucy wasn't alone. Then she called the local police. They said they'd send an ambulance crew to the hut, to make sure. She didn't think Lucy would have got it wrong, but they insisted. Her heart sank as she realised that would mean big boots and mess, strangers clattering about Kitty's precious home. Her heart sank further when she told herself that Kitty would never know it was happening.

An hour later she was making her way out of east London and into motorway traffic. Once she was safely ensconced in the fast lane, edging ninety and on her way, she let out a long, pained roar. It surprised her with its vehemence. She concentrated on the road. She thought anger was probably safer for the drive than tears, and she was certainly angry. Kitty had been a nurse for decades; she must have known what she was doing, that it would work. She must also have known that one of them would find her.

When she arrived and parked, she called Lucy. Beth and Tim were still an hour or so away. She walked along the narrow path down to Lullaby Beach, a path she knew intimately in all seasons, all weathers. She prepared herself to face an empty hut. A home devoid of Kitty.

She could see Lucy down on the beach, at the waterline. She was glad, wanting a moment to herself anyway. She had her own set of keys in her hand and was about to go inside when she heard a shout and two paramedics came running down the path.

'Wait!'

She stopped and let them catch up with her.

'Sara Barker?' the young man asked.

'Yes,' Sara answered. 'I thought you'd have been here before now – the police said ...'

'Sorry.' The woman with him nodded, 'There was an emergency, another fire, no one hurt but we had to go there first. We're the only team in both towns now and, well, you know ...' Her words petered out, she didn't need to say it.

An old woman, a suspected suicide; living people were more important.

'If you unlock the door, we'll go in and just make sure she's . . . '

'Dead.'

'Yes.'

Kitty was definitely dead. They let Sara go into her bedroom to take a look but made her promise not to touch anything until the police arrived.

'It's pretty obvious, but you know . . . ' the young man said.

Sara didn't know, but she had been picturing it since Lucy's phone call. The bottle of whisky, the blister packs empty of pills, Kitty laid out on her bed, one hand resting on her chest, the other stretched out, still holding the glass. She stood at the door to Kitty's bedroom and thought how staged it looked, how unreal.

When the police arrived a few minutes later, Sara confirmed that this was Kitty Barker's home and that the woman lying on the bed was Kitty Barker. She confirmed that she and her sister were the only other key holders. The policewoman told her they would need to take Kitty's body and no one would be allowed into the hut until they said otherwise.

Despite their assuring her it wasn't ideal to watch, Sara asked to stay at the door as the two paramedics picked up Kitty's body and manhandled her into the body bag. Sara took after Kitty in looks; they were the same height, and even as Kitty aged, she'd still been tall, but the bag seemed surprisingly small and the sound as it was closed was brief, zipping up a life. They took her away and the policewoman escorted Sara outside and watched as she locked the front door. Then Sara handed over the keys so the police could come back for whatever else needed to be done, whatever else mattered less than the latest arson in town.

When they were all gone, she walked down to the water. She joined Lucy and held her as she cried. When Beth and Tim arrived and Lucy was safely with her parents, Sara did the only thing that made sense to her: she took off her trainers, her jeans and T-shirt, wading into the water in her bra and knickers. She swam out without looking back.

Kitty was dead.

Sara swam into the tide as fast and as far as she could, and when the orange buoy came into view, she slowed her strokes, finally coming to a rest. She lay on her back, toes splashing out of the water, arms moving slowly at her sides, bobbing with the uneven rhythm of the sea, and looked back to the shore. Much of the seafront was boarded up, massive hoardings signalling the development that would run the length of the front, from the main beach where the old amusements used to be right down to the smaller bay where Lullaby Beach stood out from the derelict and abandoned original double row of huts.

When Kitty was a girl, the huts were loved, the seafront busy and noisy with children running in and out, mums and dads enjoying pints of cockles and winkles, nanas sitting on the deck knitting up a storm for the next generation. Kitty's hut was right at the end, where the bay turned into marsh-land, and the council had held it back when they sold the others in the 1930s, keeping it for the workers to brew up their tea during long days shovelling up pebbles and stones with great flat spades, shoring up the groynes. It was a good shelter on rainy days and the men named it Lullaby Beach.

The name stuck, even when Kitty's father did a deal with Councillor Nelson. 'Paid the crafty beggar well over the odds to get the place and all.' He was happy enough when the work was done. Lullaby Beach had running water, a bedroom with built-in cupboards and a serviceable little bathroom; it was useful when they ran out of rooms at the guest house, and Kitty eventually made it her home.

In the seventies and eighties, when Eastmere, the bigger town three miles to the east, was on the rise, with a new port for container ships and a lovely little marina with restaurants and bars, Westmere was left to crumble. Eventually only the handful of huts closest to the town centre stayed in use; those in Kitty's bay were left empty for years on end. Once the marshland was declared an area of natural interest, the council were even less keen to spend money on the end of the bay. To them and to the developers, Kitty's hut was an eyesore that stood in the way of progress and a beautiful new eco-friendly car park to welcome green tourists.

Kitty kept turning their offers down, and in turn, they made it harder for her to stay. The last three springs she had stood on her deck for half the night in the full moon, her heart in her mouth and hoping for the best. Every year as she watched the tide threaten her home, she worked out again how much it would cost to pay someone to come in and raise it on two more cinder blocks, a foot higher for a peaceful night's sleep. Then the tides ebbed and her carefully allocated nurse's pension would only stretch so far anyway, and the hope of certain safety receded to a whisper.

Sara floated on her back, looking inland to the hill that rose up behind Westmere beach, right along to the row of tired old houses on Marine Parade above the front. At the very end of the tall, curving line was the house she had grown up in, the guest house that had been in their family for decades. First run by Kitty's parents, when they died her brother Geoff took it on and then he left it to his son, Sara's father. Sara's parents had struggled to make a living from the place, and when her mother first became ill with the cancer that killed her, they converted the upstairs into two flats, hoping that renting property would be less daily work than keeping an empty guest house. Now Beth and Tim and their daughters lived in the ground-floor flat and rented out the two flats above – when they could find anyone wanting to live there.

Tim had welcomed the regeneration at first, glad of the work, but already it was going wrong. More holiday homes for rich out-of-towners wouldn't make any difference to the schools or the shops or the future of Westmere, or to the zero-hours contract jobs that Tim had in construction and Beth in catering.

Kitty was dead.

Sara let her head fall back, felt the water slip over her hair-line, into her ears, over her eyes, mingling with her tears. Kitty had been the go-to for her joys and sadness since her mother's first illness. Later she'd been there for broken-heart stories and worse. She'd been there for Sara when the dark nights and darker days descended and there was no reason not to let the waves of depression pull her under, no reason to fight off the feelings of uselessness and foolishness. If she didn't hear from Sara at least once a week, she would call. Sara kept a landline purely for the one person she knew would ring and ring until she answered; she kept it because Kitty had once been her lifeline. She couldn't count the times Kitty had told her she was dafter than a brush and twice as dense. It was a brusque love delivered with a good whisky and a hot scone if she was lucky, but it was love all the same.

Now Sara was swimming out from Lullaby Beach and no one stood on the deck to watch her, no one waited for her to come back to the hut shivering from cold and exhilaration. Sara was so used to Kitty watching out for her, shining her back to herself, that losing her was like losing her reflection. Kitty was not just dead, she was suicide dead. Certain dead, killed-herself dead, did-it-the-right-way dead. Sara's tears

23

were as much anger as they were sadness. She was utterly bereft and she was furious that Kitty had done this and not said goodbye. Kitty had refused to let Sara hide for more than a week at a time, and now she had chosen to take herself away for ever. No note, no explanation, nothing. Kitty had gone and taken the lifeline with her.

Six

Westmere, May

Beth finished putting away the dishes, crying again. The day had been long, exhausting and horrible since the call from Sara. They had rushed back to Westmere, raced down to the hut, drawn up sharp at the police tape across the door and the sudden, awful knowledge she had been trying not to take in. Kitty was dead. Kitty had killed herself.

She and Sara had gone through the motions, answered questions, sipped and put aside countless cups of tea. They got through dinner, dealt with Lucy and Etta's shock and questions, but now Beth was ready to collapse. Sara was in the empty middle flat upstairs, making phone calls for work. A freelancer looking after social media for more than half a dozen different charities, there was only so much she could leave unattended. Etta was on her way to bed, and all Beth wanted to do was sit on the sofa with Tim and have a good cry, but Tim had gone to sort out a job with some mates so he could have time off later for the funeral and wouldn't be back for a while.

At least Lucy had been helpful and stayed in to keep her little sister company. Ten years younger, Etta had been Lucy's baby doll in many ways, but recently their relationship had soured, Lucy had turned very grown-up all of a sudden and pushed Etta away all too often. The shock of losing Kitty seemed to have undone some of the teenage surliness she'd adopted since the end of last year, and Beth was grateful for a respite from slammed doors and moody glares, however long it lasted. She felt the tears rise up again, almost like a wave of nausea, and squashed them down; she had to hold it together until Etta was asleep. She shook her head, almost hearing Kitty telling her to step up.

Beth had been with Tim since they were at school. As teenagers, Tim had seemed more knowing, fiercer, stronger than her. He'd had to be. He'd been one of just a handful of black and Asian kids, and their school had had its fair share of bullies who shouted horrible names and then claimed they were only joking. Beth first experienced it herself when they started dating at fifteen. Sly whispers and cold glances that built to outright nastiness, culminating in brief and fierce violence one afternoon in the girls' toilets. She'd given as good as she got, but there were more of them than her, and when she got away she raced straight to Kitty.

Kitty was still working as a health visitor then, so Beth waited on the steps of Lullaby Beach until she was home. Kitty raised an eyebrow at her great-niece, battle-scarred and furious, made her a cup of tea with a splash of whisky, then opened her bag and cleaned and taped up the grazes on Beth's knuckles, the scratch under her eye.

'Not much I can do about this,' she said, lightly fingering the bruise rising beneath the swelling on Beth's cheekbone.

'It was three against one,' Beth said.

'Of course.'

Kitty waited until Beth had finished her tea, 'Now hear me out, Elizabeth. I know people pussyfoot around when they're talking about things to do with colour—'

'We say race, Kitty. Or ethnicity.'

'Exactly,' Kitty said with a curl of her lip. 'But I hope you know I mean it right. Look, you're a white girl going out with a coloured – sorry, black – lad. That's unusual round here. Stupid people pick on what's unusual. To be honest, smart people do too. Tim's had his whole life to get used to it, and I'm not saying it's all right, I'm just saying he's had more practice.' Beth tried to interrupt, but Kitty spoke over her. 'You can't fight every little tart who mouths off, you just can't. If you two stay together, you'll get far worse than this, believe you me, so get used to it and step up. Work out when it's going to make a difference and when there's no bloody point. That means saving your punches for when they're needed most.'

Beth had stepped up. Now, in her grief at the loss and her anger with Kitty for not confiding in her, for letting Lucy see a suicide as her first dead body, guilty that she hadn't seen it coming, she just wanted to lie down and give up. Instead, she went to find Etta, hoping she had answers for the inevitable questions.

Half an hour later, she found Sara upstairs in the middle flat, her work spread out in the bedroom they'd shared as girls.

'So, Etta had some good questions.'

Sara pushed aside her laptop and papers to make space for Beth on the floor beside her. 'How was it?'

'Better than I expected.' Beth sank down, taking the pillow Sara offered her and making herself comfortable on the faded carpet. 'She asked why and I managed not to say fuck knows.'

'Well done.'

'I thought so. I said we thought maybe Kitty decided it was time to die. I said she'd had lots of life and then I had to stop because I found myself wondering if that was even true.'

I mean, Kitty worked her whole life. It wasn't as if she was off on cruises and old people's holidays. All those years as a nurse and then a health visitor and working with the women's clinics, she never bloody stopped.'

'We always talked about it like it was so impressive how hard she worked.'

'It was, you are ... Look at all this,' Beth waved her hand at Sara's files and laptop. 'You're even working now.'

'I have to. I don't get paid otherwise. Kitty, though, she did all that other work for free. She never stopped.'

Beth nodded. 'Yes. Anyway, there I was, barely holding it together, when Etta put out her hand and said, "I expect she'd just had enough, like when you tell Dad he's had enough crisps and you take the bag away." So that was it, tears and snot rolling down my face and laughing out loud at the same time.'

Sara smiled. 'Then she knows Kitty's not coming back?'

'As much as a seven-year-old can. I'm not sure I know it yet.'

'Me neither.'

They sat together in silence, caught up in the horror of their day, fighting the time when they'd have to go to bed themselves and there would be no further distractions from the truth. They were also both aware they were tiptoeing around a potential minefield, something that was certain to come up in the following weeks.

Last Christmas, a simple chat about the fact that Kitty was finding the path down to the hut harder to negotiate had led to Beth and Sara's worst argument since their teens. The weather had been horrible all through Christmas Eve and Christmas Day, and when Boxing Day dawned clear, Tim suggested a walk to shake off the Christmas excess. Lucy wasn't interested, but the adults were keen, and Etta agreed to come when Sara said they could pick Kitty up on the way.

When they got to Lullaby Beach, Kitty had insisted the girls see how well she went up the hill – 'To shut you up with your panicking about me and my stick, thank you' – and they'd followed her to the highest point above the bay. They stopped for breath at the top, and while Kitty made the sisters agree they wouldn't mention her difficulty walking again for at least a few months, Tim pointed out the work for the new development along the front.

'Those foundations look like they're getting closer to your place, Kit,' he said. 'What is it, five hundred yards?'

'Seven hundred and fifty metres,' Kitty corrected him.

'You've checked?' Tim asked, laughing.

'I have,' Kitty responded, her face dark. 'Nelson's have been on at me to sell for over a year. Cheeky sods even sent out their best-dressed young lass, some fancy tart just finished at university and all full of her "sustainability degree", whatever the hell that is. They've gone from telling me I'm stopping the full regeneration of Westmere to saying I'm damaging the chance for the world to access our greatest bit of marshland because I won't let them turn Lullaby Beach into a blasted car park.'

'You'd get a good price for it if they're that keen,' Tim said.

'I'm fine, thank you,' Kitty replied sharply, taking a long drag on her roll-up and picking a strand of tobacco from her lip. Her eyes narrowed as she looked down to Lullaby Beach. 'Mark Nelson himself came around a few weeks back, all butter wouldn't melt. Said they'd pay me four times the going rate for the place.'

Sara grimaced and Beth whistled. 'Bloody hell, that's a lot for a car park.'

Kitty took another drag on her roll-up and growled as she blew out the smoke. 'Which is why I think he's lying through his teeth. I imagine you get a lot of help to make an eco-friendly car park these days. But they're not having it. It's my home. When I'm gone, you girls can do whatever you want, just as I've always said. But not before.'

'We're not trying to get you out of there, Kitty,' Beth said, putting her arm around the older woman and noticing how small she seemed. Sara took after Kitty in height and colouring; Beth was more like their mother, fair and small. Feeling Kitty closer to her own height saddened her. The tower of their childhood was shrinking. 'We just want you to be comfortable.'

Kitty shook Beth's arm away, 'I'm not an armchair, so none of you need worry if I'm comfortable. I use this damn stick to knock seagulls off my deck more than I do for balance. Like I've always said, it's yours when I go, to keep or to sell. All I ask is that you clear the place out first, rip the whole lot out and make sure there's nothing left for anyone to pry into. I don't want anyone knowing my business. Rip it all out.'

With one hand out for Etta and the other carefully using the stick she derided, Kitty headed back down the winding path to the beach. As they walked off, a mismatched pair, the sisters heard her begin a story for Etta. 'When Kitty was a girl, when Kitty was a girl ...'

The argument bubbled up late that night. Etta was asleep, Lucy was out with her mates, the table was covered in the detritus of ham, cheese and Christmas cake, and wine had given way to a bottle of Kitty's sloe gin.

Tim groaned as he tried to stuff the last leftovers back into the fridge. 'Don't take this the wrong way, but when Kitty goes to whatever version of heaven will let her in, there's a long list of improvements we need on this house: a new fridge for one.'

'And new windows,' Beth agreed, looking at their kitchen window covered in cling film to keep out the draughts.

'Roof first, then floors sanded throughout,' Tim added.

'Crap carpets gone, brilliant,' Beth added.

They were dreaming up new colours for the hallway when Tim noticed Sara's face. 'What?'

She lifted her hands as if it was obvious. 'We're not selling Lullaby Beach. It's been in the family for decades.'

'Yeah, sure,' Tim said, 'but as a glorified beach hut, it's one thing . . .'

'As an investment, it's way more.' Beth finished his sentence, making it clear they'd not only thought about it but made up their minds.

'Your girls love Kitty's place,' Sara countered. 'Lucy would never forgive you. I know she's more interested in her mates than anything else right now, but that'll pass. Etta talks about moving in there when she's an old lady like Kitty.'

The argument quickly shifted to the impossible subject of money. Sara wouldn't let Beth placate her with an explanation about the difference between their finances; she already knew the difference and it was arrogant of Beth to suggest she didn't. Tim leapt to Beth's defence and inexorably, inevitably, the whole thing segued into an almighty row about Londoners and their ignorance and small-town people and their insularity, leading to the argument all three had been trying to avoid since Sara first packed her bags to leave Westmere.

The next morning they avoided each other until it was time for Sara to drive home.

Tim spoke first as he put Sara's bag in the boot. 'Let's put that down to drink and Christmas tiredness, yeah?'

'Yes please,' Sara said, grabbing her brother-in-law's arm in gratitude. 'Etta's already asked me three times what's wrong, and I haven't the heart to tell her what a bloody cliché we are, fighting at Christmas.'

They hugged, uncomfortably at first and then more easily.

31

Sara looked up and saw Etta watching from the front steps with a smile of relief. She also saw the peeling paint around the windows and the cracks in the pointing, the huge amount of work the old guest house needed if it was ever to make a difference for Beth and Tim.

The little bedroom was dark. Beth and Sara had been sitting in silence for too long.

Sara reached out and turned on the bedside light, then took Beth's hand. 'Let's get the official stuff out of the way first – the funeral and everything – and then make a decision about the hut.'

Beth smiled at her little sister. Of the two of them, Sara was always going to wade in, speak up. It had got her into trouble many times in their childhood. Beth was grateful to her now for daring to say it. 'Yes, thank you. Later.'

They kissed goodnight and Beth went downstairs. Tim would be home soon.

Later, in bed, Beth told Tim that Sara had mentioned their argument about selling the hut. 'We've agreed to talk about it later, not yet.'

'Yes, it's too soon,' Tim said quietly. 'But I'm not going to lie and say it hasn't occurred to me today.'

'No, me neither,' Beth agreed. 'Not to you, anyway.'

She lay still and listened to the night. High up here on Marine Parade, the sea was a constant backdrop to their days, but it felt more real at night, the rhythmic wash amplified in the dark, sea-smoothed stones clattering against each other. Beth had been on holiday to inland cities, stayed in places where there were hills and lakes, and none of them quite felt real. The shore, the shifting line between land and sea, was where she knew home.

She stretched out, measuring herself against Tim as she had done for over two decades. She loved the way her body fitted into his, her head resting below his chin so that when they held each other she could feel the beat of his heart against her cheek, the width of his chest as a comfort. His physical strength had been a stumbling block early in their relationship, when Beth was taken up with her mother's illness, the cancer that came and went and came back to kill her when Beth was pregnant with Lucy. Their father was lost in his own loss, Sara went away to university, and in the initial throes of her grief, Beth mistook Tim's physical strength for deeper wisdom. She soon found that he was as fumbling and uncertain with mortality's outfall as she was. Even so, she couldn't deny the comfort she found in his size and strength. She knew it was as much to do with childhood clichés about princesses and hero princes as it was with their relationship, and she fell into him anyway, grateful for his holding.

As so often, the falling turned to touch and kissing, reaching and sex. Turned to making love. When Tim had first called it 'making love', wanting to impress her with his genuine care, Beth had giggled and then clamped her hand over her mouth seeing the hurt on his face. She and Sara were far too cool for such old-fashioned phrases; they said fucking, shagging, having sex. But Tim persisted with the phrase, and making love became something Beth understood to be real.

All the times they had made love replicated in each new time. At first, his skin against hers and the two of them gentle, careful, finding where to fit and how to join, a deep seam of every time before. Their youthful bodies when they chose to become parents before any of their friends. That first time round, making Lucy, they had been so sure this was exactly what they wanted; why not start now when they were so happy? But then when Beth saw the line on the stick and the sudden reality of a new life set in, she began to worry. All through the pregnancy she was shaky and unsure, and when their mother died at the beginning of her third trimester, no amount of Tim's height and broad chest could soak up her fear.

When Lucy's birth was uncomplicated and she fed easily, slept often, it seemed that they might have turned a corner, but nine weeks in, Beth began to tumble down. Her world became confined to their flat, everyone amazed at how well she was doing, especially with Tim up in London on that hospital construction site, away for eleven hours a day. Only Kitty suspected that Beth's capability was a mask and banged on the door for twenty minutes when her great-niece failed to turn up for lunch as expected, insisted she let her in to the chaos of the flat and Beth's messy despair, sobbing that she didn't want anyone, not Kitty or Sara, she just wanted her mum, only her dead mum.

Kitty helped and Tim gave up the job – they didn't need the money that much, or they did but it didn't matter – and time passed and grief passed, again, and Beth returned. The surprise pregnancy with Etta brought more fear, Beth worried the whole time that she would feel the same as she had done after Lucy. Then she was so grateful when none of it was as she had felt before; this was a new baby, a new person, all new. Last year she had turned thirty-nine, in a few years she would be older than their mother ever was. All the layers of Beth as she lay with the only man she had ever slept alongside.

Tim had been through his own metamorphoses. The teenage runner became a twenty-something boxer, then a mixed-martial-arts adherent, and now, almost forty, his back bore the brunt of the gig economy. He had two zero-hours contract jobs for two different firms and tried to work as hard as the lads half his age. Now he stretched every morning to alleviate the pressure on his back, made sure to remember his knee support for a long run, and held out for the day when he did not have to reach, lift, carry, slog for work. Tim tried not to think about his body too much. He tried to just do and take care and keep on.

Reaching to each other with the same bodies, feeling the rich sediment of so long together, and then – only this moment. Tim's eyes on Beth's body, her face lit by a streak of sodium orange through the thin curtains, Tim seeking her out. Beth both here now and gone to something that was body and not, something that was her core. It was a look that she knew showed all of her. It was the look Tim had searched for in the long, slow months of her depressions, the first after Lucy, the others since then easier to recognise if not easier to live through. It was the look that assured him that yes, they were broken and mended, anxious and alive and here. Which was enough for now.

Tim slipped into sleep. Beth looked at her watch. It was almost one fifteen. A brand-new day, the first whole day without Kitty; the first whole day to wonder why she had chosen to kill herself.

Seven

London, 1956

Kitty waited until summer was over, when her parents wouldn't need her quite so much. She broke the news on the day after her eighteenth birthday. Her father brooded in silence for days and harboured a lingering desire to follow Danny Nelson to a dark alley and make him see sense. Her mother bided her time, waiting until she and Kitty were alone, making up the four beds in the family bedroom on the top floor.

'I've given you more leeway than many a parent round here, your dad has too, can't remember the last time he raised his hand to you—'

'I was twelve,' Kitty interrupted, 'and you told him you'd seen me and Sandra Wright smoking on the promenade.'

'I had.'

'You didn't need to tell him.'

Her mother shrugged then, almost as if she agreed it had been wrong to tell him, wrong of him to hit Kitty. Problem was, her husband had never had the words he needed to follow through with an argument; sometimes his frustration got the better of him and he lashed out. Not for years now, but once or twice when they were first married, when the children were younger. Her mum had told her just to turn the other cheek, what could you expect, anger got the better of blokes. She said to love him anyway, love him out of his moods when words wouldn't work. It had been largely successful, sometimes she thought she'd trained her husband better than she had her daughter. She tried words now.

'But you don't need to leave home. You can see Danny and stay here. We haven't stopped you, have we? He's older than I'd like, but when you're both in your twenties it won't seem such a lot. If you go up to London ...' She faltered, shook her head, stuffed the pillow into the starched pillowcase and continued, 'There's no getting round it, people will think you're sleeping with him. They'll think you're a tart.'

Kitty pulled up the candlewick bedspread on the single bed beneath the gable window. She ran her finger along a line of the pattern, followed the loop between two tufted rows of faded pale green. She wanted to tell her mother that they had slept together, that it was amazing, terrific, when they slept together she felt so happy in her body and alive. She smoothed the bedspread and pulled it up over the pillow. Her mother was proud of these new pillows. Kitty never wanted to be proud of pillows.

'I can't help that. They're all horrible gossips round here, that's another reason I need to get away. What if I was going off to nursing school or a secretarial college? I'd be leaving home then.'

'But that's not what you're doing, is it?'

Kitty ignored her mother and went on, 'London's not so far away. I'll be home for visits all the time. It's just, it's the city, isn't it? And I can't work in Woolworths for ever, can I?' She laughed as if the very thought was ridiculous and of course her mother would understand, then went for a cuddle, trying to snuggle into her arms the way she had always done, but she was pushed away.

Her mother held her at arm's length, fingers digging into her upper arms. She had to lift her face to look Kitty directly in the eye and she had a look Kitty had never seen before. 'You've always thought you were better than us, haven't you? I blame myself. I wanted you too much, made too much fuss of you. Let's see if you make a go of it in your blessed London or how long it takes for you to come crawling back to us, tail between your legs.'

She let go of Kitty's arms and picked up the pile of dirty sheets and pillowcases they'd thrown into the middle of the room. She stopped at the door and without turning said quietly, 'I know you're not a virgin, Kitty, I can see it in your eyes, too damn knowing by half. You just watch yourself.'

Kitty sat in the bedroom for another twenty minutes, her heart racing, a fierce, stabbing twist just beneath her breast bone. How could her mother possibly know? Did other people know?

She was gone the following weekend, and whatever she'd left behind, whatever they all thought of her, spoken aloud or not, London would be worth it.

Danny made the appointment with the landlady. 'I said you're my cousin coming to get work and a sense of the city, see if you like it.'

'What will she think when you stay over?' Kitty asked.

'Nothing. It's London, half the rooms have whole families living in them. That's why the building trade's on the up and up, the war did us a favour knocking down all those old slums. Anyway, I told her you're a good girl, just in case.'

Kitty went to meet Mrs Kavanagh, presenting herself as one of the new breed of girls who knew that women had done so much in wartime and had no intention of fading into the background now. She stood ramrod straight in her best frock, nice shoes, gloves and handbag. All she needed was a hat and her mother would have been happy as Larry. Kitty didn't like hats, they made her hair go all flat and she was very proud of her dark waves. She wasn't going to chance a hat spoiling her looks.

The Irish landlady looked her up and down. 'All right with you leaving home, your mother and father?'

'They're worried about me, of course.' Kitty knew that telling some of the truth was useful, 'but they know I want to make my way. London has so many more opportunities, doesn't it?'

Mrs Kavanagh frowned. 'It's got that all right, opportunities to make a mistake as well as get it right and hard to tell which way to leap some of the time. Still, I've met Danny a few times and if he says you're a good kid I'll give you the benefit of the doubt. Only tell me.' Mrs Kavanagh stepped closer and lowered her voice. 'You're not in trouble, are you? I don't want a baby in my house. Babies make the other tenants nervous. They make me nervous too. Girls stop working once they have a baby and then how am I to get my rent?'

Kitty clasped her white-gloved hands together in the neatest way possible, speaking clearly and politely. 'No, Mrs Kavanagh, I'm not in trouble. I know I'm young and I'm well aware it's not that usual for girls to take on their own room—'

Mrs Kavanagh snorted at this and Kitty stalled for a moment, taking in the implications, then gripped her hands tighter still, glad the gloves were masking the sweat dotting her palms. She went on, 'I'm from a good family. My parents have a guest house down in Westmere, so I know about renting rooms and wanting the right sort of person in your house.

There are plenty of girls making their own living now, just as lads have always done, and I'm one of them. I'm modern.'

Kitty pronounced the last word with emphasis and the landlady's heart ached for her. Mary-Kate Kavanagh could have said she'd heard it all before, could have said she'd used similar lines herself not that long ago, although at thirty-seven she knew Kitty would think her an old woman. She nodded, took the folded notes Kitty held out, counted them carefully. Then, unlocking a drawer with the key she took from around her neck, she pulled out a rent book and put the notes in their place.

'Saturday morning, on the dot. Pay on time, keep yourself to yourself, no smelly cooking and no noise after nine at night. We'll rub along just fine. Now, if you've got a crown, I'll give you five bob and that'll start you off for the meter. I know you young girls think candlelight is ever so romantic, but we saw enough of fires in the war, thank you very much. I'd rather not be entertaining firemen at two in the morning if I can help it. It's the meter or you sit in the dark, you understand?'

Kitty nodded meekly and Mary-Kate Kavanagh decided she'd put the girl out of her misery and hand over the key.

Kitty thought Room 7 was quite beautiful. The plaster was cracked in two jagged lines that splayed right across the ceiling, the once-vibrant wallpaper of yellow roses and green ivy was peeling in the corners and dotted with soot smuts from Waterloo station just half a mile away, the windows rattled and shook whenever a bus went by, and that happened at least two dozen times an hour, but it was all hers and she and Danny would sleep here together and therefore it was beautiful. The two big windows faced north-west and beyond the row of houses opposite was the back of the station and the river, the West End and Soho just across the bridge.

It didn't take long to unpack. She put her things into the top drawer of three, making sure to leave lots of room for Danny. Even part-time in London he'd need to have some clothes here, and men's clothes were bulkier, weren't they? She hung up her frocks and her coat in the old wardrobe smelling of camphor and cedar; someone had taken care of their clothes before her. At the bottom of the wardrobe she carefully placed her two pairs of shoes, one for work, one for best. Her mother had given her an old Chantilly scarf when she turned twelve and she draped that over the back of the middle mirror on the dressing table, angling the two side mirrors just so. She smiled at herself in the mercury-speckled glass as she put her make-up and talc behind the green gingham curtains that covered the shelves beneath. Finally she laid out the embroidered cloth her mother had given her, placing her hairbrush and comb on top alongside the little jewellery box with the ballet dancer who had long since stopped spinning.

There was a small sideboard with a few bits of crockery and pots and pans inside and a burner with two gas rings sat on top. The cupboard beside it was set into the wall, the plaster and a couple of bricks removed at the back, and wire mesh covered the opening out into the street. Kitty thought it was a smart way to keep things cool, but she'd also need newspaper to stuff in those cracks come winter. On the top shelf she put the quarter-pound of tea and the sugar jar shaped like a copper's helmet she'd brought from home. On the bottom shelf she laid out a twist of salt, half a pound of lard, a few rashers of bacon, a big potato and two eggs. She'd picked them up at the market along The Cut and had loved the feeling of getting her own shopping, ready to look after her fellow.

Mrs Kavanagh had shown her the saucepan, the frying pan and the teapot when she talked her through how the electricity meter and the gas worked. All she needed was a pint of milk and they were set. She picked up a bottle of beer too, Danny would like that. There were two glasses, not matching but that didn't matter, a couple of chipped plates as well but at least they had the same pattern, two spoons, three knives and, for some reason, half a dozen forks. As soon as she got a regular job Kitty would go back to the market and get a proper set of cutlery, maybe some new glasses, and she'd buy herself a vase. Flowers would set off the little table just right.

She made the bed with the sheets and pillowcases Mrs Kavanagh had given her and then she lay down on the eiderdown, tracing the patterns of the coving around the edge of the ceiling and the central rose where the wire hung down, ending in a bare bulb. She'd get a nice lampshade too. Mrs Kavanagh said the big ceiling cracks were bomb damage, they were damn lucky to have kept the house at all. Kitty felt damn lucky herself right now. It was just gone four and the afternoon sun was flooding in, a deep golden light twisting in past the rooftops and chimney pots and all the noise and jumble of the streets outside, the trains and the buses, so many people, and here she had her own room, her own bed, all of it as full of promise as the light itself. Kitty fell asleep smiling, full of the promise of Danny. He'd said he would get the six-fifteen train; he'd be with her for the evening and the whole night.

When she woke, she was cold and alone. The luminous arms of her little travel alarm clock told her it was gone ten and the room smelt damp. She turned on the lamp by the bed and pulled the curtains, heavy and dark red. Mrs Kavanagh said they'd been left over from the war, proper blackout curtains. Kitty felt the grime ingrained in the cloth. She washed

her face, put the kettle on, made herself a cup of tea and settled herself in the window between the red curtain and the
nets. She waited.

It was just gone midnight when she saw Danny across the
street. She waved to him, slipped down the stairs as quietly
as she could, a smile on her face when she opened the front
door, the smile she'd been practising for hours, a smile that
didn't ask why he was so much later than he'd said, wasn't
demanding, wasn't needy. Back in the room, she poured him
a drink. It was cooler outside now and his coat was damp to
the touch when she hung it up. He took off his shoes and
she listened as he told her about his day. The idiots he'd had
to deal with, the paperwork taking too long, the daft bitch
at the town hall, the insurance bloke who was a right bastard and all.

'It's a wonder anything gets done in this bloody country.
You'd think we lost the war the way we're carrying on.'

Kitty had heard the same story many times. How Westmere
was on the up, no question, but the real money was in the East
End and south of the river. The docks and boroughs all along
the Thames had been the target of awful bombing and now
they provided rich pickings for developers and builders, for
the well-spoken architects with their dreams of social housing
that would better the common man simply by giving him an
indoor bathroom fifteen floors up in the sky.

Danny said those architects didn't know the first thing
about the common man. 'Truth is, Kit, most blokes I know
aren't that fussed about a fitted bathroom and indoor lav.
Their wives might be, of course, but what we'd really like is
some of that cash those bastards are raking over with all their
fancy plans for the future. I've got to be here, in the thick of
it all, to make that money.'

'I know, Danny.'

'The bastards in charge have us right where they want us. That's why I've got to do better. You and me, kid, we'll make it together.'

He sat back on the bed and pulled her to him, his head soft against her breasts. Kitty's shoulders relaxed, her breathing slowed. She loved him like this, needing her.

Long after Danny fell asleep, Kitty lay awake imagining the days and weeks to come, the nights to come, just like this, the first time that she hadn't needed to bite her lip to stop herself squealing out in joy. She had surprised both of them when she'd bitten his shoulder too just now. Danny didn't mind, said he liked a girl with some spirit. She was dead lucky in all sorts of ways. Danny always used a rubber, for instance; he wasn't like some lads, saying it wasn't his problem.

Maybe she'd get a washing set like the Victorian ladies used to have. Her nan had had one, a lovely jug and bowl, covered all over in painted sprays of lily of the valley. Kitty was horrified when her nan told her what those ladies had really used them for, after doing their duty by their husbands. Kitty's mum was furious with her mother-in-law; she thought Kitty was too young at thirteen to know any of those goings-on, but as Nan had said, 'If she's old enough to look after her own rags, she's old enough to know how to take care of herself. The girl might as well learn what's useful. Not as if any boy is going to know, whether she's a ring on her finger or not.'

Kitty was keen to learn. She was grateful for the little her mother had told her and the bit more she'd gleaned from her nan, but even if Nan had still been alive, she didn't think she would have gone to her with questions about how to look after Danny in bed. She wanted to do it right for him. He was patient with her lack of experience and had been kind, even careful, the first few times, but feeling him sink into sleep, the ease of his hand heavy on her thigh, she wanted to give him more. Of course he was tired and a bit grumpy tonight, but from now on he'd always have her to come home to, ready and willing to ease his worries. She'd get a job too and help him out with the money. It was all to come.

Eight

Westmere, June

The wait for the funeral felt interminable. It was difficult to loathe the thought of saying goodbye while also knowing they were desperate to get on with it. The coroner was an especially thorough young woman, recently appointed to the job and taking no chances. The police had taken photographs of Kitty lying dead on her bed and of the empty blister packs and bottles of the drugs she'd taken. Kitty had made sure everything was in the right place to allow her suicide to be quite obvious, and the toxicology report was clear that the amount of drugs in her body and alcohol in her bloodstream, give or take a number of hours, perfectly matched the number of pills missing, the whisky drained from the bottle. The lack of a suicide note written in Kitty's own hand, however, and the months since she had last seen a GP, as well as the new coroner's desire to get her first suicide just right, contributed to a slow and methodical process that took almost three weeks.

Finally Kitty's body was released to the family. In her verdict the coroner also noted that Miss Barker had obviously known her narcotic contraindications very well and taken great care to ensure she ended her life rather than tragically damaging it and causing further grief for her family. Sara could just imagine Kitty's face at the backhanded compliment for her decades of undervalued work in community nursing.

Beth and Sara were edgy and anxious in the wait, needing each other in a way that reminded them of their childhood. Reaching out to each other on a dark night in a shared room became reaching out by phone across sixty miles of dark land; childish needling became an unfounded adult irritation at their grief not quite connecting, empathies misfiring. Beth thought she should have noticed that Kitty was stockpiling drugs, that she had a plan. Sara was angry, with herself for not seeing what was happening, with Kitty for leaving them with no explanation, with the world for letting Kitty die alone. They took to calling each other at night as they had when Etta was tiny, when Beth would be up in the middle of the night feeding and knew her insomniac sister would be awake.

'It's not your fault, how many times have I got to say this?' Sara was sharp, irritated with Beth for going on about her guilt, 'You're doing what people always do with a death, making it all about you.'

'I am not,' Beth replied.

'Do you want me to say it is your fault?'

'Go on then, explain it to me. Fix it.'

'I can't fix it, that's not what I'm saying.'

'Then what are you saying?' Beth was exasperated. 'I tell you what I feel and you say I shouldn't feel it.'

'But it's all bollocks. We love Kitty and she's dead and instead of thinking about her, we're thinking about us.'

'No, that's not it. I'm thinking about me in relation to Kitty,' Beth said. 'I'm thinking she lived twenty minutes from

47

here, I saw her two or three times a week, and still I had no idea this was going to happen.'

'I talked to her two or three times a week and I had no idea either.'

'God knows what was going on.'

Sara agreed and then started to laugh, 'What would Kitty say if she heard us now?' She mimicked their aunt's tone when she was mocking the girls, a lisping child's voice that she used when she wanted to shake them out of bickering or whining. 'Why did Kitty do this? Why did Kitty do that? Once upon a, once upon a, once upon a Kitty ..." She'd be very mean.'

Beth snorted with laughter. 'And so irritated by our questions.'

Her snort turned into a choke and then a coughing fit. Sara waited in the silence of her London flat until it had subsided. She waited until Beth's deep breath was clear, half sigh, half moan.

'What are you drinking?' she asked.

'A sizeable whisky in Kitty's honour and because Lucy promised to get up early and take Etta swimming. Even though she's been breaking promises constantly.'

'She's a teenager. She's experiencing her first death. You're just going to have to wait it out.'

'She's my daughter, Sara, I know her,' Beth snapped before she could stop herself. 'And I know there's something else going on, but to be honest, I just haven't got the energy to dig into it right now.'

Sara chose not to bite back. Instead she lit a cigarette, taking a long drag. 'I'm so pissed off with Kitty that I've started smoking again.'

'Way to make Kitty see sense.'

There was silence between them then, Beth's kitchen clock

ticking, the fridge humming, sirens at the end of Sara's busy east London road.

'I thought she trusted us,' Sara said.

'I thought she loved us,' Beth whispered.

'She did.' Sara was crying.

'Then why? I hate that we don't know why.' Beth's voice petered out and the line was silent again.

Eventually Sara answered. 'I hate it too. I mean, surely she would leave a note? She was always telling us what to do, explaining stuff. It feels all wrong.'

'I am so bloody angry with her.'

'Me too,' Sara said.

They were both crying long after the call was ended.

The funeral was almost a relief. As they followed the coffin into the dark, heavy-Gothic crematorium, Sara breathed a sigh of gratitude when she saw the building was almost two-thirds full, 'Thank God for that. Imagine if there'd been no one to see us all frocked up,' she whispered to Beth.

Beth shook her head in mock horror, but she was also smiling. Lucy had overcome any signs of moodiness and thrown herself into helping with the preparations. She'd come down an hour earlier to make the cavernous room look brighter with the flowers they'd chosen for Kitty. Decked out in wildflowers it looked far less gloomy than they had imagined.

Kitty's friend Ernestine spoke of the young woman both Sara and Beth wished they'd known, and one of Kitty's health visitor colleagues and a dear friend spoke of her passion for the NHS and the later work she'd done with women's centres and refuges. The sisters were moved to hear Kitty's fierce politics summoned into being by a woman of eighty-three who, if she couldn't quite match Kitty's disgust at the decimation of their once-proud health service, certainly had the same love for the institution itself, and most especially what she referred to in her eulogy as 'women's health'.

Sara whispered to Beth, 'Kitty would be so grumpy at that phrase!'

'I know,' Beth agreed. '"It's abortion and contraception, girls, not bloody women's health, and don't you forget it."'

Their father had come home from Spain for the funeral, and they looked on in pride as he surpassed himself with a short speech about the aunt he'd been lucky to have as a child and how much she'd done for them all when the girls' mother died. Lucy took on the task of reading Helen Dunmore's 'Glad of These Times' and sat down proud of herself for sharing the strong lines without a stumble. Then Tim took Etta up to sing the crocodile song that Kitty had taught them all when they were tiny. No one had had the heart to suggest that a crocodile-eaten lady might not be the best image for a funeral. As it turned out, it was a funny, silly moment that lightened the tone, especially when Beth and Sara's father joined in, singing along and doing the actions. Finally Sara stood up to speak for herself and Beth.

Beth had been adamant that she would run away if she was asked to say anything beyond 'thank you for coming' and 'more wine?' at any point during the day. Sara unhooked herself from her sister's grasp and made her way to the lectern, thinking how many times in their childhood she, the little sister, had spoken for both of them, Beth both pushing her forward and annoyed that she was getting the attention. Thinking how absurd it was to be here in front of all these people, five feet from Kitty's body, Kitty still so very dead.

They had chosen not to lie. The children knew the truth, the coroner's verdict had been in the local newspaper; Kitty would have hated any obfuscation. She steadied herself against the lectern and looked out at the room of upturned faces.

There was Ernestine, bowed at the loss of her old friend, Etta cuddled tight between Tim and Lucy, her father watching with faith that she would hold it together. Sara wondered if their choice about honesty was quite right. It was one thing to shame the devil, as Kitty liked to say, quite another to pour salt into a gaping wound. She looked to Beth, who nodded, and she took a deep breath.

'We are not happy with Kitty. We are not happy with her at all.'

She was gratified by the little shake of the shoulders and smile she saw on Ernestine's face, by Tim's quiet laugh and Lucy's silent applause.

'As most of you probably know, "I am not happy with you" was a Kitty phrase. Kitty's love and friendship was fierce, uncompromising and very strong. Her displeasure was equally ferocious. Beth and I are so grateful that we had her in our lives. When our mother died, she was the rock on which we beat out our grief. It's fair to say that we were not delicate in our loss. I think we have Kitty to thank for that. We have never been delicate girls. She let us wail and roar and rage about Mum's death, encouraged us to take it right to the edge. And then she told us when it was time to get on. Kitty told us to keep going, to live alongside our grief, to live with it. Not to deny it and definitely not to buy into what she called the "time heals everything crap", but to allow ourselves to grow while grieving. It was the best thing anyone could have done for us back then. She let us have our pain.'

Sara paused. 'And here we are. Grieving. Remembering that she taught us to do it. Remembering it's OK to be angry and hurt with our grief. It's OK for grief to be noisy and loud and messy, just as there are also times when it is quiet and small.'

She looked down at the words on her page, what she and Beth had agreed she would say next. She took a breath, tried to speak, and nothing came. She tried again, and then tears came instead, a gulping, unexpected sob. The room became painfully silent as she tried to hold in the tears and her body refused to let her, another sob opening the floodgates to heaving, shaking grief.

Beth, their father and Etta almost knocked each other over as they all jumped up to race to her aid. After a rush of hugs and more tears and to the palpable relief of those still sitting, Sara picked up her page and started again, this time with her father on one side, her sister on the other and Etta perched precariously, proudly, on the edge of the lectern.

'The thing we really want to say, shaming the devil in the way Kitty taught us, is that we're bloody annoyed with you right now, Kitty. We are not happy. You could have told us, any one of us here today. You could have asked for help. You could have let us know you had made a choice. We all know how damn stubborn you always were, how sure of your path. We might not even have tried to talk you out of it—'

Ernestine sucked her teeth and muttered, 'I would!'

And a dozen voices joined in with 'oh yes', 'amen to that'.

Sara and Beth laughed, their father shook his head.

'Yeah, perhaps we'd all have tried, but even so . . . ' Sara went back to her speech. 'The hard bit now is how much we don't know. What was going on that you, of all people, chose to stop. That's the worst bit, Kitty, none of us ever wanted you to stop. It's impossible to imagine there being no you. We love you and we're really sorry that you made this choice, and even though we know it was your life and you're the one who taught Beth and me that we are in charge of our own lives and we get to make our own choices, we are not happy with you, Kitty. At the very least, we'd have liked to say goodbye in person. This way is far too hard.'

*

Two hours later, Etta was playing outside in the sunshine and Tim and their father were holding court in the makeshift bar, where Beth was pretty sure they were drinking almost as much as they were pouring. It was a funeral; of course they were going to get pissed. Ernestine was presiding over the little kitchen, churning out tea, coffee and food, directing Lucy to deliver them to this needy person or that.

Sara and Beth were both exhausted.

'Yay us,' Beth said.

'Yay us,' her sister replied. She pointed to Etta. 'I'm going to the loo, why don't you go outside? Get us both a glass of wine from your tipsy husband and I'll come and join you. We'll have to clear all this up soon, let's get some vitamin D before we do.'

Sara was coming out of the toilets when Lucy grabbed her.

'You OK, Luce?' she asked.

Lucy shook her head. 'I need to tell you something.'

'All right,' Sara answered, her dream of cool wine and a quiet moment in the sun tantalisingly close and yet so far. 'What is it?'

Lucy took a deep breath and then spoke very fast. Clearly she'd been holding on to the words for a while. 'I should have said and I didn't. I know it's wrong and I didn't say anything at first because I was in shock or something and then because I couldn't believe I'd done it. Then there were the police and the coroner and everything and I knew I'd get in so much trouble, but you were really upset today and I've never seen you like that and I'm really sorry, Sara, I'm so sorry.'

'What are you talking about?' Sara asked, worry making her tone sharp and her face hard.

Lucy was holding an envelope and Sara immediately understood. She opened it and removed the piece of paper inside, strong cream paper, carefully folded. Even before she unfolded it, she knew she would see Kitty's handwriting.

Sara read the piece of paper several times. It was all she could do not to grab Lucy and shake her. She could hear Beth through the high window, calling her name.

'Get out there and tell your mum I'll find her outside. Tell her I'm having a cry and want to be by myself.'

'But she'll come and look after you ...' Lucy tried to protest.

'Then stop her.'

'I don't know how. What shall I say?'

'For fuck's sake, Lucy, I can't do this right now. I'll talk to you later. Grow up.'

She pushed Lucy out of the toilets, ignoring her look of wounded horror.

When Ernestine saw Lucy standing alone in the corridor, she put both hands on her shoulders, holding her at arm's length.

'That's not just the face of grief, now is it? Trouble?'

Lucy nodded.

'And have you told someone?'

She nodded again.

Ernestine sighed, pulling her close to her. 'In that case, my dear, there's nothing more to be done. You come and help me in the kitchen. There's been too much drink taken on empty stomachs, time we gave them something else to eat.'

When one of the guests mistook Ernestine for Lucy's grandmother, ordering her about in the kitchen, they both smiled and neither bothered to correct him.

Sara locked herself in a cubicle. She thought she might throw up.

She unfolded the piece of paper again. Kitty's hands had

made these creases, Kitty's tobacco-stained right forefinger had run along the lines that folded the paper into three sections. Sara's own finger followed the lines and she turned her head so that her tears didn't fall on the paper. Kitty's writing was less contained than usual, the backward slope more pronounced, but it was definitely hers.

The top half was a list of the medications she had taken; they matched with those that had been on the bed beside her. It started with a huge amount of painkillers, then there were a number of antidepressants. Sara didn't have to look them up, she'd been on them herself. She didn't know that Kitty had too. Then the final and certain dose – twelve of one kind of sleeping pill, ten of another.

The bottom of the page held four dates, the handwriting even more shaky, petering out on the final line, the year a blur.

Christmas Day 1956
12 May 1957
30 April 2004
12 May

The last was the day Kitty had killed herself, weeks ago now and it still felt like no time at all. The two dates in the fifties didn't mean anything to Sara, but the reason she was so shocked wasn't just that Lucy had kept the note from them; it was because of the other date. The thirtieth of April 2004 was a day that Sara had tried and failed to forget for years.

Nine

Westmere, 2003

The summer that their mother had been dead for an impossible six months, the summer of Beth's post-natal depression, the summer their father's grief was an impassable barrier neither Sara nor Beth could penetrate was also the summer Sara started an affair with a man twenty years her senior.

In the two months between leaving school and going to university in Newcastle, she took an office junior role at Nelson Construction. She and Beth had both worked in the guest house as long as they could remember, but Sara's hunger to get away extended to her holiday job as well, and Nelson's was the only place in Westmere with any regular work. The boys at school often joined their fathers and brothers in building or scaffolding gangs over the summer, but girls were relegated to office or shop work.

Sara was lucky that that year was also a big time for the Nelson family. It was the year that old Charlie Nelson finally retired, with a massive party at the Eastmere Yacht Club, a front-page spread in the local and county papers as well as mentions in the *Times* and the *Daily Mail*. Danny was aching to tell his old man how much it cost to get the diary people to put those pieces in, but when it came to it he couldn't really begrudge the old bastard his pleasure in finally seeing himself in a broadsheet. Besides, it didn't do the business any harm, and anyone who mattered knew that Danny Nelson had been pretty much running the firm for the past two decades anyway.

Danny had no children of his own and had taken his nephew Mark on in his teens. Now that Charlie was finally out of the way, the company was rebranding as Nelson Developments – development was far more millennial than construction – and Sara's job was to go through the website as well as all the company's printed matter, digitally archiving anything that was not to be updated, noting changes anywhere else, ensuring all new print material was ready for their changeover date. The work was concentrated, pressured and tedious. Nelson Developments were launching the new look at the beginning of September, which meant that everything had to be signed off at least a fortnight before. It was perfect timing for a summer job and she could have plenty of overtime if she wanted it. Plenty of overtime working with Mark Nelson late into the night.

His first overture was so subtle it was only later that Sara recognised it for what it was. She was so used to the fumbling clumsiness of boys at school that a man in his thirties, middle-aged as far as she was concerned, suggesting they go out for a meal and a drink, 'to keep us going while we tackle the proofread', seemed like the kind of sensible thing any adult would do. No amount of revising for exams had prepared Sara for the exhaustion of tedious office work, six days a week and up to twelve-hour days. She desperately wanted to seem grown up, and so she said yes.

The next week she said yes to lunch, and then to a take-away in the office when there was no time to leave the

Portakabin that had been given over to the archive. If she was surprised when Mark turned up with a bottle of his favourite red wine and two glasses, she didn't say so, simply took her glass and raised it in cheers, hurriedly getting back to work and glowing at the attention he showed, the interest he said he had in her university plans. After three years underscored with disease and death, with grief a part of her everyday life, she was desperate for light, for fun and for play.

The first time they kissed was far from romantic. It was coming up to midnight, three weeks before launch. Mark's nerves made him brusque and exacting. By now Sara had admitted to herself that she was infatuated with him. She was not infatuated with him as an angry boss.

'You're going to have to do all of this again,' he said, waving his hand over a big pile of documents.

'Can't I just fix the mistakes you found and then it's done? There's only a couple of things wrong,' she added.

'Bloody hell, Sara, there's no guarantee I've found all of your mistakes. I'm twice your age.'

'How is that relevant?'

He shook his head, 'It means I'm bound to be more tired than you.'

Sara sat up straight from her place on the floor, amid the mess of documents. 'You ran a marathon in the spring, you're training for another triathlon, you're fitter than most of the boys I went to school with, there's no reason for you to be so much more tired than me.'

He started to speak but she didn't let him get a word in. The one thing her mother had always been determined her girls would do was speak their mind, and Sara heard her mother and Kitty urging her on as she spoke over his denial.

'I screwed up, I'm sorry, I'll fix it. But stop being so bloody grumpy and give me a break. We've had a nice time these past couple of weeks. I know you're nervous about the launch, I'm terrified about leaving home. Everyone gets scared of change. But it's exciting too. We can be scared and excited at the same time, you know.'

She was terrified he was about to storm out or launch across the desk and grab all of her work, kicking her out along with it.

Instead he smiled. 'Scared and excited at the same time. Yes. Exactly.'

Then his look changed. He left his desk, she stood up, the papers were ignored and four hours' worth of careful filing was destroyed as they rushed for each other.

It was exciting and scary for both of them. Sara's previous relationships had been teenage standard: fumbling, halting and punctuated by uncomfortable silences, conversation an impossibility. With Mark there was easy chat, sexual skill, interest in her, and there was also the delicious lure of the secret, the hidden, the wrong. For the last month she was in Westmere, neither Mark nor Sara pretended they were having anything but an affair. Short, illicit, thrilling, because they could.

Part of the joy for Sara was keeping it to herself. United in their grief, the sisters diverged strongly when it came to relationships, and Sara knew that Beth would not approve. At twenty-three, Beth and Tim had been married for two years and they already had Lucy. While Beth had some vicarious interest in Sara's previous relationships, she had also been slightly censorious. Sara loved exploring the whole new realm of her body in sex, it was less about the boys she had gone out with than the possibility of what might be ahead of her. If this was how she could feel, at eighteen, from sex in stolen moments, in secret meetings, what might her body do for her when she had a room of her own, new people to choose from, people she hadn't known since she was five years old in primary school?

On her last night at home, the big suitcase already in the downstairs hall, a smaller backpack in her bedroom awaiting the last of her toiletries, they had a family meal at the local pub. Their father managed to say how proud their mother would have been, how proud he was, and did so without making the girls feel like they needed to look after him. When he finished speaking, he exchanged a little look of thanks with Kitty, who had coached him for the past few days. He gave Sara her mother's watch as a going-away present, and both girls knew how much it cost him to part with the memento that had sat on his bedside table since her death.

Kitty made a speech too, with her customary sharpness. 'You make damn sure you know you're heading off to study as well as play, madam.'

'Yes, Kitty.' Sara smiled, with a kick to Beth beneath the table.

'Kick her later, listen to me for now,' Kitty went on. 'Always buy your own drinks, change your sheets at least once a fortnight, never go out without a tenner in your back pocket.' She handed over a ten-pound note, which Sara took gratefully. 'And also make sure you throw caution to the wind and rip it all up every now and then.'

She raised her glass and they toasted Sara's future.

Late that night, unable to sleep, Sara went downstairs and found Tim in the kitchen. He and Beth were staying with her father at the guest house while Tim did some work on their little flat, wrenching it into the twenty-first century.

'Beth's snoring got you again?' she asked, closing the door quietly behind her.

'Lucy's grizzling, teething maybe,' Tim answered. 'I thought a cup of tea might help Beth chill too.'

Sara joined him at the window looking out into the dark back yard, 'Yeah, my sister's rubbish when she can't sleep.'

'She's worried about you. We both are.'

Sara smiled. She had always enjoyed it when Tim played the big brother. 'I'll be fine. Once I'm settled into my accommodation—'

'Mark Nelson,' Tim interrupted.

Sara could feel herself blushing, caught out. She hadn't intended to tell Beth about Mark and had only done so as they walked home from dinner earlier, her excitement and sadness all mixed up with nerves and gin, whispering the story because she was about to go away and didn't want to leave with a secret between them.

'It's not because he's married,' Tim said.

Sara didn't believe him. Tim was old-fashioned, it was one of the things Beth liked most about him and Sara found sweet but irritating. Of course he'd think it was wrong. She wasn't really sure what she thought about it herself, other than that it had been huge fun and maybe she'd never have done more than kiss him that night in the Portakabin if she hadn't already been leaving, with a finish line in sight.

'Don't tell me off. It was only ever going to be a fling. No one else will ever know.'

'Beth didn't tell me,' Tim said.

Sara frowned. 'Really? Then – what?'

Tim's response was sharp, 'Rosa McCready saw you two kissing.'

Rosa was Mark's secretary and was also a bit of a joke between Sara and Mark, her two-decades-long service to the company plainly due to a passion for Mark rather than any genuine excitement about the company itself.

'Shit.'

'Yeah.'

Sara was quiet, and then she shrugged. 'It'll be OK, she adores Mark. She's not going to want to get him in trouble, right?'

'She told me.'

'She told you because she hoped you'd do exactly this, get me to end it. Do you think I should tell Mark that she knows?' Sara asked.

'And give him another reason to treat her like shit?'

'He doesn't.' Sara bristled.

'He knows she fancies him. He uses it to do what he wants and get her to cover up for him. He's done it for years. You don't think you're the only one, do you, Sara?'

Now Sara was on safer ground, she and Mark had talked about this. 'I know I'm not the first affair he's had and I won't be the last. I'm sorry we screwed up and sorry Rosa saw us, but if she didn't say anything the other times, she's not going to start now.'

Tim half laughed. 'It's not about being found out, it's about not doing the crap thing in the first place. It's about not doing the crap thing with a man who doesn't give a damn about anything or anyone. Listen to what you're saying about him, you know he doesn't.'

'It was fun.'

'Fun with a man who doesn't care about his wife and kids, who screws around not for love or some great passion, but just because he can. Why on earth would you want to be with someone like that?'

He left the kitchen then, and Sara stood for a few more minutes, her heart pounding. She wanted to race after Tim and tell him he didn't know what he was talking about, he didn't know Mark at all. And somewhere, in the small of her back, the pit of her stomach, she thought he was probably right.

The next morning, Tim had left for work when her father helped her load her bags into the car, ready for the long-awaited new start, leaving Westmere, getting on with her life.

Ten

London, 1956

It took just three days for Kitty to pick up a job at the station café. When Danny went down to Westmere, she took herself out and walked the length of The Cut, up and down the little roads leading north and south, noting the Old Vic and the fire station as her landmarks. She made a note of the pubs and tea shops on the way, peeking in to have a look at the clientele, imagining herself bringing a bacon buttie to that old bloke, serving those three lads a well-poured pint, offering a cup of tea to the old girl who'd made such an effort and got herself all dolled up to go to the market, wearing a hat that had seen better days long before the war. There were a few pubs she wouldn't chance, loud places where dockers were easing their way back into the world after a long day's work that started at four in the morning.

It was all exactly as she'd hoped, and a spit from the Festival of Britain site as well. She was in London to make her own future, just as those designers had dreamed up the future of the country after the dark years of war. Never mind that old Churchill had been dead set against it and made them pull down the Skylon before she'd had a chance to set eyes on it; she was here and that was what mattered.

On her second day alone, Kitty went down to the Elephant and Castle and then walked another mile south and thought herself very fine indeed when she made it back by an entirely different route, crossing the Old Kent Road and coming to her next landmark at London Bridge itself. She found Waterloo by following the curve of the river, past the Oxo Tower and the docks, the empty spaces between studded with rubble.

On her third day, she put on her tidiest blouse and skirt, her good shoes, swept up her hair into a neat bun to make herself look older and went off to find a job. She was no end of pleased when, after trying two pubs – both of which took her name and told her to come back next week – she asked at the café just inside the station and was offered a job there and then. It was as if London was doing its best to show her how welcome she was. The sun was shining, even the broken buildings looked charming in the right light, and people were awfully nice when she said she wanted to get to work right away. It wasn't all that different from home, everyone liked a worker. They said that London welcomed anyone prepared to graft, and it seemed they were right. At least that was what she thought until she got to know the girl in the room below and heard how much harder she'd found it to bag a job.

Ernestine was Jamaican, coming up twenty-three, a trained teacher, and she had been in London for four months. Since she arrived, she had taken three part-time jobs, all of them washing or cleaning, and as yet she had found nothing she could rely on from week to week. Kitty was glad of the company when Ernestine knocked at her door and suggested they go out for a wander. She said a drink would be more welcome, and Ernestine laughed and told her that she'd been assured English ladies drank only tea, yet perhaps that wasn't the whole truth.

Kitty smiled. 'I imagine even my mother would think a saloon-bar shandy was perfectly acceptable.'

They sat in a quiet corner and Kitty asked Ernestine about her trouble finding work. 'I don't understand; you've got so much more behind you than me. I was awful at school and I've no real references to speak of.' She took a sip of her gin and lemon.

Ernestine raised an eyebrow and laid her arm alongside Kitty's. 'You don't see this?'

Kitty looked down. Ernestine's dark brown skin made her own arm look more pink than white.

'Of course.' She blushed, started to speak and then stopped herself.

'Go on, say it,' Ernestine said.

'It's just, I was brought up not to point out things like . . . '

Ernestine's voice was light but her eyes were wary. 'Not pointing it out doesn't make it go away, Kitty.'

'But you've got proper qualifications,' Kitty persisted. 'Exams count for something, they matter more than you being . . . you know . . . '

Ernestine smiled. 'Dark will do. Not English. Jamaican. And as British as you. We were told England was crying out for trained teachers. That's what they said when I booked my ticket, but now I don't know.'

'I could ask at the station caff?' Kitty volunteered. 'They want another waitress, and it's close to Corngate Street.'

Ernestine laughed. 'Thank you, but no. I believe I will find a teaching position. I'll keep on with part-time work until then. I am well trained and have very good references. Something will come my way. I have faith.'

'You go to church?' Kitty asked, surprised. She and her own friends had long since discarded God, along with Father Christmas.

'I do,' Ernestine answered, 'but no, I meant I have faith in myself.'

They raised their glasses to something coming their way and then went back to Corngate Street, Ernestine for another day of knocking on doors and cold looks, whispers behind her back and much worse than she told her new friend, Kitty to get a good night's sleep, because tomorrow was Friday and tomorrow Danny would be back.

Danny had his own routine. Monday to Thursday he worked between his father's company office and their three building sites across Eastmere and Westmere; on Friday afternoon he came back up to town. On Friday, Saturday and Sunday nights, he and Kitty went out with the rich men he hoped would invest in his plans.

Danny explained, 'There's so much building going on in London right now, they're not looking anywhere else. Rolling in money and the lazy buggers just dump it on the first developer that comes along. That's usually these East End or south London bastards, crooks the lot of them, tied up with gangs and all that malarkey.'

'Then shouldn't you steer clear?' Kitty had asked.

'No, love, that's why I should get in. If every other bloke outside London is scared off by the gangs, it leaves an in for me. Truth be told, the work my old man has lined up is too small for most of them to be fussed with. I need to make it sound a bit bigger than it is. He's got too much of the Westmere fear in him. Not like us, Kit, we'll pick up half a dozen backers in no time. There's got to be someone who sees that the future isn't all bloody London.'

Their nights out with potential investors quickly took on a pattern. First a drink in a Soho pub, then off to a restaurant, Italian or Chinese or French to show how cosmopolitan they were, prove to these big-bellied, gold-ringed rich men that

Danny knew his way about. After dinner they'd go to a club for a few hours more, often they didn't get back to Corngate Street until gone two in the morning. Having spent so much on entertaining, on whisky and sodas, cigars and smiles that made their cheeks ache, they'd walk south across Waterloo Bridge in the dark, Kitty half skipping to keep up with Danny's pace. The skirts and frocks he liked her to wear were well fitted, and matching his big strides was difficult if she didn't want to rip the seams. Clothes rationing might be over, but costs were still high, and she knew for a fact that Danny didn't think make do and mend would work much magic on the men they were trying to charm.

Danny was the life of the party while they were out, all joking and geniality, but once the night was over he wanted his bed, and fast. Kitty would make him a cup of tea and take it to him in bed while he made notes about the men they'd wined and dined, writing in a shorthand Kitty was just beginning to decipher. He talked about it as a general might describe the manoeuvres on a battlefield, while Kitty eased herself out of her frock, her girdle and suspenders, feeling her body come back to itself, breasts and stomach softening, the deep grooves cut into her skin by the tight elastic slowly filling out after hours of being pulled in and pushed up. She rolled her feet on the cool lino, arches aching from the new shoes Danny liked her to wear, even though she could almost match his height in them. She'd give him that, he had no problems with a girl who could look him in the eye in her heels.

She watched herself in the mirrors of the dressing table, slowly cleaning her face with cold cream, three angles of Kitty. Her hair combed out, lashes and eye make-up off, she saw herself go back in time from the twenty-five she pretended to their guests to the eighteen she really was. When

Danny was finished with his notes, she turned out the light and climbed into bed. She was happy to hold him, let him roar and fuck out his frustration or hope from the night. She was grateful to be his girl. She believed she could make him happy just being herself.

When Danny was down in Westmere, Kitty got up at half past five to get to her job at the station, took her time pottering about her little room, had a cup of tea to wake herself up and a quick wash in the shared bathroom on the landing below. When Danny was with her, she tiptoed from her room, dressed in the bathroom so as not to wake him and headed straight out to work. Her shift started at quarter past six and she worked right through until a half-hour break at two, then joined the cook in cleaning out the kitchen before she knocked off at four. By quarter past she was slowly walking up the stairs to her room, her feet aching, her hair coated with the grease of hundreds of plates of the much-loved Station Special. Danny hated the smell on her and she tried to wash it from her skin, brush it out of her hair before she saw him. Sometimes one of the other tenants was in the bathroom or there wasn't enough hot water, other times he was lounging about the room, annoyed that she wasn't waiting for him, even though he knew what time she finished work.

'I'd have thought you'd know to expect me by now,' he said one day, stretched out on the eiderdown, shoes off, arms behind his head, hair and skin glowing with good looks in the pale-golden sunlight of the late-autumn afternoon.

'I do,' Kitty said, glancing at her alarm clock, 'but my shift goes on until four, and it's not quite quarter past. Give me a minute and I'll be right with you.'

'Couldn't you have got away a bit early? I made an effort for you.'

Kitty grinned, thinking he was joking. The effort he'd made was entirely for the man whose money he hoped to reel in this evening.

'What?' he asked.

'Nothing,' Kitty said, grinning, unaware of the change in his tone. 'Close your eyes and pretend I'm not here. When you open them again, I'll be lovely Kitty, not Kit from the café.'

She didn't see him leap off the bed and she didn't see his open palm close into a fist, but she felt the smack against her ear, and her head, neck and then her body rocked sideways with the force. She was so shocked that she laughed out loud. A high, brittle sound she had never before heard from her own mouth, it echoed inside her head, ringing. The second time he hit her, because she'd laughed, a backhander across her mouth, she stood still in shock, and then, as she edged away, the tears began to flow.

'Stop crying,' he said. 'I can't bloody stand a crying woman.'

She couldn't stop. The tears were involuntary, as was her stance, hanging on to the dressing table with one hand, the other over her mouth, somewhere between an angry dog and a cowering child.

'Kitty, leave off. It was just a smack. Give it a rest.'

He reached out both hands and Kitty didn't know what she was meant to do, move away or move to him. Was he threatening another slap or did he want her?

'What . . . I don't know . . . What did I do?' Her words were stammering, her breathing shallow and unsteady.

Danny dropped his arms then, defeated by her ignorance. He was all contempt, his voice hard. 'If you don't know, love, there's no point my explaining, is there?'

He picked up his wallet and keys, walked out of the room, leaving the door open behind him. She waited as he rounded the landing at the top of the stairs, heard him whistling as he took the steps two at a time as always. Three floors down, the front door creaked back on its hinges and then slammed shut, a shivering silence in its wake. From outside, through the broken sash window that didn't quite open, didn't quite close, she listened to the tip-tap-tap of his toecapped shoes as he walked off down the road, the sound merging with the bus idling at the stop, the chatter of children playing on their way home from school.

After a while Kitty crossed to the door, closed it quietly, her forehead pressing into the chipped paint of the door jamb. She ran her fingernail back and forth over the key in the lock. When she slowly turned the key, she savoured the smoothness of the action as the bolt slid into place. She looked around, trying to work out what she had done wrong. The room had no answers for her. She sat down on the old rug in the middle of the floor. She did not cry. She would need to remember to unlock the door in a bit; he'd hate to have to knock.

When Danny came back, he was in a great mood. He bounded up the stairs and bumped into Ernestine, who was on her way out.

She took a small step back, looking at the bunch of roses in his hand. 'Peace offering?' she asked.

Danny grinned. 'You want to get a life of your own, love. Taking too much of an interest in other people's business might be all right where you lot come from, but we're a bit more civilised here.'

Ernestine raised an eyebrow. 'Civilised? Is that what you call it?'

'I'll call things what I want in my own country, thank you very much. I don't need the likes of you coming over here and—'

Ernestine raised her hand and Danny surprised himself by shutting up. 'I've heard it all before, Mr Nelson. If you don't mind, I have work to go to.'

She clipped past him in her heels and walked smartly down the stairs. Danny watched her go, wondering how she had so easily made him feel suddenly small. She had something of his old man about her, that one. He frowned and shook it off. Kitty would make him feel better.

Danny threw open the door, a wide smile on his face. He handed Kitty the roses, so dark they were almost black. When he leaned in to kiss her, she could smell the beer on his breath, the cigarette he'd just put out. She kissed him back and he held her very tight, crushing the roses between them.

Kitty tried out the line she'd been practising for the past half-hour. 'I'm ever so sorry, Danny.'

He leaned his cheek against hers, spoke quietly. 'What are you sorry for, Kit?' Then he stepped back just a little, put his hand under her chin and lifted her face. He stroked her jaw-line and cheekbone, bent his head again to lay soft nuzzling kisses against the cheek he had slapped.

Her words came slowly. 'I know I look a mess when I get in from work. And you might think the blokes are all over me, but honest, they're just interested in their food. The grease gets in my hair and I don't smell elegant or sophisti-cated like you like, so I'm sorry. I want to be here ready for you, I do.'

He shook his head and she thought for a moment he was going to go for her again, then he stepped back, took the roses from her and put them in the sink. He was whistling as he unwrapped them and poured water into the tallest glass she had, pushing the stems down into it. Kitty thought she would cut the ends of the stems later. She'd meant to get a proper vase but there never seemed to be a moment free. She would put a bit of sugar in the water, they'd be dead in no time otherwise.

He broke off whistling to say, over his shoulder, 'You're as daft as they come sometimes, Kitty Barker, you really are. I'm not fussed about you working. I'm proud my girl wants to pay her way. We're a team, you and me. It's not about your job, not a bit.'

He set the roses down on the scratched old worktop and she hoped they wouldn't topple, shatter the glass, send water all over the floor.

'Try again.' He turned, his face clear and eyes direct. 'Why are you sorry?'

Kitty stared at him, opened her mouth and closed it again. She stuttered, stammered and stopped. She had no idea what to say.

Then Danny burst out laughing, 'My word, your face. I had you there!'

'Wha ...?'

He bounded across the room and spun her around. 'I'm the one who should be sorry, that's why I brought flowers. I don't give a damn about the smell of the fry-ups. I miss you something awful when I'm back in Westmere. I just want to be with you, love. I'm a rotten bastard and I'm sorry. Forgive me?'

And his eyes were so wide, his touch so gentle, his words so sweet that Kitty tumbled into him, her whole self reaching towards him. She still had no idea what she had done wrong. It didn't matter. Danny wanted her now.

Over the next few months, Kitty became accustomed to hiding the stain of a slap beneath a sweep of hair or a thicker layer of powder, long-sleeved blouses to cover the bruises on her arms or wrists. Bruises she felt odd about, both interested and distanced. She was drawn to touching them during the day, feeling the weight of her fingers on a sore point, like touching the brown dent in a bruised apple, a sense that she might go through her skin if she pushed hard enough. She felt thin, brittle.

Danny often told her she was too sensitive, that he was only joking, that she took everything too seriously. Some days, some nights, she did everything right and then he was her Danny, who loved and needed her. Other times nothing she tried made him happy, and as his worry about the need for investor commitment grew deeper, the line between pleasing and angering him became harder to judge. Then touching the bruise became a talisman. Kitty could push against the shaded place and feel the sick-sweet sense of an ache just beneath her skin. In hurting where Danny had hurt, she could feel herself.

Eleven

London, 1956

It was late on a Wednesday evening. Work was easing off with the bad weather and Danny had come up to town early. They had been out for chips and then to the pub for a quick drink. The night was cool and there was a real sense of winter in the air, the smell of coal fires mingling with the acid of the vinegar and aspirin factories. It seemed that the weather in London turned properly cold sooner, the fog was certainly thicker, sickeningly so some nights, when Kitty thought she could almost feel it clogging her nose and throat. Even so, there was a sense of excitement in the air. As if the mischief that took place under cover of darkness in warmer months was rubbing its hands at the thought of the long nights to come, many hours more to play.

For once there was nowhere to go but the house on Corngate Street, no one to please or entice, and both Kitty and Danny felt more relaxed than they had in weeks.

'It'll be grand staying in London come Christmas time, Kit; you've not seen anything like the way they make up the shop windows. We'll go up town and walk round them all. They go to an awful lot of trouble, but you should see how it brings the crowds in. That's what I'll want down in Westmere, sparkling stuff that draws them to have a look and then tempts them through the doors to spend their money.'

He was naming the shops he'd seen the year before and the stories they'd had in their windows, real works of art he said, his arm warm around her waist, and Kitty leaned into him, excited for the future he was talking into being. This was the Danny she'd fallen for at home, all bright eyes and enthusiasm, far from the worried lad he became whenever he thought too much about the nagging need for money, his growing eagerness to get out from under his old man's thumb. With this Danny she could see ahead, imagine them making a life together. She would be the one to help him stay calm when things were difficult, buoy him up when he was down and, one day, celebrate beside him when their hard work came to fruition.

They turned the corner at the far end and Kitty heard a series of barks, followed by a strange, high-pitched yelp and then a whining cry. Danny saw what was happening before she could quite make it out, and he was halfway down the road and on the bloke before she could call him back. Not that she wanted to. A man was laying into a dog; he had the animal by the scruff of the neck with one hand and was beating it with the belt he held in the other. The dog, poor creature, was whimpering and yelping in distress at his feet. Every few licks of the belt the man would stop to get his breath, but instead of running off, the dog would turn, cringing beside its master, abject in its wanting.

Danny grabbed the man around the neck and pulled him off the dog, wrenching the belt from his grasp. Kitty was just on the pair of them when the dog, seeing his master attacked, lurched from his spot on the pavement and, teeth bared, prepared to go for Danny. It was only Kitty's piercing whistle, distracting both Danny and the animal, that gave the older man a chance to pull himself free. Danny stepped back, his hands up to show the dog he wasn't harming his master, and the man, grinning, slowly took back his belt and returned it around his waist.

'Stupid flamin' thing.' The man was drunk. He was telling Danny but also talking to himself, his slurred words both reason and excuse. 'Can't train it, can't get rid of it. Follows me round begging me to pay it attention, won't do a bloody thing it's told no matter how hard I beat it. Daft as a brush, aren't you, Samson, eh? Stupid as a woman and twice as ugly.'

He ran a hand over the creature's muzzle and Kitty wanted to weep watching the dog wince in terror and reach up to the man at the same time, trying to lick his beer-red face, a painful dance of fear and wanting. They walked off down the road and left Kitty and Danny looking after them, the dog's tail curled under its hind low to the ground, the man every inch his master.

Later, when they were in bed and in the slow lull of warm limbs and gentle dozing that Kitty so enjoyed after they had made love, Danny turned into her, pulling her arms around his shoulders, making himself small against her breasts, reaching in. Usually he fell asleep right away afterwards, stretching diagonally across their three-quarter-sized bed, complaining she was too hot or too cold so that she huddled herself against the edge to make way for him, marvelling at his ability to go from ferociously active to out cold in no time. Sometimes, though, a different Danny emerged from the sex, not the man hungry for power, but a boy asking to be held and caressed.

Kitty waited a while, letting him find his way to her, snuffling against her skin like a blind kitten seeking the mother cat's teat, and when he was finally still against her, she asked, 'What is it, love?'

He shook his head, a silent sigh breathed into her skin.

She waited a few moments and tried again, her voice even softer. 'It's all right, Danny, it's going to be all right. We're here now, you and me, we're in our room, our bed.'

He mumbled into her breastbone, 'How'd you know, Kit?'

'I don't, not for sure, but I get that way too sometimes.'

'How d'you mean?' His voice was gentle and Kitty's heart slowed to hear it. She could have whispered like this with him for ever, warm and quiet.

'I feel unsafe, all churned up. Like all the bad things that've ever happened are coming again, only now they're coming from inside.'

She felt Danny's head nod against her chest and his voice was soft, very low. 'My old man was like that for years, like the bloke with the dog. He'd lay into me soon as look at me, right from when I was small. I thought it happened to everyone, you know?'

Kitty gently stroked his shoulder to let him know she was listening, he could go on.

'Then I went to school and I can't even remember what it was, this lad was after me to do something – play the wag or smash someone's window, we were only kids – but I said to him, "Oh no, I can't. My dad'd give us such a belt." The lad looked at me strange, like I'd, I don't know, Kit . . . ' His voice petered out.

'Like you'd told a dirty secret?'

'Yeah. Just like. Only until then I hadn't even known it was meant to be a secret or that it was dirty. I thought everyone got a thrashing whenever they annoyed their old man. I mean, we all got a smack around the ear sometimes and we got the strap or the cane at school like everyone did, but I was nine or ten before I worked out that there was only me and one or two other kids who'd been thrashed within an inch of our lives. And more than once. Much more.'

Kitty kissed the top of his head, the smell of him making her want to weep, hair oil and aftershave and cigarette smoke. 'My mum used to say, "I'll beat the living daylights out of you."'

'But she didn't do it, Kit, did she?'

'No. She'd never have done it.'

'Nor my mum neither.'

'Oh, my Danny.' She stroked his hair, her words more breath than sound, and felt his body shake. Danny never cried; she couldn't imagine what it would take to make him cry. He laughed, he raged, he was bored, he could be wickedly sharp if he thought she was being dense, but sorrow seemed like an emotion too far for him. The few times he'd talked to her of being little, the twice before he'd begun a story like this, he'd always backed off, the words refusing to come, somehow angry with her for letting him feel so much.

He started speaking again. 'My mum, she just stood back and let him lay into me. I used to think she was scared he'd have a go at her, but I never saw it. You know, the only time I saw her get between him and the target of his fists was when he tried to belt our dog.'

He reached away and unrolled himself from the small space he had made against her, and even in the moment he was stretching out his spine she missed him there, missed her arms around him, holding him tight.

'Bloody hell, pass us a fag, Kit,' he said.

She reached for the packet and the lighter that sat on the bedside table. Danny lit both of their cigarettes, and they lay on their backs in the bed, sagging into the middle, small red lights glowing bright against their faces, dim again at arm's length.

'I can't even remember where we were. I don't think it was Westmere, not our beach. We might have been at the reservoir, the old man used to like going there sometimes. Mum'd make a packet of sandwiches and a thermos and we'd drive over. She'd sit in the car with her knitting or a magazine and he'd take me for a walk. He was always trying to get me to take an interest in the birds, the trees and reeds and whatnot, but I didn't have it in me to tell one thing with a beak from another, nor the different leaves – honest, Kit, they all look the same to me. To my mum too, and I think that riled him even more, that I took after her. He wanted me to be his lad, his son.

'Anyway, the dog took off. Blue, he was called. Half retriever, half God knows what, a soppy big old mongrel and I loved the sight of him. He'd caught scent of a hare or a rabbit and off he went. The old man went mad, whistling and yelling for him. It went on for half an hour or more and I was trailing after my father and trying to call out for the bloody dog as well. I knew what was coming, I just wanted the dog to come back and get in the car with me, warm and muddy and wet.' He handed Kitty his almost finished cigarette to put out. 'That smell of wet dog fur never leaves you.'

He was quiet for a moment, and when he went on, his voice was even softer, slower. 'He came back eventually. We were by the car and that dog came bounding back like he'd never been away, tail wagging, tongue hanging out from running so damn fast and his mouth had all blood round it, so he'd caught something all right. When the old man saw the blood, he went mad. Lunged for the dog and had his belt off so fast. I'd only ever seen it from in front of him, with his one hand round my neck, the other on his belt. This time I saw how it was done. There's a real skill to holding a creature so it can't run and getting your belt off one-handed, you know. A real skill.'

Kitty held her breath as she waited for what was coming

next. She heard the rain begin pattering on the window pane, a grey day tomorrow, the slow and steady tick of her alarm clock.

'And what do you know? My mum was out of that car like a shot, threw herself between my dad and the dog. It must have taken the old man every ounce of strength to hold back, but he did. He stopped himself beating the breath out of that dog because my mother begged him not to. Begged him not to hurt the dog. The flamin' dog, Kitty.'

Danny didn't say any more and Kitty didn't ask him to.

Twelve

Westmere, June

Lucy went up to her room as soon as they all got home from the funeral. Sara knew her niece was avoiding her and decided to let her be. Tomorrow she would ask her to come for a run, make her explain why it had taken her so long to share the note. And after that, she'd have to find a way to explain it to Beth. They were all exhausted, now was not the time to get into an argument about Lucy coming to Sara first with her secrets, yet again.

Lucy was not sleeping. She was taking photos of herself, her face in shadow, her body a corpse beneath the sheet. She took a few dozen before the form was right, playing with the edit until her shape was illuminated, defined.

She shared the final images in her social media stories with the repeated caption Look at me. Open your eyes.

In the morning, she hoped to wake to a slew of hearts, a forest of little fires, disembodied hands applauding her from the ether. The praise of strangers cushioning her from fear closer to home. What she actually woke to was Sara storming into her room just half an hour later.

She was holding up her own mobile with Lucy's images shining out. Her whisper was harsh. 'Delete these bloody photos, Lucy.'

'What?' Lucy mumbled.

Sara carefully closed the door and turned on the light, ignoring Lucy's groan.

'The ones in your story. Delete them. We've only just been allowed to have a funeral for Kitty and you go and share photos of yourself looking like a corpse laid out on the bed? How do you think that makes me feel? What about when your mum sees them?'

'She won't, she doesn't understand the internet.'

'Don't be such a bloody teenager, of course she does. Just get rid of them. Now.'

Sara waited while Lucy deleted the photos from the app and then from the phone itself.

'I'm sorry, Sara,' she finally volunteered.

'About the photos or the note?'

'Both. Everything.' Lucy's whisper was a wail, 'I'm sorry I'm such a mess.'

Sara shook her head. She was incapable of maintaining her anger in the face of her niece's upset. She sat on the bed and pulled the girl to her, thinking how small Lucy seemed, so different to the cool, sharp mask she had adopted over the past year.

Lucy cried and mumbled into Sara's shoulder, words stumbling out in half-sentences broken by sobs. 'I saw Kitty and then I saw the envelope and I knew she was dead. I didn't want it to be real. I've never seen a dead person before and it was ... I felt really mean, Sara, but I didn't want to be with Kitty like that. I didn't like it. I didn't like her.' Her face morphed into the tragedy mask of a heartbroken three-year-old, all tears and snot and her mouth slowly twisting, her jaw involuntarily widening to let out the howl she'd held in all through the previous weeks.

Sara sat with her until the muffled sobs subsided a little, then she quietly said, 'But that doesn't explain why you took the envelope. Or why you didn't tell any of us later.'

'I knew people would go through Kitty's stuff and I thought it was private, whatever was in the envelope. So I took it. I meant to show it to you or Mum, but then that night I thought I'd be in trouble with the police, or the coroner or—'

'Let's just concentrate on the trouble you're in with me, OK?'

'All right, but you didn't make it easy. You and Mum were so upset, and everyone has been so angry with Kitty – I hate that you've all been angry with her.'

'I do too,' Sara said. 'But I also hate that she chose to leave us and didn't even call to say goodbye, didn't give me a chance to persuade her not to do it.'

'Which is probably why she didn't call to say goodbye.'

'Yes, Luce, I do get that.'

'So I knew you'd be furious and it just got later and later and then with the inquest and everything it felt like I'd left it too late and . . . I screwed up. I know.'

Sara sighed. What could she say? Lucy had made a mistake and admitted it; there was nowhere left to go.

'Are you going to tell Mum?'

Sara frowned. 'Tell her what Kitty wrote or that you didn't tell us about it?'

'Either. Both.'

'I'll have to, somehow.'

'She's going to be really annoyed that I told you, not her.'

'Yes, she is. Thanks for that.' There was a pause and then Sara asked, 'Lucy? There wasn't anything else with the note?'

Lucy shook her head. 'No. Promise.'

Thirteen

Newcastle, 2004

Newcastle was everything Sara had hoped for and more. It was so much bigger than Westmere, but with none of the fuss and tat put on for tourists that she'd seen in her few trips up to London. She had grown up with an ever-present knowledge of the coastline at home, now she homed in on the Tyne for her bearings. However lost she found herself in the first few days, marking out a new geography, the river would always be there eventually, down a hill, down the steps, down to the water. Even so, losing her way occasionally felt like a badge of honour, it gave her a sense of pride to think she had been brave enough to take a turn that could be a shortcut or might go nowhere at all.

She chose to learn her new city on foot. In walking the city into her memory, her body changed with the new topography: calf muscles became stronger, waist tighter, eyes wider to take in all the new possibilities. She began to see her height not as a drawback, but as a boon, striding new streets and enjoying her body as she did. She quickly discovered that for the few moments she felt homesick for a long line of horizon, there was the sea, Whitley Bay and an ice cream a bus ride away.

By the end of her first term, she had traded in her place in student accommodation for a shared house with six new mates crammed into four bedrooms. Two of them took the little box rooms and the others divided the vast double rooms with screens and pinned-up sheets. They were all still teenagers, all in their first year. Tony was almost twenty and had come home to the north-east to study after eighteen months backpacking around Europe and India, Yulia was the youngest at just seventeen, a maths prodigy with a Finnish father and Geordie mother. It was Yulia who provided violin accompaniment to their late-night drinking sessions. Her parents only lived over in Jesmond, but their wild-child daughter had long outgrown both the parental home and their patience. The six flatmates developed separate lives in their various courses and came home to share stories of hope and despair, filtered through an adequate supply of cheap drugs and drink. By the middle of the second term, Sara and Yulia were also sharing a bed.

There was no coming-out drama, no big fuss. Yulia had told her parents she was queer in her early teens, Sara had assumed she was probably bisexual since she'd first imagined herself with someone else, but in the same way that none of the boys at school in Westmere had interested her much, neither had any of the girls. Yulia was exciting, demanding and quite often draining. Their relationship was exactly as thrilling, fraught and explosive as Sara had dreamed a passionate love affair might be, and after two months of secretive meetings with Mark, it was a special joy to be open and public in their desire.

Yulia and Sara were being exceptionally public in their desire as they walked home from the local pub, hand in hand, eyes to eyes, hip to hip, when Mark stepped out of his hire car and called Sara's name. He had hoped to make a grand entrance, demand she reply to the calls she'd been ignoring, but three hours of waiting in the car in the cold and his shock at seeing her arm around an elfin beauty as opposed to the gauche northern lad he'd been expecting made him stumble and stutter.

'Sara, what the . . . ? Sara! Shit. Christ.'

He came to a halt in front of the two young women, righted himself and glared at them both. The sodium street light behind the girls bounced off his forehead, and for the first time, Sara noticed his receding hairline. She took in the softening angle of his jaw, the way that even pulling himself up to his full height could not disguise the signs of ageing she knew he hated. He stood in front of them blustering his need to hear from her, his demands masked as concern, his insistence she tell him what was going on, and she suddenly saw him as Tim must have seen him. It was not an attractive sight.

Yulia held out her hand to him, speaking in her soft Geordie accent. 'I'm Yulia, Sara's lover.'

Sara saw him take in the tattoo that ran from Yulia's thumb to her inner arm, the tattoo that moved when she played the violin. For now it was exposed only as far as the cuff of her jacket, but in that moment Sara saw a shift in Mark, from anger to interest. She noticed that when he took Yulia's hand his grip was gentle, his eyes direct.

'I'm Mark, I'm Sara's . . .'

He turned to Sara, waiting for her to finish the sentence, and she shook her head. Yulia laughed, pulling her hand away, not at all taken in by Mark's change of tone. 'I'll leave you to sort out who you are. You can wake me later,' she said to Sara, adding 'if you want' with a cheery grin, and ran along the street and up the steps to their front door, a bounce in her step. Yulia loved a drama, but only if it was her own.

'Get in the car,' Mark ordered.

'Piss off.'

'Sorry, no, I didn't mean it like that. It's cold. It's bloody freezing up here.'

'I like it.'

Mark took in her long charity-shop coat, 'At least you're dressed for it, but I'm really not, so please, sorry, get in the car and we can have a chat. Catch-up?'

Sara sighed but followed him to the car.

For the next ten minutes she listened as Mark complained. She hadn't been in touch, she'd worried him hugely, he had no idea what had happened to her, he'd been forced to come all the way up here to check on her.

'Why the hire car?' she asked.

He had the grace to look embarrassed, 'Angela pays attention to the mileage on mine. And hers.'

Sara wanted to say of course she did, it was a way to keep tabs on him, find out what he was doing, who he was shagging. She let him go on, his expectations of her, his idea of what was going to happen when she went away, how none of it had gone according to those plans.

She was taken aback. Mark hadn't said any of this to her before; in fact he had been delighted when he knew, right from the start, that she was going away in September.

She shook her head. 'You always knew I was leaving home. You said it was good.'

'It was, it is. You're living your life, I just … I want to be with you, Sara.' His eyes were pleading, his hands grasping. 'I didn't expect to feel this way, but I thought, well, maybe we could …'

Sara stared at him, 'Could what? Are you leaving Angela? Leaving your kids?'

'No, of course not, I just—'

She shook her head in disbelief. 'You just thought you

88

could have me on the side, when you wanted. We never said anything about having a future together, never.'

Mark tried another tack. 'You do look amazing, you know, Sara. Getting out of Westmere has done you a load of good.'

Sara smiled. She'd let her hair grow longer and had stopped straightening it since she'd been with Yulia, she'd begun to find a dress sense of her own, somewhere between charity-shop chic and unapologetic Amazon. She really did feel she was becoming herself, whoever that woman might be. That self was no longer impressed by compliments from Mark Nelson.

'Thanks, Mark.'

She said nothing more, surprised at herself for putting the onus of conversation on him.

'So you're gay?' He spoke out of what was for him an uncomfortable silence.

Sara shrugged. 'Does it matter?'

'No, but I didn't know. You never said anything about that.'

'It wasn't relevant. And I'm not sure anyway. Bisexual maybe. Probably. I don't care, I don't need it to have a name. And it's got nothing to do with you.'

Mark ran a hand over his face. When he looked back at her, he was smiling.

'What?' she asked.

'Oh, you know.' He shrugged. 'Every red-blooded man's fantasy . . . '

'Seriously? Yulia would eat you alive. And not in a good way.'

Sara got out of the car. Yulia was many things, but patient was not one of them. Mark might find the idea of her fury exciting, but Sara had seen it in action and Mark would need a full windscreen if he was to drive away safely.

She leaned against the door, frowning. 'Look, I'm sorry

you came all this way and I'm sorry I'm not what you wanted. Or I don't want to be what you wanted. But you have to go, Mark. I'll see you later, when I come home. We can have coffee or something. Maybe. Bye.'

She closed the door quietly and stepped away, forcing herself to walk casually the few hundred yards to their house, not to run up the steps, not to slam the front door behind her.

Much later that night, after Yulia had told the story to their incredulous flatmates over several bottles of wine, mercilessly mocking Mark's behaviour until Sara challenged her with 'Why are you so surprised that someone fancies me that much?' After they had made love and laughed it off, with Yulia asleep and breathing lightly beside her, Sara lay awake, annoyed with herself. She was not sorry that Mark had driven so far, she was not sorry she had not been in touch with him, she was not at all sorry that she was not able to be what he had dreamed she was. She was angry. And she wished that anger had come more readily than apology.

She had an opportunity to try out the alternative a fortnight later. Walking home from a late lecture, the sun long gone and a biting Arctic wind whipping her hair into her eyes, she stopped to pin back the offending strands. As she paused, she turned and looked back along the quiet road. She'd taken a shortcut home. This road was long and mostly deserted, old and narrow. The two-up, two-down houses on either side were boarded up, slated for demolition, anti-development posters she recognised from university noticeboards taped to the doors and pasted across the metal-shuttered windows.

Usually she went the longer way around if she was by herself. Much as she was in love with her new city, excited by all it had to offer, she was still wary of walking alone in the dark. She strode down this street without a care when she was with

Yulia, but now she felt uneasy, the empty houses like walled-up lives waiting on their last breath. The few occasions she'd walked here alone she had always made sure to do so in broad daylight. Tonight she was already late. Yulia was making a special meal to celebrate some Finnish spring festival and the menu had sounded delicious when she had explained it at the weekend. It was also very complicated and Sara was needed as sous chef, so the shortcut had to be taken.

She turned back in the right direction and yelped in shock. Mark was standing directly in front of her.

'I didn't mean to scare you.'

He was smiling, as if his presence on this street was perfectly normal, as if they'd arranged to meet here. He was holding out a massive bunch of spring flowers. Sara stepped back, and even then she could still smell the sweet, sickly scent of narcissus.

'Jesus, Mark, what do you want?'

'To apologise.' He lowered the flowers, hung his head. 'I'm so sorry, Sara, I shouldn't have surprised you before.'

'You bloody well shouldn't be surprising me now.' She spat the words, furious, and happy to allow her anger out this time. 'If you wanted to apologise, you should have sent a card. Go home, Mark.'

'No.' He stood in front of her, too close. He was not shamefaced now.

Sara could smell his aftershave. Back in the summer, she had thought she might miss it, a smell that had been specifically Mark: cedarwood and something a little citrusy. The scent had settled deep in her brain as a sign of an interesting man, a man nothing like their unhappy, grieving father or the boys at school or the building-site blokes in Mark's company. Now it was too close, the cedarwood cloying, the citrus burning, clashing with the too-strong narcissus, too early for so far north. She could smell Mark's breath too, coffee and decades of red wine, impossible to mask with mints. She could feel his hands on her. The flowers were on the ground. He pulled her to him, sharp and fast, and she remembered how different he was.

Yulia was strong, her arms and legs finely muscled, her breasts almost too large for her small frame, but because she was shorter than Sara, when they held each other Sara allowed herself to feel a little protective, her height and larger build encompassing Yulia's slight body. She had never said this to Yulia, of course, who would probably have laughed and challenged her to an arm wrestle. Even so, she liked the feeling of looking after, caring for. She also knew, her body knew, that she had enjoyed being held by Mark in the same way. Summer felt a very long time ago now, but her body had a different memory. Her body felt the extra warmth of his and it was intensely disturbing to be here, in this hold, her body not disliking it, her mind furious, her heart racing, her self pushing away.

Sara knew this was not an embrace. It was different and shocking because he was holding her and she did not want to be held. Her body almost yielded and suddenly Sara was glad of the coffee stink of his breath, the cloying perfume on his skin, the smell of narcissus, because they reminded her that she did not want to be here and did not want him to hold her.

She turned into him more surely now. He was murmuring pleasure and his heart was pounding against his ribs, she could feel it as he held her tighter still. He was bending his head down, his lips pursing to kiss her, and she twisted her head away, forcing him to kiss her hair instead. He was groaning now, trying to push his erection against her and as she leaned away to get a better angle he whispered that he loved her when she was a tease, always had.

Then she brought her head round in a raging burst, smacking his cheekbone and then his pursing lips so hard she could hear his teeth crack against each other. Mark growled in pain. As he tried to grab her again, she kneed him in the groin, feeling the rush right through her body at the moment her knee caught his balls and brought him to the ground.

She stood over him, writhing on the empty street, and her words were a torrent of rage. 'I don't want to see you. I don't want your flowers. I didn't say you could hold me. I didn't say you could kiss me. Leave me alone.'

Sara jumped around him and raced the rest of the way home. She was flying, she was roaring, she was thrilled with her anger and her action, and underneath all of that, she was scared. Mostly, though, she was really bloody delighted with herself for not saying sorry.

Fourteen

London, 1956

The build-up to Christmas meant that more potential investors were in town, more reasons for Danny to show off the
gorgeous girl on his arm and for Kitty to be the beautiful
attraction, the tempting bauble he dangled before them.
Many more reasons for Danny to be seething by the time they
reached the south side of the Thames. That night, a fortnight
before Christmas, he grabbed her just as they got back into
the house at the railway end of Corngate Street. He shoved
the door closed, and before Kitty could whisper to him to be
quiet, they didn't want to wake Mrs Kavanagh, he reached
for her arm and yanked it high above her head, pushing her
back against the hall wall.

'Danny, what—' but his mouth was against hers, shutting her up.

He kissed her with such force that she couldn't kiss back;
there was nothing to do but receive the pushing of his face
into hers, their teeth clashing, his tongue probing her mouth.
One arm above her head, the other pinned between her body
and his, Kitty's shoulders were pushed into the tired plaster
of the wall, her hips jammed against the dirty old wainscot,

the thin wooden ledge where the wainscot met the tired wallpaper jabbing into her back.

He pulled away just enough to rest his heavy head against hers, then he whispered with his mouth right against her ear, his breath full of the night's wine and brandy, 'You're too bloody good at this game, girl. Too bloody good at it by half.'

'But I don't know—'

Again she tried to ask what he meant, again he shut her up. This time he clamped his free hand over her mouth, and now she tasted the sweat from fingers that had formed a clenched fist as he barrelled home, smelled tobacco from his roll-ups and the faint scent of the hair oil he'd used before they went out. He shook his head and groaned and she held her breath. She stood, pushed hard against the wall in the hall, and understood that she was here and now and she was also thinking ahead to somewhere else, to a time and place where this wasn't happening. She was in this night and she was on Christmas Day.

Her parents' guest house was always overheated at Christmas time; they prided themselves on their few winter guests never having to complain about the heating, never having to ask for an extra blanket, another hot-water bottle. Kitty might travel down to Westmere in a polo neck, but within ten minutes of her getting in the door her mother would be asking why she was all covered up. In a quiet, careful part of her mind, Kitty took note. From here she could watch herself and make sensible choices, like tempting Danny's hand away from her throat. She knew that blouses might hide marks on her arms, but she was not a button-to-the-collar girl, never had been.

Danny was whispering urgently in her ear, 'God help me, I get so jealous, Kit. I want you all for myself. I know I'm an idiot, I just can't help it. I get in such a rage and it's so damn hard to hold it in all night.'

'But Danny, you want them to look at me like that. That's the plan, isn't it?' She was almost laughing now, her fear washed away by his need, back inside herself.

He shook his head. 'Yes, only I don't like it, I don't like it a blind bit.'

'Flippin' heck, I'm the one who doesn't like it. I do it for you, love, for your work.'

'Promise?' he whispered. 'Promise me faithfully? I need you to be my girl.'

Kitty melted then, melted into him, the last of her fear draining away, and all she felt was his upset and her ability to soothe it. Pinned to the wall by Danny's longing, she soaked in his need. It was something, the power to be the one he needed, the one he wanted, the one he was scared to lose. She had something.

'You make me mad, Kitty, you really do.'

Kitty edging them upstairs and Danny's hand on her cheek, almost a tap, almost a slap.

'You drive me crazy, Kit, my lovely girl.'

Fingers twisting into a pinch on her upper arm.

'God, but I can't get enough of you.'

The pinch now a punch, light, almost playful.

'All mine, Kit, all mine.'

The day before Christmas Eve, Kitty came back from her shift to find a note pushed under her door. It was from Ernestine, asking if she'd like to join her for a drink. She turned the note over in her hand, wondering if she could. Danny was down in Westmere for his family's big Christmas party – his mother would have his guts for garters if he didn't turn up – and Kitty was due back at her parents' guest house early on Christmas Eve afternoon.

Kitty frowned at the note, written in Ernestine's beautiful

copperplate writing. She'd love to go out for a drink, it was Christmas after all, but Danny had turned up unexpectedly before now and he always hated it when she was out, treated it as if she'd disappointed him on purpose and either sulked for half the night or took it out in nastier ways. Kitty had learned it was easier just to stop in. At least she thought it was, but then the last time it had happened he'd been quite different. She'd come in a bit merry from a night at the pictures and a quick port and lemon down the road with Ernestine, and as she put her hand on the door to her room, she had a sudden knowledge that Danny was there, waiting. The light was off and she could see the little red glow of his cigarette from where he sat on the bed on the other side of the room.

'Danny?' she asked, worried.

'You're all right, darling,' he answered.

As she was lifting her hand to flick on the light, he spoke quietly from the dark. 'Come over here, lovely girl.'

She crossed the room, slipping off her shoes as she did. The port and lemon turning in her stomach, her breath held. He'd burned her once before with his cigarette, swore blind it was an accident, though she hadn't been sure. She wasn't sure now.

'I'd have stopped in if—'

He cut her off with a laugh. 'You're your own woman, Kit, that's one of the things I like about you.'

Kitty didn't know what to make of it. He reached over to put out his cigarette in the heavy glass ashtray on the bedside table and stretched out for her hand in the semi-darkness. Danny pulled her to the bed, laid her down beside him and kissed her slowly and softly for so long it felt like he was wooing her all over again. In her hunger for him, for his lips on her mouth, his hands on her body, Kitty forgot how unpredictable she knew him to be, all she knew was how he

97

made her feel, awake and alive and as if all was right with the world.

Later, after the kissing, after making love, after the gentle slide into each other, curled as one, she whispered, 'That was different.'

She could feel his slow smile against her forehead, his lips forming a kiss. 'I'd hate to be predictable, Kit,' he said, his breath warm and whisky-scented against her hairline. 'Best keep you on your toes, eh, girl?'

She remembered that night as she stood there holding Ernestine's note. How pleased he had sounded with himself when he said 'best keep you on your toes'.

Two hours later, Kitty was on her third whisky mac and Ernestine was slowly working her way through the version of rum punch she'd concocted from the glasses of white rum, dark rum and bitter lemon she'd ordered and the orange she had bought especially at the market in The Cut.

They were drinking at a pub near the Elephant, much further from Corngate Street than the dozen or more around the station, but it was somewhere Ernestine felt more comfortable, 'I prefer not to be the only one in a room if I can help it,' she'd explained to Kitty.

The White Lion, run by two queer blokes, welcomed blacks, Irish, women drinking alone and even dogs, as long as they weren't what the landlords called 'soppy little snivelling lapdogs'. Kitty thought the landlords were awfully tough for a pair of poofs, not at all like the queer couple who had a guest house on one of the side streets in Westmere. Her mother had warned Kitty and her brother – Geoff especially – away from that house when they were little, telling them not to talk to the two gentlemen who owned the place, and certainly not to engage with any of their guests. Obedient as ever, Geoff thought no more of it and went a different route down to the bus stop, but Kitty took her mother's prohibition as a challenge and spent a good few months staking out the corner of the street to get a glimpse of the danger lurking behind the dark-blue door with the shiny brass letter box and glorious orange and yellow chrysanthemums in blue-glazed pots that ran up either side of the front steps.

Mostly the only people she saw were men in plain suits like her father's when he went to visit the bank manager, they parked their nondescript cars and walked up the steps with their heads down and suitcases tightly held. Her waiting was finally repaid when a smartly dressed man pulled up in a green sports car and ran around to open the passenger door, his shoe taps clipping the cobbles of the side street as he did so. He opened the door and out stepped a lady who looked the spit of Lauren Bacall. When they got to the top of the steps, the man rang the bell and the lady turned to look along the lane. The door opened and then, just before she went in, the lady waved at Kitty, who was ten years old and staring in wide-eyed admiration at her golden shoes and golden dress. Kitty held that image of the lovely shiny lady in her mind for months, the kind of lady she wanted to be one day. It was several years later, remembering what she'd seen, that she understood that the gentleman who'd opened the car door with such panache had also been a lady.

Kitty told Ernestine the story of the two ladies and the sparkling shoes and the sports car and they decided they might as well make a night of it; it was Christmas after all and they ordered another round of drinks.

Back in Corngate Street, Ernestine invited Kitty to her room for tea. Kitty loved Ernestine's room. It was smaller than hers but so much more comfortable. Ernestine was not only earning less than she'd expected, she also sent money home every month to help her family with the younger children, yet somehow her room was warm and inviting. There were cushions made from old clothes bought at a jumble sale and stuffed with older clothes cut into ribbons, and crocheted throws on everything – the bed, the two chairs, and even two hanging on the wall.

Kitty ran her hand along the throw on the bed and asked, 'Is this what your house in Jamaica looked like?'

Ernestine shook her head as she poured out their tea. 'My mother's house is light and bright, windows open on the yard. There are plenty of flowers, she grows her own vegetables and herbs. Here, well, I don't mean to be one of those people who complains about English weather all the time—'

'I don't see why not,' Kitty laughed, settling in the old arm-chair. 'English people do. Danny moans about the weather most days.'

Ernestine brought over their tea. 'I'm sure he does,' she said lightly.

Kitty looked at her friend. 'Don't start.'

'It's no good, Kitty. I have something I have to say.'

Kitty pulled the cushion out from behind her back and held it to her chest, a barrier to her heart. 'Go on then, spit it out.'

'I am fond of you, Kitty. We are friends, I think? Good friends?' Kitty nodded and Ernestine continued, 'You under-stand that I am a few years older than you, I have had a few more years around men.'

Kitty started to open her mouth to make a joke about the polite and strait-laced Ernestine having been 'around men' but thought better of it as she took in her friend's expres-sion. 'Go on.'

Ernestine took a sip of her tea and then she started. 'It is hard for me, Kitty, to see you wasting your time on a lad like Danny. Hear me out. You're clever and bright and you have a lovely figure, very pretty face. You come from good people,' she held up her hand to stop Kitty's protests, 'even if yes, your town is terribly boring and there is so much more you could do with your life. I've taken it all in. Westmere is no longer on my list of great English seaside destinations.' She smiled, took a deep breath and went on, 'You are not me, Kitty, you do not have to make the best of it. You do not have to take a small and damp room in a terrible part of town where everything is dirty and falling down, where you have to cross the street to avoid tramps or drunks or worse—'

'It's not that bad,' Kitty interrupted.

'It is and you know it is. The only reason you do it at all is for him.'

'For Danny?' Kitty answered, irritated, 'Why not? He's ambitious, excited about his life, our life.'

Ernestine raised an eyebrow and Kitty wanted to laugh at how teacherly her face was, how serious, but Ernestine was not joking. 'You may say "our life", but where is the engagement ring? The proposal? I'm your friend, Kitty, I don't judge you, but I do have to ask, what's in this for you?'

'I'll tell you what's in it for me,' Kitty snapped, hurt and angry. 'Someone with some gumption. You and your mates off the boat, you're here, you're doing something with your lives. I know it's tough for you, honest I do, but you're giving it a go. You're all giving it a go. You know I was telling you that Danny has a party at home? How his mum wanted him to be there?' Ernestine nodded and Kitty went on, 'Well, that party happens every year in Westmere and every year my parents don't get an invitation. They're not the great and the good. My dad is fine with it,' she was stumbling over her words as she warmed up to her story, 'but it's never been enough for my mum. She's always said she wasn't interested in a do like that, but she'd love it, she'd love to be invited, just once.

'When I was a girl, she wanted to buy the house next door, knock the two into one and make our place a proper hotel, with a lounge bar and everything. There'd have been loads more business, but my dad wouldn't have a bit of it. My father's got no ambition and it's my mother's life that's been stifled.' Kitty shook her head. 'My dad used to say I was too much like my mum, that's why we fought like cat and dog. I couldn't see it when I was at home, but I can see it better now. You're right, Danny's not easy. And I don't have any promises, no ring, no proposal. But maybe that's the price I have to pay for a lad who dreams big, who wants more than the path marked out for him. At the very least, I'm not going to repeat my mother's mistakes. My father is a good, kind man, but their life ... it's nothing, Ernestine. And that scares me more than anything, giving in to a life like that.'

Ernestine sat quietly, letting Kitty's words ring around her room. She waited until Kitty was sitting back in her chair, her flushed cheeks a little less red. When she spoke, it was in a quiet but firm voice.

'There's no guarantee Danny will give you a better life.'

Kitty smiled, grateful to her friend for her care, no matter what. 'I know, but he is a way out for me. You did it, you took the only way out you could. You're battling every flamin' day when people say bloody awful things and you can't even get a job you're properly qualified for—'

'I know how hard it is for me, Kitty,' Ernestine said sharply, her quiet words holding back none of the truth.

'And I want more too,' Kitty said. 'I'm not as smart as you, I was breaking my neck to leave school. I have to find my exciting life alongside a bloke who's prepared to graft for it.'

'And when he hurts you? Is it also worth it when he hurts you?' Ernestine asked, her fingers lightly touching the bruises on Kitty's arm, her tone unambiguous.

'He loves me,' Kitty said, as if Ernestine had asked a different question.

102

Fifteen

Westmere and London, 1956

Kitty went home just for Christmas Eve and Christmas Day, citing her job as the reason Danny was taking her back to London straight after they'd had their dinner.

'It's the sales, Mum, you know what it's like.'

Her mother shrugged. 'Can't remember the last time I went up to town for the sales. More bother than it's worth if you ask me, all that pushing and shoving. London's not all it's cracked up to be, no matter you might be breaking your neck to get back to it.'

Kitty's mother was torn between hurt and worry. She'd seen that Kitty was subdued, compliant almost, and yet determined to head off right after their dinner. They stood at the kitchen worktop preparing the vegetables. The turkey had been in the oven for three hours already and the giblets were simmering on the stove. The windows were covered in condensation, and from the guests' sitting room Kitty could hear the sound of Geoff and their father joining in a game of cards with the sad regulars who came to Westmere every year for Christmas, nothing better to do with their special day.

'It's not that bad, Mum. I'll stay for the washing-up, that's the worst bit of the day anyway.'

Her mother grunted assent, and as a fleeting look of disappointment crossed her face, Kitty felt a rare pang of genuine warmth towards her.

'Come on, leave the sprouts for a minute and give us a cuddle.'

But Kitty's mother was not one to show her vulnerability to her own husband, let alone the daughter who thought she was so much better than her own family that she needn't spend Christmas evening with them.

She shook Kitty off. 'Don't be soft. I'm sure you'll be happier up in London than with us anyway. Let me get on. You know it's no good for your dad's stomach if he has his tea too late, not when it's as rich as all this.'

Kitty tried once more. 'Honest, it's just that the station will be heaving tomorrow. With everyone coming up for the sales, my boss needs me and we're promised a bonus for the day.'

'Best to be where you're needed, Kit,' her mother said, carving a cross into the stem of another sprout, her words as sharp as her knife. As Kitty gave up and turned back to the mountain of potatoes, her mother added under her breath, 'We all like to be needed.'

Kitty was telling the truth about her boss needing her in for the Boxing Day shift, but the extra work wasn't her only reason for heading back early. Danny had a prospective investor lined up, someone in from America.

'The Yanks think we're all like bloody Churchill, kowtowing to them left, right and centre. We'll show him another side of London life, none of your stuffy Westminster nonsense. We'll give him a proper night out. Throw in a bit of your English-rose charm and he'll be begging to come in with us.'

'I'm not sure I count as that,' Kitty said, worried he was expecting too much of her.

'Then work on it,' he'd said sharply. 'I'll pick you up by the weighing machine on the front. Which reminds me, don't eat too much Christmas dinner, don't want to spoil your figure.'

When Kitty came downstairs to kiss her parents goodbye, Geoff surprised her by offering to walk her to the front. She couldn't very well say no, so she left her mother with a kiss, told her father she didn't need the few bob he offered and let Geoff carry her little overnight case down the hill.

Geoff launched in the minute the door was closed behind them, the dusty plastic Christmas wreath banging against the door knocker. 'I don't like this, Kitty, I'm worried about you.'

'You used to complain I was lazy, now you're annoyed I'm going back to work?'

'I don't mean that. I'm glad you have a job, I just hope you keep your pay safe.'

'What are you on about?'

Geoff stopped. The sea lay cold and grey below them. Kitty looked at her watch. They had five minutes to get down to the front. Danny hated to be kept waiting, but Geoff wasn't moving.

'For God's sake, Geoff, what?'

He shook his head and put down her bag, reaching for her hand. Before she could stop him, he had pushed up the sleeve of her coat and her jumper beneath, his hand tight on her wrist as he turned it over. Even in the street light, the bruises on the inside of her arm were obvious.

'This.'

'Like I told Mum, it was a bloke in the caff. Stupid bugger grabbed me as I was hurrying past, too keen on Mildred's bubble and squeak by half.'

Geoff looked as if he might cry, and Kitty's stomach lurched.

'How about the bruise on the back of your neck? The one that looks like you were pinched there, and damn hard at that? What about the ones on your upper arms? What about those marks, Kitty? Is the whole of bloody London that desperate for a cup of tea?'

'No.' She shook her head, caught, stuck. 'I—'

'We know it's him, Kitty. Mum, Dad, we all know it's him. You're bloody lucky I stopped the old man last night, he was all ready to go off and crash that party and beat the living daylights out of Danny flamin' Nelson. I've half a mind to do it myself, right now, when he comes to meet you.'

Kitty could feel herself burning, the horror of her family knowing, the impossibility of making them understand. She was also shocked that anyone might hurt Danny, least of all on her behalf. Somewhere in that tangle of emotion there was also a sense of pride, joy that her family cared. All her feelings, contradictory and simultaneous, along with the absurdity of her gentle father or her quiet, serious brother lifting a hand to a man like Danny Nelson. She wanted to cry at their care, laugh at the absurdity. Shame won and she let her body take her away from the truth.

Kitty picked up her suitcase, pushed Geoff aside and ran off down the steps to the front, breathing hard to stop herself crying. Geoff called something after her, but she didn't hear, didn't want to hear. She kept running and arrived breathless and almost giddy just as Danny pulled up. She didn't even give him time to turn off the engine; just threw her bag into the back and dived into the passenger seat, wrapping her arms around him.

'Now that's a nice welcome,' he said, grinning under her hail of kisses.

'I missed you so much. It's all so airless here, bloody Westmere.' She waved ahead of them to the pier, 'Look at

106

it, shut up and dark on the one evening most people would rather be out, anywhere but sitting at home with the same lot year after year, stuffed full of the same awful dinner everyone's had the whole country over and now slowly dying in front of the telly.'

'There it is,' he said, still smiling, putting the car into gear and heading back to the main street that led away from the front.

'What?'

'The whole truth. Admit it, some of that lovely welcome was really because I'm giving you a ride the hell out of Westmere.'

'It's both,' Kitty said, lighting cigarettes for both of them and looking out at the dark streets they were leaving behind. 'I've always known this wasn't enough for me, only I never met anyone else who felt it until you. I love you for wanting more than this.'

Danny looked across at her, mock indignation on his face,. 'You only love me for my ambition?'

She laughed, easing off her shoes and lifting her stockinged toes to the dashboard, settling in for the drive, warm and happy. 'You are your ambition, Danny Nelson, and well you know it. I see how hard you work at what you want. I love that too.'

He nodded. 'We're peas in a pod, Kit,' he said, pulling out onto the main road that took them out of Westmere and right up to London.

The roads were clear and quiet and they made it back to Corngate Street in record time, pulling in just after six. Danny stopped off at the payphone on the corner while Kitty went up to the room. They weren't meeting the investor until nine, so they had a few hours, and she wanted to surprise

Danny. She closed the curtains against the cold drizzle, lit the gas fire and lifted a clean white tablecloth from her case, taken from her mother's pile of Sunday-breakfast best. She took out her two glasses, rubbed them both over with a clean tea towel and set them on the table alongside the two bottles of bitter she'd set aside for tonight. Then she carefully unwrapped the four glass baubles she'd taken from the old silver tinsel tree at home and laid them on the table. With only the fire and the bedside lamp turned on, the room was warm and the red and gold decorations shone against the heavy curtains. She heard Danny coming up the steps, leaping two at a time as he usually did, and positioned herself just beside the table, warm and lit, a sprig of mistletoe in the hand she held above her head.

Danny was slower in bed, more gentle than usual, and Kitty luxuriated in the heat of his body against hers, the contrast between the warmth of their skin and the chill of the worn sheets. They found themselves relaxing into making love in a way that surprised and delighted them both.

'That was different,' she whispered, her head on his shoulder.

Danny turned into her, kissing the mess of her hair. 'Good different?'

'Very.' She was smiling, a wide sated grin right across her face.

They laughed and Kitty caught herself in the soft drop between waking and sleep, a delicious sense of letting go. She nuzzled closer to him and allowed herself to fall asleep, happier than she'd been in weeks.

When they woke, the room was cold. The gas fire had gone out when the meter went; the drizzle outside had cleared, leaving a freezing fog. Danny was more his usual self, brisk, businesslike, determined to make a good impression. The cold had them racing through washing, dressing, Kitty's make-up swiftly applied as Danny polished his good black shoes.

'Looking forward to tonight, Kit?' he asked, his eyes on the shine of the leather.

'I am,' she answered from her place at the mirror. 'I've never been out on Christmas night before. Usually we're in bed by ten.' She looked at the delicate wristwatch her parents had given her for her fifteenth birthday. 'Twenty past eight, nearly ready.' She finished her make-up, a touch more powder and the new lipstick Danny had given her, carefully shaping a deep red bow that was beautifully set off by the midnight blue of the sheath dress she had poured herself into. It was a dress she hadn't yet had the courage to wear, but he had insisted it was exactly right for tonight. She put on her shoes, adding three inches to her height, and turned around slowly. 'Will I do?'

Danny grinned, put on his second shoe and jumped up, clicking his fingers in appreciation. 'You'll do just fine.'

As they walked across the bridge, Kitty thought she'd never been happier.

Marty Gilbert was funny and charming. He was excited by Danny's plans and grateful to them for giving up their Christmas night to show him a good time in London. He lived in Manhattan now, but his mother was from Virginia and that, he said, explained his impeccable manners, the way he called Kitty 'ma'am' and pulled her chair out for her, helped her on and off with her coat as they went from bar to restaurant to club. He worked in London often enough to know better than to expect a great deal of the evening – it was no New York City – but Danny and Kitty excelled themselves. If this was the kind of offer Danny Nelson wanted to make to the poor people of Britain as America helped them out of the shadow of that godawful war, then Marty Gilbert was their man. He was in.

Marty leaned across the table, shook Danny's hand. 'I think we have a deal, young man. You sort out that nightcap and I will very happily sign your papers in the morning.'

He went off to find the bathroom and Kitty turned back to Danny, her eyes wide and her whisper of joy edging towards a shout. 'He's in!'

Danny nodded. 'That's what he said.'

Kitty frowned. 'You think he didn't mean it?'

'No, he meant it. It's just ... ' Danny shook his head. 'Kitty love, when he said "nightcap" ... Well, it's something he asked me before, when we talked about tonight. About the deal.'

Kitty knew what Danny meant before he said the words. His kindness and care in bed earlier had been about this moment. His choice of her dress and the strong red of the lipstick. The way he had been singing her praises to Marty all night. Danny didn't usually make an evening out about her. As Marty Gilbert came back from the bathroom and laid a proprietorial arm on her shoulder, Kitty understood that she was the nightcap.

For a moment, all she knew was the heat of Marty Gilbert standing close to her, a sudden understanding. She could have walked away. She could have removed Marty's hand from her shoulder, ignored the pleading in Danny's eyes, left the club and walked straight back to Waterloo. She could have locked the door on him, packed her bags, gone back to Westmere on the first train in the morning. Kitty could have done all of these things, but she couldn't see herself doing any of them, saw no way to go other than the route Danny had mapped out for her. There were many options and, somehow, only one choice.

She sat at the table, she laughed with Marty and played along, making Danny happy, being his best girl. He'd often called her his greatest investment; now she would prove it. There was a strange fizzing feeling at the top of her stomach. She couldn't place it, didn't know what it was. She was scared and nervous and she realised she was not surprised. This was where it had always been heading, what so many of the potential investors had angled for and none had been allowed. Kitty now understood, sipping the sweet bubbles, that the men who'd come before simply hadn't put enough money on the table.

It was a long time later that Kitty understood the fizzing feeling to be anger. That night, Christmas 1956, she assumed it was fear. It took years for her to tell the difference.

Kitty followed Marty and Danny from the restaurant, waited while they exchanged details about their next meeting – a meeting where Kitty's presence was not required. She accepted Danny's kiss and the couple of quid he slipped her for a cab home later and then she took Marty's hand as he helped her into the taxi that would take them back to the big hotel on Hyde Park. Throughout the fifteen-minute journey she paid attention to detail. The brim of Marty's hat, the fur collar on his woollen coat. His hand was warmer than Danny's, heavier. The cab driver was balding, his manner ingratiating when he heard Marty's American accent. He knew there would be a good tip.

It was just coming up to midnight on Christmas Day and the hotel lobby was heaving. There were groups of people on their way from one party to another, some speaking French or Italian, others with American- and Arabic-accented English. Kitty studied the colours the women were wearing: silver and gold, deep red and emerald green, midnight blue and royal purple. Fur coats were carefully slipped on as women prepared to go out into the cold, shrugged off and handed heedlessly to the concierge as other women hurried inside, décolletage and shapely waists to show off the minute they were indoors. Kitty wondered how many of the women were wives and girlfriends, daughters and sisters; how many were women like her. Women like her. She felt it as a body blow and caught her breath. Then she felt Marty's arm across her shoulders, steering her towards the lift, and she let the feeling go.

They were silent in the gilded lift, silent as he led her along the carpeted corridor. She had been to hotel bars with Danny and his investors, had been sent to meet the wealthy men in the lobby, standing out in their camel coats, their new hats, or to pick them up from the shiny hotel cafés that were a world away from the caff in the station where her shift started at a quarter past six in the morning. Marty was less talkative now. Perhaps he was nervous. Perhaps he didn't usually do things like this. He had told them of Barbara, his happy housewife with a beautiful new refrigerator, and their two sons who were keen baseball players, not as good at algebra as they should be, as he wanted them to be. The boys were eleven and nine. He and Barbara had been married for fifteen years in spring. There was a mirror in the corridor and Kitty saw herself gliding along beside Marty, his arm around her shoulders still, holding her close, containing her.

He unlocked the bedroom door and ushered her in, turning on the light just as she stepped ahead into the dark. She thought it might have been easier in the dark. It was harder to keep noticing, her mind reaching for solid objects. The room was full of them. Bed. Armchairs. Small settee. A desk. A radio and television unit like those she had seen in American films, like nothing she had ever seen in

Westmere. Everything was oversized, with flounces of fabric adding to the sense of scale. It was a room that made her feel like Goldilocks; all of it just right for someone else, anyone else, none of it right for her. It was not her room, it was his.

Marty was even quieter now, there was none of his earlier joviality, no laughter. He opened a narrow cupboard and took out two glasses, a bottle of whisky. He handed her a drink without asking if she wanted it, without offering a toast. Cheers were redundant.

'I'm going to the bathroom, then I'll have a shower. Join me.'

It wasn't an invitation.

Kitty waited until he called again. When she walked into the bathroom, it smelled of shit, Marty's shit. He made no apology from behind the shower curtain. She needed to wee but nothing came. She took off her midnight-blue dress, her stockings and suspenders, the bra that crossed her heart, her pants. Perfunctory, simple. The mirror above the sink was fogging up, so she ran a hand across it. She looked at herself, looked at her face, her eyes, her body. Took in the deep line where the bra had cut into flesh, the better to offer up those breasts. She looked back at the face in the mirror, watching until the steam covered that girl's face.

Kitty was thinking of herself as she, looking at herself as she. She noticed this and was interested. She was interested in the bedroom, interested in the bathroom. She had not had a shower before. They were in the films too, showers for wealthy Americans in elegant houses or fashionable apartments with shiny big cars, soda fountains, junior high schools and girls who were cheerleaders. Another world. Kitty was at the door to another world. From behind the fog in the mirror she watched herself step into it, climb into the shower with Marty.

*

Afterwards, as she left the hotel, as she hurried along Hyde Park, turned down into Piccadilly, Kitty noticed the empty streets, the sharp colour of the street lights, the Christmas glitter in the shop windows, still sparkling. She hailed a taxi just after Fortnum's. The cabbie, another balding man, did not ask where she had been. He was not interested. He had a daughter of his own safe at home, safe in bed, this one's age give or take a year. This carry-on wasn't what he had gone to war for, not at all. He dropped her off on the corner of Corngate Street and thanked his lucky stars. Then he forgot the girl, just one more fare before he went home for his breakfast and a kip. It had been a long night, always was, bloody Christmas.

On the threshold of Mrs Kavanagh's house, Kitty watched her hand turn the key in the lock. Inside, in the semi-darkness of the downstairs hall, she felt herself take off her shoes, and then the cold as stockinged toes walked up the old stairs, the lino colder still on the landing halfway up. At last her feet felt the old carpet on the landing outside Kitty's room. Her room, she reminded herself. Kitty's room.

She unlocked the door and, grateful for the dark, for the midwinter morning that offered no light, she took off her midnight-blue dress, her stockings and suspenders, the bra that cut into her body, her pants. She was clean. She had had another shower afterwards, as Marty first dozed and then snored. She had stayed under the gentle water for a long time. The hotel soap smelled of lavender. She had washed under the flow of water, soothing arms, ribs, breasts, lips, places so recently touched, newly touched. With the hotel flannel she had wiped off what remained of her make-up – lipstick and mascara staining the cloth. A cleaner would deal with it in the morning. That was what Marty had said when he grabbed her and pulled her to him in the room, knocking the drink out of her hand. What he'd said as he held her under him, semen spilling onto the sheet, telling Kitty how he loved hotel rooms, why he loved them.

'The girl will make the room up in the morning, like we were never here, this never happened.'

She got into bed alongside Danny. She was cold, shivering, and she did not want Danny to wake, ask how it had gone. She stilled the shivering with force of will. Kitty was amazed at her mind, what it could do, where it could go. It was an hour until her alarm would go off for her shift at the caff. She lay and waited for the click that came before the bell. Danny hated being woken by her alarm. Luminous hands turned closer to morning.

Sixteen

Westmere, June

Two days after the funeral, Beth and Sara went down to Lullaby Beach to begin looking through Kitty's things, daring themselves to consider what they might keep and what would go to charity shops. It was Sara's idea; she had to get back to work next week. She wanted to get on with something before she returned to London, make a start.

'Come on, you and me, we need to do it sometime. We don't have to make any decisions, just ... have a look?'

Beth went along with it, even though all she wanted to do was stay at home. She had enjoyed feeling close to Sara in the run-up to the funeral, loved how her sister had spoken for them on the day, and wanted nothing more than to keep everything light, chatty, warm. It would be hard to talk about clearing out the hut without also talking about whether they would sell or keep it. She agreed because there was no good reason to put it off.

They had just unlocked the door when Sara said she had something to tell her.

'That sounds ominous.'

'It is a bit. I've been trying to get a chance to talk to you alone, but there've been so many visitors, so many of them wanting to tell us about Kitty, and all those annoying people scared to actually say the word "suicide"—'

'So you don't want to clear the hut?'

'I do, but I need to tell you this first. And I needed to tell you alone.'

'Just say it, Sara.'

'OK. There was a note.'

'What?'

'There was a note. Lucy took it.'

'A suicide note?'

Sara nodded.

'Lucy took it?'

Sara nodded again, and Beth wanted to shake her and stop her stupid nodding.

'What the hell?' she said.

'Kitty left a note. It was on the bed. Beside her. Lucy took it. She told me about it after the funeral, at the end of the day.'

Beth wanted to say a dozen things at once and knew she would say none of them. Instead she stared at the sheet of paper Sara had lifted from her backpack, taking it from her slowly as if it was fragile, precious, dangerous.

When she had read it four times over, she muttered, 'Give me a minute.'

It wasn't a request and Sara let her be.

Beth went outside to sit on the steps. She wanted to lean back on the warm wood and drink a glass of wine in the sun and hear Kitty inside, grumbling about the government while she gutted the fish she'd caught that morning. She wanted to be alone so she could let out the rage she felt at Kitty abandoning them. She wanted to scream at Sara, all the words she was ashamed to say.

Beth stared at the piece of paper in Kitty's handwriting, the list of dates, listening to her sister tell her about her daughter.

'She gave it to you at the funeral?' she asked.

'Yes.'

'And you've waited two days to tell me?' Her voice was cold.

'One day really. Just yesterday. And I didn't know what to tell you. Lucy's mortified. She doesn't know why she took it. She's really upset—'

'Yeah, thanks,' Beth interrupted. 'I do know my own daughter. Of course she's upset, she screwed up.'

Sara sighed. 'I was just trying to explain.'

'Right, and making a big thing about you and Lucy understanding each other so well that when my daughter steals the suicide note from our aunt's deathbed, you wait several days to tell me and then break it to me as if it's an afterthought.'

'Not several.'

'It might as well have been a week. Why the hell didn't you tell me right away?'

'Because I had other things to worry about. Because it's not all about Lucy, it's not even all about you,' Sara snapped back. 'I really don't want to fight with you, Beth. I just don't. It's not about who is closest to who, that's not relevant right now.'

'It feels pretty bloody relevant to me.'

'I know, but . . .'

Sara stopped. They had been through this so many times before. Beth believed that Sara had been closer to their mother during her illness and death, closer to Kitty later. It infuriated Sara that her sister minded so much. When their mother was dying, Beth and Tim were newly married, Beth was pregnant with Lucy. They had other things to worry about. Sara had been younger, still living at home. Of course she had spent more time with their mother. While Beth was getting on with raising a family, Sara had been through

118

a series of unsuccessful relationships, and so she and Kitty had more time to spend together, a shared understanding of being single in a world that preferred all women coupled and procreating.

'What?' Beth asked, her belligerent tone striking against the warmth of the day, a calm sea quietly rolling in.

Sara leaned against the front door, the old paint flaking in tiny crackles as she rested her back against it. She shook her head. 'Does it really matter who told who and when and where? You know now.'

'It matters to me,' Beth answered. 'You think I'm just jealous, I feel like you're leaving me out. We both keep coming back to it and it never shifts, but that's not what I'm upset about, or not only what I'm upset about,' she added, conceding.

'What then?'

'Kitty left us a message.' She shook the paper. 'She must have wanted us to know that those dates mattered to her. We know what happened on the twelfth of May, but the others mean nothing to me. I mean, I was in a complete blur back in April 2004. Mum was dead, Lucy was what? Four months? I suppose something might have happened that mattered, but I doubt I'd have noticed. Only they must have meant something to Kitty. These dates might explain why she did it. She must have wanted us to know.'

Sara stared towards the sea. The yachts had been out an hour or so ago, rounding the point from Eastmere, bright sails of fluorescent pink and green and yellow in amongst the more regular white. Most of them had turned back when the wind began to drop, but there was just one still out there, beyond the orange buoy, slowly and laboriously struggling in. It was how she felt now, grasping uncertainly forwards.

Beth turned and saw that she was crying. 'Do you know?'

Sara shook her head. 'I don't know anything about what Kitty did in the fifties, only that she went up to London for a few months and didn't like it. Same story she told both of us. She came home and she moved in here. Remember? She just used to say London wasn't half as shiny as it was made out.'

'Then what is it?'

'One of those dates is mine.'

Seventeen

Newcastle, 2004

'Are you finished?' Sara asked, her tone flat, her voice quiet.

'Oh yeah, sorry,' Mark answered, moving unsteadily and lifting himself off her body, staying close. Too close. 'I was nearly asleep there for a minute. It's a bloody long drive up here, you know.'

He stretched, his arms above his head, his heavy legs weighing down, pulling the duvet away from her cold back. She didn't care. Cold was fine. Cold was good. She did not want to be warm, cosy, not now.

'You should go,' she said.

'Yeah, you're right. Angela was asking all sorts of questions this week. Where was I going, what route, how long did the drive take? On and on. She's not at all sure about these trips away, doesn't understand why I need to talk to a firm in the north-east. And the lad is playing football now on Saturdays. I ought to make an effort to go watch him some time.'

'Just go,' she said, her voice a little louder, her tone more strained. Sara felt the catch in her throat, saliva welling in her mouth, wondered if she might vomit. There was nothing to throw up, she was empty, felt herself both within a void and holding one, her skin was a thin membrane between the two. She took a breath, another, long and slow. Somewhere in her breathing she could smell the perfume of this room, beyond the smell of him – something of Yulia – and it was suddenly a nostalgic scent, as if it took her back to a time very long ago. This morning, very long ago.

Mark turned on his side to look at her, genuine concern in his words, his eyes already moving on, heading home. She hoped he was heading home.

'Are you all right, Sara?' His face offered a lopsided grin, half hidden in the pillow, a fleck of dried spittle on his upper left lip, moving as he spoke. 'Hope you're not coming down with something. Not sure what I'd tell Angela if I caught a cold on a business trip. Mind you, I could always blame it on stopping over at a service station. Bloody filthy places, like planes. You don't want to breathe in any of them if you can help it.'

She could feel the fire rising, bile and fury. She looked at her watch. It was just gone three in the afternoon. She didn't want to risk her flatmates coming home, ready to party their Friday night into a weekend of excess. Yulia had a class that finished at four, followed by her Friday-night shift at a bar in town. She sometimes came home between the class and her shift. If she didn't start talking after the class – twentieth-century philosophers, so getting caught in conversation or argument was highly likely – if she ran all the way, she could almost make it. Yulia said it was worth leaving an argument unfinished to come home and get changed, to dress in neutral colours, quiet clothes, to get through the night in the bar as a server of drinks, not someone to be interested in, looked over, reached for.

Sara didn't want to shout and she didn't want to fight. She just wanted Mark gone. He still lay there in the bed. Her bed, her and Yulia's bed. Now it was the bed, any bed, a bed.

She thought she'd try to explain, perhaps he might even understand. 'You need to go.'

'I need to get on, yes.'

'No, you need to go. I want you out of here.'

He smiled. 'Oh, you've got the guilts.' He shrugged, a self-deprecating smile. 'Yeah, it's a toughie. How do you think I felt all summer?'

'I wasn't your first affair.'

Sara was surprised she was engaging in conversation, surprised she could form whole sentences. The rage inside had no words, no phrases, no way to move her mouth around it and create coherent sound.

'Fair point, I've had more practice, but honest, it's OK. You'll get used to it.'

'No.'

He stretched, made himself comfortable. He was still in the bed. She couldn't believe he was even in the house, let alone the bed. Couldn't he feel her disgust? How could he be here, so close to her fire, and not feel it?

She tried again. 'I didn't want that. I didn't say yes to that.'

He yawned, bored now. 'None of us say yes to feeling bad afterwards, but it happens. We're not thinking about the afterwards, are we?'

He reached a hand towards her and she reared up, backing away from his touch. 'Sara? What's going on?'

There was a chink in his imperviousness, she took a breath. Tried to explain, 'Listen to me. I'm not talking about guilt. I'm talking about this, this . . . ' She didn't have the words to say it, or she did but she didn't want to use them, not those words. The sweep of her arm took in the room, the bed, the duvet he lay beneath so easily. She swallowed, opened her mouth, let the words begin to form in her throat, on her tongue, but even then she couldn't bring herself to say them.

'Babe?'

One syllable. One little word. The fire filled her chest, her eyes, her brain. She did not see red, she saw orange, yellow, deep scarlet, colours that spread to her hands and turned her fingers and nails into hooks, knives, flashing scissors, made bullets of her toes, axes of her legs. She reared up and turned on him, slapping, kicking, scratching, hitting. She felt her toenails make contact with his shin and was delighted at the howl of pain as she dug in and ground down. She punched and kicked and she punched again. Every action was an individual release. She felt as if each part of her body was working autonomously, separate from her and from itself. Left hand, right hand, left foot, arm, elbow, a body held together only by rage and disgust. There was also, she noticed, the thought coming from far away like a high note rung on a distant bell, an experience of pleasure. It was pleasurable to kick out, to dig, to gouge. Enjoyable to hit and to hear the sound of her knuckles grazing against his jaw, his ear, his brow bone. The hollow clunk as her fist smacked his skull.

'I didn't want it. You wouldn't go away. You said one kiss. One kiss and you'd leave. You said one. Then you wanted more. You promised you would leave and you didn't. I said no more and you didn't listen. You wanted it so you pushed and pushed. You pushed yourself in me. I didn't want it. I didn't want you. I said no. I. Said. No.'

'What do you mean, you didn't want it? What are you on about? What the ... seriously? What the actual fuck?'

Mark scrambled to the far end of the bed, stumbled over the sheet, one foot tangled against the other, looking down in disgust and horror at the blood dripping from his shin.

'Jesus Christ, Sara, what are you doing? What's wrong with you?'

She stared at him. What was wrong with her? Did he not

know? Had he not heard? She looked at him grabbing for his shirt, pulling on his boxers, angry and yes, a little bit frightened. Worried.

He was shouting, furious. 'What the hell do you think you're playing at?'

Playing. How could he say that? Here and now? Who was mad, him or her? Sara didn't think she was mad. Angry, yes, more incandescently furious than she'd ever felt, but she didn't think she was mad. She was sure she knew what had happened in the past hour – she looked at the clock on her bedside table. Less than an hour, much less. No more than twenty minutes since he'd said, 'One last kiss.' Everything had tilted in such a short time.

She wasn't mad. She would make him understand. She tried again, the words clearer, slower now. 'I didn't want it. You said one kiss. You didn't leave. You pushed. I didn't want to. I said no.'

He sighed, pulled on his socks, shook his head. She wondered if she was speaking aloud. Maybe the words were all in her head. How could he not know what she was saying?

He was staring at her and she was looking back. The space of the room was an abyss between them and the only place to go now was in and down. Sara knew that unless she made him understand, there would be no way back.

She could feel her face frowning as she looked at him, trying to understand his confusion. Then suddenly she understood him and that was even more strange, weirder than how her body felt right now, alive and numb, wide awake with anger and also shut down, silenced. He really didn't know. He didn't know what he had done, he didn't understand her words and he genuinely didn't know why she was doing this, hitting out, pushing him as far from her as she could. He didn't know why she wanted him out of her room, away from her home, from her body and her mind. Away from her memory. Why she wanted to hurt him back.

He was half dressed, vulnerable, standing opposite her at the end of the bed, scrabbling into his pants. His cock and his little paunch both hanging down. Had he stopped going to the gym since summer? He looked older than thirty-six. Maybe she didn't know what thirty-six looked like. Some of their lecturers were in their thirties and forties, most of their teachers at school had been around that age. Right now he looked older than any of them. Maybe they would all look older if they were as he was now, uncertain, bruised, worried.

Mark lifted his palms, a gesture of surrender that was also an appeal. He seemed genuinely confused. 'What is all this?' he asked.

She watched him show first shock, then horror, then utter incomprehension as she answered simply, 'No one has ever forced me to have sex with them before, so I'm not sure what's going on, what I'm doing. But I think I'm doing what any woman would, if she could, to the man who forced her to have sex when she didn't want to. I'm hitting back.'

She heard the words and was so proud of herself for saying them and not screaming them, for saying them not swallowing them.

Then she heard his litany of denials, the righteous anger, so many how-dare-yous. The fury as he tugged on the rest of his clothes, slamming about the room she had created with Yulia, their room, their bed, their little home. He pointed out the shabby curtains, the mess of perfumes and make-up on the dressing table, the pile of jumbled earrings. He said they were children playing, little girls pretending to be grown women.

After he had picked apart the room and their things, his tone shifted from anger to bitterness, nasty now, Well of course she thought he'd forced her. That's what she thought

126

proper sex was. She'd probably decided real sex – between a man and a woman thank you very much, the real thing – she probably thought it was bad now, didn't she? Now she was a dyke she'd decided all men were the bad guys, wasn't that right? For pity's sake, was she that much of a cliché? This wasn't Greenham bloody Common, this was the noughties or the new millennium or whatever the hell it was called, women could fuck men and it could be a good thing, a fine thing, they were adults and they could fuck and no one needed to feel guilty, all right? No one. Didn't she know? Maybe she couldn't remember, perhaps she didn't recall how hungry she'd been for it, for him, all those weeks of summer. Practically begging him to shag her in that bloody Portakabin on the site. He'd wondered how he'd keep up with her, half his age, but he had, he'd kept up with her all right, done his damnedest, made the effort. Look how hard he'd tried, coming up here to see her. That bloody drive, all this way. He was knackered, but he'd done it anyway, all the way here to be with her. And this was how she thanked him. This.

Now he was fully dressed and she was laughing. It was too absurd not to laugh. Of course he wouldn't agree, say yes, you're right, you told me quite clearly that you didn't want to have sex, you told me I could only come in for a coffee, and that was the third time I'd come all this way, when I'd demanded that you at least speak to me, it wasn't fair not to speak to me. Yes, you insisted you were happy with Yulia, but I pushed and pushed, and when you didn't hit me away as I leaned in to give you a goodbye kiss, the kiss I had promised was a farewell kiss if you'd only give it, the kiss that promised I'd never follow you on your street again, then I pulled you to your feet and into the closest bedroom, and what good fortune it was yours, and I wouldn't leave and you knew this was the only thing that would get rid of me, one last fuck, you knew that, and so you let me push you down onto the bed, you let me pull down your jeans, your pants. You were silent and not moving and I shaped your body to make it fit mine and I raped you.

Of course he wouldn't say that.

And because he would not say that, she had nothing else to say. So she laughed.

He left, shouting behind him that she was mad. Stark raving fucking mad.

Yulia didn't come home between her class and her shift. After an hour of sitting cold on her bed, Sara picked herself up, stripped the sheets, remade the bed, tidied the room. She had a shower and stayed under the water until she stopped shaking.

It was just gone seven thirty on the evening of Friday 30 April 2004.

Eighteen

Westmere, June

Beth had listened quietly. When her sister finished speaking, she reached out her hand and was grateful that Sara leaned into her, allowed herself to be held.

After a while, they sat back and Beth shook her head. 'I don't know where to start. I'm ... ' she shook her head again, 'I'm sorry that happened to you. So sorry. It's horrendous.'

'Yes.'

'And I'm pissed off that you didn't tell me years ago.'

'I know.' Sara smiled, allowing Beth's hurt.

'And I'm still bloody furious that Lucy stole Kitty's note, and it's all kind of mixed up. You not telling me about this, Lucy not telling us about the note ... ' Beth broke off, her fists tight balls crunched against her forehead, pushing into her head. 'I'm sorry. Go on – you told Kitty what had happened to you?'

'Yes. Do you remember when I came home, around Easter, my first year at university?'

Beth shrugged. 'Sorry. Barely.'

'Which is why I didn't tell you then. Lucy was a baby, you weren't OK. I know it was a tough time for you. You don't have to remember.'

Beth nodded. She was battling a raft of emotions, horror at what had happened to Sara and real hurt that she hadn't told her, that she had told Kitty instead. She also remembered feeling intensely jealous of Sara. Her sister had swanned off to Newcastle, was having an affair with another woman, being so interesting and different, while she was at home in Westmere, struggling to remember what had seemed so attractive about marriage and motherhood. Worse, the baby she had so wanted now felt like a burden.

'I think you all thought I was just exhausted from typical student behaviour, shagging, drinking, no sleep. I was exhausted, but ...'

'Not for those reasons?'

Sara shook her head. 'I was depressed. Depression is knackering.'

'It must have been so hard for you, and all I remember is thinking you were so amazing, having this exciting life. And your girlfriend – Swedish?'

'Finnish. Half. Yulia.'

'There I was, barely coping, not coping. Thinking I was a rubbish mother, that nothing would ever change, and trying not to be jealous of you.'

'Same,' Sara whispered. 'Trying not to be jealous of you.'

The sisters spoke together.

'I'm sorry I didn't tell you.'

'I wish you'd told me.'

Sara sighed. 'I didn't want to tell anyone. I wanted to pretend nothing had happened, but a few days afterwards, I got really sick. It was an STD of some sort. God knows who he'd been shagging between me leaving home and him following me up to Newcastle.'

'His wife?' Beth asked before she could stop herself, wincing and bringing her hand to her mouth. 'Sorry.'

'And that is one of the other reasons I didn't tell you. You and Tim were so ...' She paused. 'It really doesn't matter. We've all changed and it was ages ago.'

'It was. And we were scared young marrieds, barely managing. I was in the depths of post-natal depression, trying to pretend that it was so easy to be together for the rest of our lives and never ever want anything else. I understand why you didn't come to me and I'm sorry.'

'I was an idiot too; all that "Westmere is so boring" crap.'

Beth shrugged. 'But it is.'

They both laughed then.

'Are you OK to talk about it now?' Beth asked.

Sara lifted her hands, equivocating. 'Yes. No. It was so long ago, but sometimes it feels as if it's still really recent. And then Me Too came along and it was in all the news, both the stories and people saying it was so long ago, why does it matter any more. Sometimes I just hate feeling so defined by something so crap.'

'Do you think that's why you went into the work you do? With those women's charities?'

Sara frowned. 'I hope not. I care about my work, I enjoy it and I'm good at it. I hope I'm not only doing it because that happened to me.'

'Wanting to stop it happening to other women isn't a bad reason,' Beth said.

'I know, but I'm not sure it's enough.' Beth's reasoning was too close to some of Sara's own worries late at night, when she tried to pick apart her actions from her intentions and found they were often closer than she'd thought. 'I've wondered that about Kitty too, the abortion work she used to do, before it was legal.'

Beth nodded. 'I remember her telling us how women would come down to the hut and ask her for help to get to a clinic. She told the story like it was so long ago, but it wasn't really, was it?'

'I remember thinking she was so cool. Her politics about choice and all that. It was only years later that I wondered if it was because of her own life.'

'You didn't ask her?'

Sara shook her head. 'No. And typical Kitty, she didn't volunteer anything.'

'So many things we should have asked her.' Beth picked up Kitty's note and stared at it again. 'I still can't believe she did it.'

'Kitty or Lucy?'

'Both, but Lucy right now. That and the fact that she told you, not me.'

'At least I tell you, not like Kitty. Don't you remember it used to drive Mum mad that we had secrets with Kitty?'

'I do. Even more now I know how it feels to be the wicked fairy-tale stepmother who doesn't understand.'

'Not wicked, just very little.' Sara leaned over and kissed her sister on the top of her head, precisely because she knew how much it irritated her.

'Piss off and get me a drink.'

They went inside and Sara poured them both a shot of Kitty's whisky, looked at the bottle and topped both glasses up to the rim.

Beth nodded her approval. 'How much left?'

'Just enough to get us past the awfulness of having to work out what to do next and hopefully not quite enough to have a massive row while we do it.'

She raised her glass. 'I'll drink to that.'

'To Kitty and secrets.'

'Bloody secrets.'

They toasted, and then Beth spoke slowly. 'So that's one of the dates . . .'

'Yes. And the date she killed herself.' Sara sipped her whisky and allowed it to warm her mouth and throat before she went on, 'I don't know how we find out about the others. They must be around the time she went to London, then came back and started living here.'

'So maybe there's something here? I mean, we have to sort her stuff out, right?'

Sara nodded.

Beth went on, 'She wanted us to know about those dates. Maybe she left something that would tell us what they meant.'

'I can't bear it, though, getting rid of her. It makes me feel more alone, more like there's only me.'

'You have us.'

Sara knelt on the sofa, looking out to sea, away from Beth. 'When we left the crematorium, you and Tim got into your car with the girls. You drove to the wake as a unit.'

'We didn't do it to leave you out,' Beth said, her words sharper than she'd intended.

'I didn't say you did. But I don't have that. I never have that.'

Beth didn't argue further. She was well aware that Sara felt her single status keenly, more so as they got further into their thirties and the chances of finding someone she might want to have a child with looked less likely. Kitty had understood in a way Beth knew she never would.

She sat beside Sara and closed her eyes. She breathed in the scent of sea air and so many cups of tea, decades of baking and the last remaining hint of Kitty's tobacco. The tide was high and the noise of waves smacking against the shore filled the silence, the strong water scouring out stones as each wave twisted back on itself. Kitty's old alarm clock ticked a counterpoint to the sea's rhythm from its place on the bookshelf, five minutes fast as ever.

Sara ran her hand over the faded covering on the sofa. 'I feel more part of something here than I do anywhere else. I don't want to lose that.'

Beth opened her eyes to look around the room, the walls yellowed from decades of Kitty's roll-ups, hung with pictures drawn by Beth and Sara years before and others by Lucy and Etta. The bookshelves were stacked two-books deep and cluttered with medical biographies, Kitty's reading matter of choice, spanning centuries of healing breakthroughs and hundreds of lives.

'What if we feel different about here, about Kitty?' Sara went on. 'What if we find out stuff we don't want to know?'

'I think that's already started. I'm not sure we can stop it now.'

Nineteen

London, 1957

'Girl, I'm so sorry.'

Kitty's stomach twisted; she groaned inside. It was so much easier to be hurt by Danny, wounded by him. When he was sorry, he was small and pained. Every single time he vowed never again, she found herself leaning towards him, opening for him. His voice was genuinely penitent. This Danny was a whole new person, almost childlike, so different that she'd had no idea how to respond the first time he came to her that way.

They'd had a row about something, about nothing, and as he became angrier she had backed off, trying not to inflame him, not to annoy him. But her back-off annoyed him all the more and he'd lashed out and knocked her to the floor, then stormed out of the room shouting that she'd be the ruin of him. She picked herself up after a while, washed her face, went to bed with a cold flannel pressed to her cheek. She was not crying. Unlike the first few times, it was no longer shocking. It was sad and strange, but it was how he was. Perhaps all men were like this, all of them with any gumption at least. Her father had none and her mother had complained about

135

that often enough, maybe Danny's fierce determination, his raging ambition, had nowhere else to go when he was angry.

It must have been three or four in the morning when he returned. The buses were silent, only goods trains rumbling through, and she found herself turning towards him before she remembered how they had parted. When she recalled his words, his fists, she felt her body harden against him, reaching into the peeling wallpaper as if it might hide there, hide her away. Danny pulled her to him, though she resisted, rolling her over to face him, and kissed her so gently, kissing the lips he'd spat at, the cheek he'd punched.

Whispering over and over again, 'I'm so sorry, please forgive me, Kit, please.'

When she didn't answer, she had no answer, he tried again. 'I need you, Kitty, surely you know that. I need you so terribly.'

He had never before said he needed her. He'd told her plenty of times how she needed him, that she was using him to get away from her boring family and her boring prospects. She couldn't disagree that the hope of escape had been part of the attraction, and now she did need him, not in the way he meant, but because she loved him more than anything else in her life.

'I need you with me, Kitty. Please don't shut me out, don't push me away. I'm so scared.'

Kitty felt her body shift closer to his treacherous body, wanting body, seduced by his words, coming closer to him, the better to listen with her arms, her breasts, her belly, her thighs.

'I'm so scared my plans will come to naught and you'll be off. I'll be alone and there's no point to any of it without you, Kit, no point at all.'

She wanted to laugh at this change in him, the needy lad in

136

her bed. She wanted to cry because she knew this was who he was underneath the bravado, she had always known he was a soft kid somewhere beneath all that. Kitty had imagined this Danny so many times, as scared as she was, as uncertain. She couldn't laugh it away in case he thought she was mocking him, she daren't cry in case she annoyed him, so she reached out, took him in her arms and they lay there, Kitty in her nightie, Danny half dressed, half cut.

She waited until she felt him relax, heard his breathing slow, and then she whispered, knowing he would not hear, 'Danny Nelson, you daft bugger, where would I go? Who would I go to but you?'

She turned up at work the next day with a black eye and blamed herself, shaking her head ruefully at Mildred and whispering, 'I'm that embarrassed. I only went out on a bender last night and tripped over the milk bottles coming in. I knew the landlady would have my guts for garters if I broke one, so I let myself take the fall, not the bottles. Smacked right into the shoe grate on the doorstep. Let me work in the back today, will you?'

Mildred sighed, nodding Kitty away. 'There's a dirty great pile of dishes in there, you get to them and we'll sit down once the rush is over.'

Later, over a cup of tea when the breakfast crowd had gone on to work, Mildred reached out a hand. 'You know you don't have to stick it, don't you, love? No one would think any worse of you for heading off back home. You're young still, not everyone's cut out for the city, or for – well, you know how hard it can be.'

But Kitty shook her head. 'I'm fine, I just need to lay off the port and lemon and I'll be right as rain. It's not London that's the problem, it's my weak constitution.'

Mildred looked at the girl opposite her, her strong frame,

her hard-working body, her face too set for her years, and nodded. 'If you say so, but everyone's got a final straw. Mind you pay attention to yours when it comes.'

The straws began building up. The first time they went with a prospective investor after Danny had left her to sleep with Marty Gilbert, Kitty had tried to plead off, told him she was due her period, had cramps and a headache. He said she needn't come out for long, just enough to let the bloke know he might be on a promise. She went because it was easier than not, but they were both tired and irritable by the time they got home and Danny told her she'd better buck up her ideas, there would be more entertaining as they moved into spring.

Kitty knew she should have kept her mouth shut, but she couldn't help herself. 'Fancy that, who'd have thought prostitution was a seasonal affair?'

Danny's answer came with a punch to her lower back, hard, the closest place he could reach from the edge of the bed, where he was taking off his shoes. 'And what does that make me then? A bastard pimp?'

He threw his shoes down and laid himself across the bed. Kitty wondered how long it would be before he'd fall asleep, if he would hit out again or if she was safe for tonight.

'This is for our future,' he wheedled.

Kitty realised she hated the sound of his voice tonight, it drilled into her jawbone where it met her ears. She kept her mouth clamped shut so she didn't answer back.

'I'm the bloody fool who has to pretend to like those bastards,' he was saying. 'I'm the one who has to spend all night trying to get them to understand I'm a good bet, that if they invest with us we can really do something, something big. All I'm asking of you ...'

Don't say it, she thought. If he doesn't say it, I can pretend

138

he doesn't know what he's doing, what he's asking me to do.

'... is that you show willing. If he wants to sit beside you, if he puts his hand on your leg—'

'My thigh, Danny, it was my thigh. Way up here, higher than my suspenders.'

'All right, but it's a touch, that's all it is, Kitty.'

'Not always.' She was surly. 'He wanted to kiss me and you egged him on.'

'Christ, Kit, he has a packet to put into the business. Of course I did. I'd have sent you off to his hotel and all if you hadn't been sat there like some frigid schoolgirl. I'd promised him a fine evening out in London and you spent the night looking like your drink had curdled. You made me look a right fool.'

He fell asleep soon after and Kitty sat awake in the old chair, staring into the dark of her room.

In the end, Kitty's final straw was neither the bruises and cuts, nor the men Danny told her to entertain. She had become practised in leaving herself on those nights, on being purely the girl Danny wanted her to be. In the end, Kitty's final straw was the fear. So many forms of fear.

There was the fear that built slowly, over an afternoon and evening, fear that she never knew what was coming. She was able to ignore it in the morning, leaving the room clean and tidy, just in case Danny was there when she came back. For the first few hours at work she would chat with customers, laugh with Mildred and the other staff, but once the dinner-time rush was done, the fear would kick in. What if Danny was in town? What if he'd been watching from the station concourse and seen her pat that old French-Jewish fellow on the back, the one who always left her a little tip as if she was a waitress on the continent and the station caff was in his beloved Paris that he'd left at the start of the war and believed he would never see again? What if he had been and gone to the room, found the sheets not smooth enough, the curtains not pulled back properly, his teacup not clean and waiting?

She would come home from work and be surprised to see him stretched out on the bed, a day or so later than he had promised to arrive, presenting himself as a gift, a treasure. Sometimes, climbing the three flights of stairs to the room, she had a presentiment that he was already there, took time to arrange her features, ensure her tone was just the right mix of surprise and delight. Other days, after a long shift, hoping only to get out of her shoes and have a lie-down, her look of joy took too long to arrive. All too often neither the ready face of joy nor the quick fix worked and the evening was spent trying to find a happy medium between being the capable but not stuck-up Kitty he believed she ought to be and the needy girl he detested. She was always too much of one and not enough of the other. She could not win.

On the nights when a dinner guest failed to turn up, or arrived but lacked the requisite admiration for Danny's plans, the fear bubbled to the top of her chest, constricting her breath and twisting her mouth into an uneven line, scared to speak a word out of turn. Then, when they walked back home across Waterloo Bridge, Danny strode ahead and Kitty struggled to keep up, the pretty shoes pinching and twisting her toes in a foreshadowing of the pinching and twisting of her arms, her thighs, her nipples that was to come, bruises that could be hidden beneath clothing, fear that threatened to vomit up and ruin everything.

The fear was at the back of her throat even when she had judged everything just right, from dress to hair-do to the colour of her lipstick. It was there when she crept into the room close to dawn, afraid that she still smelled of another man no matter how hard she had scrubbed at herself. Even in the few nights alone in her room, listening to the wireless and knitting, there was a slow trickle of concern at the back of her neck, turning to a wave of dread like a punch to the stomach when she heard footsteps tapping up the street, no matter that she knew the last train from Westmere had come in hours ago.

Very occasionally she felt the fear ebb away enough to give her a few hours of peace. It usually happened when she went out with Ernestine. She always told Danny where she was going; he'd ask about the picture they'd seen. He didn't have time for pictures himself, far too busy, but if Kitty wanted to waste her money then that was her lookout. He said there was nothing for him to worry about when she was with Ernestine, no respectable man would look twice at her, no matter how good she looked herself, not if she was palling up with a girl like that.

The fear didn't quite leave even when Kitty knew Danny had to be in Westmere for his mother's sixtieth, away for a whole weekend of partying.

He held her on his knee and shook his head. 'I'd love you to come, but you're hardly one of the great and the good of Westmere, are you? You know my old man's a bugger about who he gives his champagne to. It'll be different when it's my concern. You and me against the world, girl. You're all I've got, Kitty Barker, you know that? All I've got.'

Kitty loved it when Danny spoke this way, she knew he meant it. It was tough with his family, always having to live up to the old man's demands. She kissed him and promised she'd be waiting when he got back, that he would get through the two days of celebrations by thinking of her, his girl, their future. When he made love to her then, ever so gentle, she almost believed herself.

He left her dozing in bed, told her how beautiful she was. She heard his steps as he lightly bounced down the stairs, the front door closed not slammed, heard him tap away towards the station and the train back to Westmere. She pulled up the eiderdown and smiled, Danny's scent on her mouth, her lips, Danny's body imprinted on hers. That night, though, she woke startled from the same dream she had most nights that she slept alone, a dream she could never fully remember right to the end. She was running away from or towards someone, and just as she reached them she would wake as if surfacing from the sea, pulling herself up and flailing for solid ground, sucking air into lungs that felt as if they might burst with the strain. She woke with tears on her face, a whimpering at the back of her throat, relieved that he was far away in Westmere and saddened by that relief.

The snowdrops were all up in the park and the crocuses beginning to show when Kitty allowed herself to acknowledge what her body had been telling her for the past six weeks. She thought she might be pregnant. She hoped it was Danny's baby, but it could have been Marty Gilbert's or one of the other men Danny had sent her off with since Christmas; none of them had taken care and she hadn't known how to ask them to. She had tried to ask Danny what she should do, but he said it riled him too much to think of his girl with those men.

'If it's that bad, I needn't do it again. If neither of us wants it.'

'What do you take me for, Kit? Of course I don't want it.'

'Then I won't do it, never again, Danny.'

He flipped in an instant. 'I'll let you know when we've done enough,' he said as he slapped her across the face.

Then he cried and begged her, on actual bended knee,

142

begged her to go along with him one last time, maybe twice. Two more big hitters, two more blokes who could add up to everything he needed. He cried and kissed her and said he was so sorry, and even though Kitty couldn't really hear the sorry any more, she did what he asked because she couldn't think what else to do.

She confided in Ernestine after the second month passed and she still didn't see her period. Her breasts were heavy and her stomach increasingly queasy in the face of three dozen early-morning station breakfasts, each fried egg a confirmation of her condition. Kitty's halting admission that there was a baby coming made Ernestine speak her mind even more plainly than before.

'I've been thinking of saying this for a long time, and now I'm angry with myself for not opening my mouth sooner. Your Danny is a lazy man, and lazy men don't change. Greedy men can learn to share, angry men can mellow – it takes years, but it happens. I saw it with my own father. But a lazy man is no good to anyone and he's twice no good to his woman. He'll send you to work for him and then complain that you're away when he wants you at home. A lazy man cannot change, the world is too much on his side.'

It was almost March. Danny had to stay in Westmere for a few days and Kitty was able to spend more time with Ernestine. They sat laughing over the possibilities for the baby's future, thinking up names, dreaming of the new world that he or she would be born into, a world of television and movie stars and rock and roll, a world where two girls laughing in the corner of a pub, one of them white, the other black, would be ordinary, not worthy of a look or a comment. It was a world neither of them truly believed in, but both hoped it might be better for the baby.

Ernestine hugged Kitty goodnight on their shared landing.

'I'm telling you, he won't change. You have to put the baby first now. We both know he can't keep his fists to himself. Don't look shamefaced, girl. You're not the first woman to put up with a man like that, but you can't risk him hurting the baby in you. It's time to move on, even if that does mean going home. And you tell your mother to keep the finest room for me, will you? Ernestine Catherine MacIntyre will not accept a back room with no sea view, absolutely not.'

In the end, it was the fear that forced Kitty to go home. When she accepted that she was now fearful for two, her next step was clear.

Twenty

Westmere, 1957

Geoff was waiting for Kitty when the train came in. There were few passengers, but even in a crowd he could always spot his sister, a head taller than most girls, a strong walk announcing her striking presence. The girl coming towards him was Kitty, but a shadow, diminished, flattened. He took her suitcase from her hand, peeling her fingers from the handle as she held onto it for dear life. Then he walked her to the waiting room, sat her down and held her as she cried, her whole body sobbing. He handed her his handkerchief and then his spare. Geoff and his father always had a spare. When she stopped, when she said she could walk, he led her out of the station. Head down, scarf around her hair, hankie up to her face, they were any reunited twosome, tears of joy at a station.

They went to the seafront. It was just gone twelve and they were lucky, it had started out a filthy day and any early day-trippers were in the arcade or the tea shops on the front, the pier virtually deserted. They walked right to the end and stood for a few moments in the shelter, looking out to a storm-hazed horizon. Kitty went out in the rain to stand against the railing at the end. She looked almost translucent, Geoff thought, hardly there. She leaned against the metal bars to look down to the swirling waves beneath, just as she had when they reopened the pier after the war and Geoff used to lift her up, holding on tight so she could sit right at the edge, pretending it was a ship and they were sailing away to adventures. He'd always check her clothes afterwards, make sure there were no paint flecks, no clues that they'd been 'reckless and wanton', as their mother called it.

She came back to sit beside him. 'I used to think I was so special, Geoff. Allowed to come down here with you when all my other mates had to go with their mums or dads. I loved that you'd bring me down to the pier.'

He nodded, cupped his hand against the wind to light their cigarettes and waited. He'd put his coat around her when they felt the strength of the sea wind and there was nothing of her. It was biting cold though, he hoped she'd spit it out, whatever had brought her home, before the tide got much higher and the spray kicked up. You could get a right drenching this end of the pier if you weren't careful.

'Then I grew up and thought I didn't need a big brother or any of you.'

'Everyone gets like that for a bit. Growing up and too big for their boots.'

'You didn't.'

Geoff shrugged, thinking of how she'd taunted him for the past five years. He remembered crying bitterly in the privacy of his bedroom, cut to the quick by some disparaging remark, the little sister he'd thought would always look up to him.

'Thank you for coming to get me,' she offered, and he nodded in response.

He didn't say he'd hardly had a choice, the way she'd sounded from that phone box at Waterloo, crying so much he had to ask her three times to repeat herself before he knew what she was saying. Halting words telling him she needed to come home, begging him not to tell their parents yet. She said she'd been calling since six, she knew he got to work early and hoped he'd be the one to pick up the telephone. He'd been late today, helping their father with one of the doors that was stuck on the second landing, hadn't got in until gone half seven, well after his usual start time. Poor kid had bought a ticket for the eight forty-five. She must have been frantic, worried she'd miss him and come back to Westmere and risk bumping into their mother doing her morning shopping. He didn't often go out at dinner time, but that made it easier to ask for a few minutes more. He said he'd a present to find, let his boss and the other lads rib him about a secret girlfriend, but he'd have to get back to the garage sharpish.

'Do you want to tell me about it?' he asked. 'What's that Mum says? A problem shared?'

Kitty grimaced. 'She also says you've made your bed and you're to lie in it.'

Geoff waited a moment before he asked, very quietly, 'Kitty, what is it?'

She took a deep breath and he watched the set of her shoulders, then a tiny nod of her head, as if she'd made up her mind about something, before she turned to him and said, 'Only that all of you were right. I've been an idiot. I need to come home and I know she won't want me. I need to persuade her that I'm sorry and I'll make it right.'

Geoff let out a low whistle. Their mother had been so angry and hurt since Kitty left, even more so since she'd given them such short shrift at Christmas. They'd not had a peep from her since. She'd missed their father's birthday in February. Now it was Easter next month, spring cleaning of the whole guest house, top to bottom, next week and here was his little sister, turned up with no warning and wanting to stay put.

'She won't go easy, Kit, you know that.'

Kitty's face fell, whatever stoicism she had squared off in her shoulders a moment earlier seemed ready to drain away. Then she shook herself and nodded. 'I know. Only do me a favour, will you, Geoff? Have a word? Tell her I'm sorry and I want to come back, that way she'll get the worst of it out before she sees me. You know what I'm like, I can only keep my mouth shut for so long and I don't want to muck this up.' She grasped his hand and her fingers were freezing, bony. 'Please?'

He did his best. He always had. Geoff had taken his role as big brother seriously since the day his mother brought his baby sister home from the hospital. He broke the news and then hurried back to work, hoping he'd saved Kitty from the worst of it when she went to the guest house an hour later.

The almighty row erupted immediately. Kitty's father insisted she was welcome at home, always. Her mother glared at him and muttered under her breath that her husband and son must be blind as well as daft.

Kitty was shaking with the effort of holding herself in, there was so much she couldn't say. The men Danny had made her sleep with, the horrible things he'd said. She wanted to tell them the truth, have them understand why she had to get away, for herself and for the baby. She couldn't say any of it. All she could say was that she needed to come home.

Her mother raised an eyebrow. 'You can stay in Lullaby Beach. Once summer's over, you can start that secretarial course you thought you were too good for. If you're able,' she added in a tart aside. 'Or maybe the hospital, they always need willing girls. They'll train you up fast and you can get a job, pay proper rent on the place too. I'll not turn you away,

Kitty, you're my own flesh and blood, but your father and I have worked like I don't know what to make this business thrive. You're not going to spoil it for us, I won't have it.'

With that, she took off her apron and left the kitchen, left the guest house.

For the first time in years, Mrs Barker went for a long walk without a scarf to keep her set from getting blown all over the place. When she came home, it was well past tea time, Kitty and Geoff had both gone up to bed and her husband was waiting for her in the kitchen, the kettle on and cups laid out.

'What's all this in aid of?' she demanded.

'You. You're a softer woman than you'd ever dare let on and I know this is breaking your heart. Thank you for letting her come home,' he said, getting her chair and cutting a doorstep of bread to slather with dripping, a treat she rarely allowed herself. Good dripping was why her guests came back for her fried bread, too nice to waste on the family. She huffed as she sat down, pushing her shoes off her aching feet, but she was grateful to him all the same and patted his hand when he set down her teacup and slice.

A week after Geoff had met her from the train, Kitty and her mother stood at the door to Lullaby Beach, looking at their work. The floor was scrubbed, windows gleaming. The walls were bare, the cupboards sparsely filled. Kitty had put away her clothes in the wardrobe and the small chest of drawers, made the bed with the candy-striped flannelette sheets she'd loved when she was a girl. What little she had was neatly in its place.

'Thank you,' Kitty said.

Her mother tutted. 'No point cleaning a place unless you do it properly.'

'I mean for—'

'I know what you mean, Kitty, and I'd rather not talk about it. We'll only fight, and I don't want that. I'll hold my tongue for the moment.'

Kitty couldn't help herself, and even though she was biting back the words as she said them, they came out anyway. 'Hold your tongue? You've made me feel like a right tart since the minute I crossed the threshold.'

The slap came fast, her mother's hand stinging across her face, and tears sprang up in defiance rather than hurt.

'Well, aren't you? A pregnant tart at that.'

Kitty felt the blush rising from her chest, her whole body chilled and steaming red at the same time.

Her mother's smile was not unkind, but it was vindicated. 'How could you think I wouldn't know? I carried you inside me. I know you, my girl, I know how you move, how you lift a cup, put down a pan. You're different. I know what that feels like.' Her words came more slowly, softer. 'I remember how it is to move with a baby inside you, quiet and growing. You can't help but change, even if you don't want to. I can see it in you.'

Kitty's answer was faltering. 'No, I hurt my shoulder, I fell—'

'Yes, love, I've seen your bruises. Pushed, more like. Or threw yourself. Old bloody wives' tale that one, about falling down the stairs, no chance of it working early on.'

Kitty just stared back, nothing to say when her mother seemed to know it all.

'Then I'm right?' her mother asked.

Kitty nodded.

Her mother seemed to deflate then, stepped into the centre of the room, turned first one way and then the other and then sat down. Kitty brought her a glass of water.

150

Her mother took it and slowly sipped. She shook her head. 'I can't tell you how much I hoped I was wrong.'

'I am sorry, Mum. I'm sorry for it all,' Kitty said, sinking to the floor.

She wanted more than anything to lean back against her mother's legs, to feel those bony knees against her own bony shoulders, to laugh as they had when she was younger about the pair of them being the spit of each other, all sharp angles, to have her mother stroke her hair with her heavy hand. To feel at home. But those times were long gone. She sat neatly on the floor, her legs to one side, listening to her mother, who, as ever, had a plan.

'I've been thinking about this. I've thought about nothing else for days, truth be told. I imagine you're determined you won't marry him or he won't marry you?'

Kitty's voice was clear when she said, 'I'd rather die.'

'So be it,' her mother said. 'The way he's taken advantage of you, we're better off having nothing to do with him. They're a brazen lot, those Nelsons, all brass polish pretending to be gold. I've said that all along, no matter how bad your father thinks it is for business. Right, here's what we'll do. You can keep yourself to yourself, no one ever heads down this end of the bay anyway. There's a home over past Eastmere you can go to when you're closer to your time. If you're anything like me, you likely won't show until you're six months gone anyway.'

'I'm not giving it up.'

'You're not keeping it, and no, you're not giving it up either,' she said, stopping Kitty's protestations with a raised hand. 'I'm damned if I'll let another woman bring up my own flesh and blood. When it's born, it can come and live with us, grow up as ours. Your father and I won't be the first couple to turn up with a late baby. Of course people will talk. You think I haven't had the benefit of their kind advice and sideways glances since you strolled off to London with the Nelson lad? But it'll take more than the mouthy snobs of Westmere to put me off my stride.'

Kitty nodded, grateful for a few months' respite. Whatever came next, she had a home and a safe place for her baby to grow.

Her mother stood up, took off her apron, pulled on her coat, taking her headscarf and gloves from her pockets.

'Mum,' Kitty said. 'Thank you.'

Her mother nodded. 'I don't think you've said thank you to me – and meant it – for a very long time. It's nice to hear.'

Kitty was crying, her face crumpled, hot fat tears falling down her cheeks. 'I'm so terribly sorry.'

Her mother pulled her to her feet and held her. They were very close and her hold was firm and strong. She whispered fiercely in her daughter's ear, 'You're mine, Kitty. Don't you forget it. I don't have to like what you've done to love you. And I'm at my best when sorting out a mess, your dad always says.'

'This is one hell of a mess,' Kitty moaned.

'It is,' her mother agreed sharply, pushing her away with both hands and looking her square in the face. 'And this is the right thing to do with a bad situation, as I'll tell anyone who cares to mention it. Not that anyone would dare.'

Kitty nodded, wiping her eyes.

Her mother spoke sharply as she pulled her headscarf tight and knotted it under her chin. 'I'm not condoning a bit of it, you know that, don't you? Not a bit.' She turned on the top step. 'And you've an appointment at the cottage hospital at eight thirty tomorrow morning. The matron is a friend of mine. She said she'll give you a job until you go to the home. I doubt it'll be anything much, but it's money in your pocket and it will keep you busy. You mind your manners when you speak to her. She's doing me a very big favour with this.'

When she had watched her mother stalk off along the path, up between the other rows of huts, seen the last of her coat flapping in the wind, Kitty came back inside. It was well past six, and neither of them had eaten since a corned-beef sandwich her mother brought down from the guest house hours earlier.

She put on the kettle and sat as she waited for it to boil. She heard the waves outside, quiet now with the low tide, the seagulls fighting each other over strands of seaweed, the odd dead fish, cracked cockle shells exposing cool flesh. The kettle whistled and she poured the boiling water into the pot, watched the leaves swirl up and then settle. She fetched the milk from the side pantry Geoff had put in for her, modelled on the one in her room at Corngate Street.

The hut was full of early-evening light. It was clean and quiet and it was hers. She was safe. She took a sip of too-hot tea and welcomed the burn on her lips. She wanted to mark this, mark herself. She needed to remember this moment. This was the second time in six months she had made a little home for herself, and it was the last one she ever intended to make.

Twenty-One

Westmere, 1957

Kitty slept well on the first few nights in Lullaby Beach. Coming home to her family had felt like the loneliest choice she'd ever made. Now that her mother was in on the secret, at least there was someone on her side, no matter how sharp she was about it or how very decided she was about the baby's future. It was a future Kitty was far from persuaded of, but that was five or six months away, plenty of time for her mother to change her mind, plenty of time for Kitty to work out what she herself wanted to do, about the baby and her life.

The job at the cottage hospital was with the dead and dying. Kitty wondered if her mother had known when she sent her off to meet the matron. The woman was kind, and remarkably sanguine about what she called Kitty's 'predicament'; she said it had happened to more nurses than she cared to count, there was no point wringing their hands and wishing otherwise, the thing to do was keep busy and be useful. Kitty's job was to help the nurses who were attending to the few terminally ill patients, taking the dirtiest work off their hands. Whenever she had a spare minute, she was to support the mortuary attendant, washing the bodies, preparing them for their families to see and take away.

Matron filled in Kitty's card as she explained, 'You'll know we're the only hospital for both coastal towns and the villages in between. The older folk prefer to come to us, so we have what you might call a steady flow of the dying and the dead. You'll be needed and welcome and it'll keep your mind off things. Stay busy, work hard, that's the way.'

Kitty was enormously busy, and to her great surprise she found that the work suited her. The nurses were glad to have her help but had far too much to do to bother with gossip or chat. They told her the tasks they wanted her to take on and left her to it. It was the same in the mortuary, though less to do with Alf the attendant's schedule and far more to do with his desire to sit outside and note birds in the notebook he carried in his overalls pocket. The hospital was built on several fields bought from a local farmer and still overlooked working agricultural land, so at any quiet minute Alf was out the back door and peering through his binoculars across the fields. He showed Kitty around the mortuary, supervised her first washing and laying-out and then declared her well trained.

Working alone for twelve hours a day would not have been her choice six months earlier, but now Kitty found that the repetitive tasks of the mortuary and the care required in doing the most menial tasks for the dying was exactly what she needed. The repetition gave her time to reflect; carefully and gently washing an old lady or a dying young man who had soiled themselves, giving them as much dignity as she could, allowed her to care beyond herself. By her third week she was trusted to do a few more exacting jobs, and Alf even allowed her to help with a couple of bodies as he prepared them for burial. There was an undertaker in the city, but for many in the fishing and farming communities for whom the boom would never happen, the small fee Alf personally charged to get the body ready for the ground was as much as they could afford. If it was a scam, it was one Matron and other staff turned a blind eye to. They were all doing their best for the community they served.

Kitty worked Monday to Saturday, came home to Lullaby Beach at eight in the evening exhausted and glad to be so. She ate well in the staff canteen at dinner time and made herself a scratch tea in the evening, egg and chips or a bit of bread and jam. Most nights, as the sun was setting, she took a long walk along the front, returning with gratitude to the safety of her little home. She could not deny that time was passing – she was wearing her mother's skirts and frocks because the few she had brought from Corngate Street would no longer do up – but the routine of the work and the simplicity of her week felt like a pause. It was a moment to catch her breath and it felt good to be breathing again.

The fourth Sunday in the hut she woke very early, before it was properly light, and stretched in the comfort of her own bed. The soft pillows and good new mattress that had held her all night were very different from Mrs Kavanagh's old bed, tired from however many people had slept in it. Even thinking about that made her shiver. She shivered more at a fleeting image of herself as an ignorant girl, hanging around the hut so that she could watch Danny at work with her father, not even a year ago. The memory of her childish infatuation and how obvious she must have been made her wince. He'd seen her coming all right. She pushed the memory away, determined not to allow the past months to poison her new start. She closed her eyes and sank back down, a few moments enjoying the quiet of the room, the soft rhythm of the waves outside.

When the building work on Lullaby Beach was planned, her mother insisted that if they were going to bother with the

156

time and money of a rebuild, it had best be done properly. She demanded that Kitty's father pay extra attention to the bed, always top of a list of customer complaints. Too soft, too hard, too low, sheets wrong, pillows wrong, you name it, they moaned about it. Kitty's father took extra pains, building the bed right into the frame of the hut, the headboard forming part of the back wall, with thick wadding as insulation between the inner and outer walls, so no one's sleep would be disturbed by a creeping sea mist. It might be just a glorified hut, but it was solid and warm. With the connecting door open, the curtains left wide in the main room and her pillows bunched behind her, Kitty could lie in bed and look right out to sea.

After a while, she got up and made herself a cup of tea, opened the front door to stand outside on the deck while the kettle boiled, the beach all her own. She counted the waves as she had done as a child, first picking out the big crashes and then noting the small waves that followed, each one beating its own rhythm, part of an unknown whole.

She washed quickly, delighted as she was every day that she no longer had to share a toilet and bathroom with eight other people. She took real pleasure in pulling on a plain cotton skirt and loose-fitting jumper. The outfit was completed with a light cardigan against the morning breeze and an old pair of her mother's shoes – 'You'll need to look after your feet, you'll see,' her mother had said. She was dressed exactly like the boring women of Westmere she had so derided less than a year ago. Now that she was wearing the costume, she felt it for the liberation it was. No man would give her a second glance dressed like this, let alone the kind of looks she had come to both expect and dread in her time with Danny and his investors: hungry, appraising, owning.

She closed the door behind her and took herself out for a

walk in the sharp, fresh air while the front was still quiet. The light was pale, the sun just above the water and yet to burn off the thin mist that hovered over the sea, the whole of the Westmere seafront looked softly washed out.

She started out picking her way over the pebbles, careful of the piles of seaweed dumped by the tide, and by the time fifteen minutes had passed, she was into her stride. When they were little, she and Geoff had known these pebbles as well as they knew the peeling wallpaper in their shared bedroom and the layers of paper beneath, stories of other years, other lives. Kitty knew how to walk on these stones, lifting her feet and planting them squarely, a broad base for the uneven surface. This was the opposite of all those nights teetering back across Waterloo Bridge, her feet could feel the sand holding and shifting beneath the rumble of stones above. She knew how to tread here.

She turned the corner where the spit led out at low tide, separating the small bay where Lullaby Beach lay and the wider bay where most of Westmere preferred to play, built up with arcades and tea shops. The pier stood out half a mile ahead, its stilt legs naked above a low tide that was almost on the turn. Kitty broke into a run, leaping across the stones, arms pumping at her sides, her long dark hair tangling in the wind off the sea. She stopped at the pier, heart racing, eyes stinging and nose running from the speed and the wind. She laughed at herself, a caricature of a child dressing up in Mummy's clothing, cardigan bunched around her waist, shoes covered in damp sand and a mosaic of tiny stones and broken shells. She turned up the incline of shingle and headed back along the paved front, the rising sun at her back, warming the breath of hope swelling inside.

That hope died as she came closer to Lullaby Beach. Danny was standing on the deck. It was impossible to see him clearly at this distance, but she knew by the way he stood, his hands on the rail, his legs apart, a ship's captain off to conquer all before him. Closer still and there was a lift of the chin, a stare that took her in, all of her. The whole time she walked towards him, one foot after the other, into his orbit when she wanted to be anywhere else, her mind was screaming that she should turn away. Instead she ran a hand over her hair, winced at the rat's tails, pulled the cardigan tighter. She was seeing herself in Danny's eyes, seeing herself with shame.

Kitty stood at the bottom of the steps leading up to the hut. Five steps, each one closer to Danny.

'You're not coming up?' His mouth was smiling, his eyes were not.

She tried to speak. She knew how much he hated it if she didn't respond. She didn't care what he hated, not now, yet at the same time, she did. Her lips were a thin, tight line. No words came.

'How about a cup of tea, Kit? You could probably do with a cup of tea, rushing along the beach like that. You'll do yourself a mischief.'

She swallowed, tried again to speak, but there was too much to say and all of it needed saying at the same time. A few words wouldn't do.

He shrugged and turned to the door. She thought he was planning to kick it in or shoulder it, had seen him do that before.

'It's open,' she blurted out. 'I never lock it, no need down here.'

He laughed, taking a key from his pocket. 'Even if you had, your dad got me to fit the locks. I thought a spare might be useful, just in case.'

He opened the door and let himself in. Kitty watched him walk into her home and wanted to cry, wanted to run. She climbed the steps to the deck, each step a world to cross. She tried to remind herself by the feel of the cardigan, the smell of the seaweed, the sound of the waves, that she lived here now, she was not in Corngate Street, she was not answerable to Danny Nelson.

'I'll put the kettle on, shall I?' He smiled, very calm, very cool.

She watched him, at ease in her home, in her life.

Danny stood in the middle of her front room, taking up all the space, all the air. He turned slowly in a circle, pointing things out, speaking to himself but for her to hear, the way he used to when he hit her, when he tried to make her see sense. He admired the new curtains, the clever way she had arranged her belongings, making the hut seem almost spacious. The bookshelf with a few novels and her first nursing textbook taking pride of place. He rummaged in drawers and cupboards, found the pot, the tea cosy, spooned out the leaves, got them a cup each, saucer too.

'Just like you've never been away. Bet your mum and dad are well pleased, your boring brother too. Bunch of no-hopers. They'll be laughing themselves silly that you've come back with your tail between your legs, wanting to be let in and a saucer of milk besides.' He looked at her and let out a disappointed sigh. 'Is that what you're after, Kitty-cat, all togged up in Mummy's cast-offs? Trying to be the good little daughter so they'll be nice to you and let you sleep in a hut on the beach? I mean, it is just a hut, isn't it? Not exactly putting themselves out, are they?'

He turned back to the kettle on the little stove. 'I know a watched pot won't boil, but you're the only boiler here, love. You don't half look a fright. Give your hair a brush, there's a good girl.'

'No.' The word came at last. Simple and stark. It came at

'love'. She shook her head. 'No. You have to go, Danny. I don't want you here.'

'Not really up to you, though, is it?'

'It's my home. I don't want you in it.'

'But Kit, you're my girl, everyone knows that.' He shrugged. 'Well, my girl and anyone else's, right? My girl and anyone else that I say.'

She was shaking, a deep, shuddering shake that came from her lower back, through her gut, forcing her breath into sharp bursts. 'Not now. I don't want you. I'm not that girl. I'm not her.'

He turned towards her properly then and the space between them shrank. The hut was tiny, a doll's house, and Kitty and Danny were the wrong dolls, too large to fit, forced into the room anyway. He reached out and it was as if his hand crossed the room and time, weeks and months contracting to nothing. Kitty could smell his tobacco, his hair oil. Her stomach lurched and she thought she might throw up. She brought her hand to her mouth and he nodded. She could tell from his smile that he thought it was in fear, but Kitty was smiling behind her hand, smiling in wonder and relief. The smell of him had made her realise that she felt no lingering desire, only a clear and deep anger. The smell of him made her feel sick. She was done with him, and it was such a relief to know this in her body as well as her mind, a visceral understanding. She felt her bones slide back into place, her heart slow down to normal, her heaving stomach come to rest. Her breath was calm, her words quiet and simple.

'I don't want a bar of you, Danny Nelson. Get out of my home.'

He left the kettle boiling. At one point she tried to reach for it, just to stop the shriek of the whistle, but he wouldn't let her, pinned her tighter beneath him on the rag rug on the scrubbed floor. He said he'd pour the bloody water over her if she moved. Part of her didn't believe he would and part of her wasn't at all sure he wouldn't. The whole time he was raping her he was talking to her. His voice was mostly calm, deliberate. He told her he was letting her go, giving her permission to go, but on his terms. He told her that he would decide when they were done. After this, after today, they would be done. He'd not been dumped by a tart before and it wasn't going to happen now, not when he'd finally signed the deal. He said this just proved how stupid she was; she'd done so much of the work towards it – on her back, he added, this back, he raked his fingers along it – what a daft cunt she was to have come back to Westmere now. Just when it was all coming together. She could have had it all, been lady of the bloody manor. But no, she'd behaved like a tart and a tart she would stay. And now, because he said so, now they were done.

Kitty lay on the floor for a long time. He had left the door open and she heard the tide coming in. The waves were closer, louder. The sea wind was chilly. At some point she pulled the rag rug around her. At some point she thought about the men and Danny, Danny and the men. There was a difference. She had said yes to those men. She had not wanted to sleep with them, not chosen to sleep with them, but she had decided to go along with it. Going along with was not the same as wanting. She had neither wanted nor gone along with Danny just now. And she had honestly been afraid about the water, boiling water all over her, he'd said.

He'd kicked her when he left. He had gone through to the little bathroom and pissed in the toilet, the sound and then the smell of his piss streaming out. She would wipe the floor later, as she had so often at Corngate Street. He didn't

162

wash his hands, Danny never did, not even when he came to her straight from a site. He came back into the front room doing up his fly, the toilet unflushed, and as he was leaving, he aimed a kick. At her stomach, she thought. Perhaps he had guessed about the baby. Or at her body, she later realised, down there, her sex. She had moved, though, turned about. She wanted to see the sea, to know for sure it was still there, the water ready to hold her no matter what. So he came back looking at his fly and not paying attention to her on the floor and his kick, wherever it had been aimed, went to her right shoulder, between the shoulder bone and her neck. She heard the crack from inside her ear as well as in the room. He heard it dulled by her skin and thin flesh, by the toe of his boot. Steel-capped; he'd stopped in to see their new building site on his way.

'Ah, fuck,' he said. It was the tone he used when he knew he was in the wrong. The more wrong he was, the angrier he became. Kitty had learned never to contradict him and damned her neck and shoulder bones for doing so now.

He paused, took a breath, perhaps the first moment he had stopped since he stepped into the hut. Then he walked around her, slowly and quite carefully, out onto the deck, down the steps two at a time, his boots crunching away across the shingle in the golden light, his whistle on the wind.

The kettle was ruined. She turned off the gas. Such a waste.

Twenty-Two

Westmere, 1957

Kitty took care to visit a big library up in London. Frightened though she was to take the train to Waterloo, to risk bumping into anyone she knew, Danny worst of all, her need was more urgent than her fear. She spoke to the young man behind the desk in the reference section, explaining her interest in women's reproductive organs, monthly cycles and pregnancy. He blushed a hot red, mumbled something about being new and pointed her in the direction of a row of shelves far from the centre of the room, a dark corner left aside for medical concerns and what he stammered out were 'women's problems'.

The books were old and many of them were terribly out of date. Kitty knew the old wives' tales about keeping your hair dry during your period and not eating certain foods, but she hadn't expected them to be written up in medical textbooks. Nor had she expected to find graphic explanations and accompanying diagrams that answered her questions. She had thought she might have to search for days to find the methods, but there they were. Several books had long lists of herbs that could be given to pregnant women as drinks or tinctures or in suppository form. The accompanying pieces said that they were recommended by medieval midwives when the baby had died before birth and the woman herself was dying of the foetus rotting inside her. The books took care to give no guidance about dosage, pointing out that many women died from taking the herbs in wrong measures, a stark warning to anyone seeking the knowledge that Kitty was after.

Eventually she gathered a stack of books and went to a table right at the back of the long room, far from the main pool of light where half a dozen people had been sitting all morning. There was an elderly man who looked as if he was in the library simply for somewhere warm to sleep; the bottoms of his trousers were ragged and his shoes had long ago seen better days. There was a small table with several young men. Kitty decided they were students with final exams looming, a fretful silence hummed around them, interrupted only by a hushed swapping of books, whispered comparisons of notes. In the whole huge room there was just one other woman, a middle-aged lady in one of the large leather chairs, quietly reading a novel. The scarf around her neck half hid a short strand of pearls, and every now and then she ran her index finger along the iridescent ridge of beads. Kitty promised herself that one day she would sit alone and read a book. All she needed to do was get through the next few weeks, the next few months. She started to make her notes.

It took her over a week to gather everything she needed. Despite the damage to her shoulder and neck, she went to work as usual. When Alf caught a glimpse of the bruising on the back of her neck, he asked her what had happened. She told him it was just a daft accident. She'd tried to climb East Cliff to bring back some of those wild irises her mother liked so much.

'I forgot I wasn't eight years old, Alf, that's all. Until I came over all dizzy and took a tumble.'

She took his advice and showed her shoulder and neck to the doctor who specialised in the broken and fractured bones of holidaying children and the old people of Eastmere's nursing home. He warned her that her shoulder might never again sit properly or her head turn easily, adding that she was lucky not to have broken her neck.

On two consecutive Sunday mornings Kitty took long bus rides to small towns she had never before visited. She went for slow walks in the woods with a small bag in her jacket pocket and a little fork to dig up plants that matched the sketches she had made from the medical books, keeping the roots intact and marvelling that the local woods had so much more variety than she had ever before noticed. Only a year ago the old paths had been nothing more than a route, now her attention was focused and sharp. She did not want to accidentally poison herself. She had been surprised at first to realise that she did not want to die. She wanted rid of anything to do with Danny Nelson, that was all, that was everything. Some part of her was still a young woman invested in a future, she had decided to train as a nurse when all of this was over. There was a person she could yet become and she needed to stay alive to become that person. There was a baby belonging to Danny Nelson she had to get rid of first.

Kitty pulled the curtains as soon as the sun went down. Her bedroom and the front room were lit only by her bedside lamp. She covered the bed with her two towels and a freshly ironed sheet, reasoning that if heat sterilised medical instruments, then perhaps it could sterilise fabric as well. She laid everything out and took extra care sterilising the knitting needles, boiling them in her one big pan for over half an hour and leaving them simmering on the little stove, ready for when she needed them.

Eventually there was nothing left to prepare, no reason to wait. She lifted the hot pan from the stove and set it beside the bed, the water still hissing. She closed the door between the bedroom and the front room. The tide was far out. With the windows shut and the curtains drawn there was a peculiar silence in the room, an absence of the uncertain rhythm of the sea.

She took off her pants and folded them, laid them on the wooden chair at the side of her bed. Somehow this simple action reminded her of every night of her childhood: the old chair with the frayed wicker seat had come from her bedroom in the guest house, the pants were plain, tired. Kitty felt plain, tired. She sat on the edge of the bed for a moment, held her shaking hands together, brought her head to her knees to hold back the dizziness.

Then she lay down on her back and pulled up her night-dress, letting her legs fall apart. Each action was a memory, Danny's hands, another man's hands, another. Kitty assured herself she was alone, these were her hands. She stared at her legs, mottled with cold despite the curtained warmth of the night. She whispered to herself that she was here in the hut, the doors and windows were locked, she was alone and she was safe.

Slowly she reached down and felt inside herself. She was surprised at how tender she was. She had felt the burning when she peed, had known herself to be scratched, scraped from his force, but she had been moving carefully because of the damage to her shoulder and neck. She had not realised quite how bruised she still was. Hesitantly, wincing at her own touch, she felt for the top of her cervix, her shoulder burning with the effort of reaching, her neck twisted to hold through the pain. With her other hand, the easier shoulder, she reached for one of the needles. It was hot from the boiling water and she chose to feel the metal burning her finger and thumb. Her skin and flesh would soak in the heat, a scar would pass, she was doing it now. Kitty could not wait for the needle to cool, to be easier to hold. If she waited even a minute, she might never do it.

Ignoring the pain, she opened herself more widely, pushing away the thoughts of Danny, the words he had said as he forced himself in. She was glad it had happened in the other room, that her bed had not been touched by what he had done. Slowly she moved the needle up and in, one hand holding, the other guiding, biting her lips against the pain that groaned within her as well as across her shoulder and neck.

She had practised with the dressing table mirror positioned opposite her body and had decided the mirror did not help. She couldn't get close enough to see properly and the light was not bright enough anyway. When she had tried to get right up to the mirror, standing in front of the dressing table with one foot on the floor and the other leg up, the pains in her neck and shoulder were too intense, shooting down her right arm. Worse, alongside the pain there was also the chance of seeing herself, looking into her own eyes. She did not want to look at herself as she did this. Somehow it was more bearable if she was not hurting herself in this way. If she was not herself.

It took several stabs, each one deeper, pushing harder, to get the needle inside her cervix. Even when she did, it did not slide through as she had imagined it might, making guesses as to the distance it needed to travel, imagining her body as the cross section in the library medical books, the length of her vagina, the length of her cervix. The needle shuddered slowly in. A push of half an inch, another push met this time with resistance. She didn't know what was resisting, her body itself or the hand she was using to push, scared to hurt, to

168

damage. After a few minutes, her hands and legs shaking, sweat rolling down her forehead and into her eyes, stinging more than the tears that had been falling for some time, she decided this was it, one last effort and she would be there. Taking her time, breathing slowly, trying to calm herself, just half an inch more, Kitty stuttered the sharp metal into her flesh, into herself and into the other self she could no longer bear to hold.

For the first few hours there was nothing but some blood, a gentle cramping, nowhere near as bad as the period pains she usually had, the period pains she had spent the past four months yearning. And then there was nothing. Kitty waited an hour more and finally gave in to a deep, dreamless sleep. She woke after seven hours, astonished that she had slept the whole night with no pain from either her shoulder or her neck stabbing through sleep to wake her. She realised she had not moved, simply dropped still into darkness. She had been lying on the doubled towels and was disappointed to see that she had not bled in the night, nothing had happened in her sleep.

She opened the curtains at the front of the hut and left her door and front window open. It wouldn't do for her mother to pop by and ask why she had everything closed up. By mid morning there was a dull ache in her lower back; by late afternoon it had grown to a fat belt of pain, encompassing her lower belly and hips in a swelling grip. She tried to eat a plain biscuit but the smell made her gag. She sipped alternately at cold tea and a glass of water, tepid on her dry lips. Beneath the pain lay a thick sediment of fear. Kitty was terrified she might pass out, that someone would find her.

Her research in the library, gathering a jigsaw of information from a dozen or more books, had helped her work out what to do to abort the baby. It had also alerted her to the deep interest the law had in her body and in punishing her for the action she had taken last night. The books also quoted the Church, its sure and certain belief in eternal retribution. Kitty did not believe in God, punitive or otherwise, but she did believe she had brought this all on herself – the brutal fire in her gut, the waves of pain that had her sweating like a pig one moment and shaking with cold the next, the retching that produced only bile, chest aching with the effort of heaving. Hours of her body reacting and the whole time she had no idea if she had succeeded in freeing herself of Danny Nelson's baby, or if she had gone too far, pierced something, ripped something, if the blood was hers alone, or hers and the baby's. In the midst of the pain, deep into that night, she no longer cared which, she just wanted it done.

The baby came away over a day later. A chunk of something that was more than blood but less than flesh, something of her and also completely alien. She bit into her fist to stop herself crying out, smothered her eyes, her nose, her mouth with her hand and remembered Danny doing the same, smelled again the tobacco on his fingers, felt the heat of his hand keeping her from breath. Finally she lay back on the bed in sweat and grief, the last of her dreams with Danny slipping out in the blood between her thighs.

She walked far out into the water that night, trying to rinse away the loss and shame, to wash away the Kitty who had wrapped up the mess in a towel, who now sluiced herself down. After a while she waded back to the shore. She stood on the beach and found nothing was washed away but blood.

Kitty spent the next day in bed. She had asked for a few days off work, called from the payphone on the corner before she started the process, left a message for the sister that she was coming down with something nasty. No one wanted vomiting and the runs at the hospital, she knew she had a couple of days to hide. She lay in her bed, bleeding, sweating, crying. The pain shifted. At first she was doubled over as if dragged inwards from both the centre of her spine and her belly button, pulling front and back into a centre that was trying to empty itself. Later, after she had forced down a cup of tea, a slice of bread, and had vomited both, the pain was a rack, stretching her out on sheets that were damp with sweat, crusted with blood.

Two and a half days after she had ironed the sheet, boiled the needles, laid out the towels, the pain began to subside. She slept for almost five hours, waking ravenously hungry, her throat aching with thirst. She stumbled through to the front room, leaving the door locked, the curtains closed; she drank water from the tap and then poured herself a fresh glass, and another. She went back to bed with the remains of a dry loaf and a saucer loaded with raspberry jam, a cup of tea with three sugars to make up for the milk that had gone off. She curled into a ball and fed herself, a wounded cat, breaking off bits of bread, dipping them in jam, sipping tea between slow mouthfuls. When she was finished, she left the cup and saucer on the floor and pulled the dirty sheet around her, the blanket over her head. She slept.

She woke to the high-pitched scream of a seagull, and opening her sticky eyes realised it was too dark for the birds, understood that the scream was in her own head, her mouth, her room. She woke to the high-pitched scream of her own loss, a keening, drowning grief, sorrow and relief in one, the deep seam of mourning opened, revealing the pain of the past year. Dreams ruined, trust broken, hope lost and, finally, through tears and sweat and blood, through her own body, truth acknowledged.

Kitty was too young to know that she could survive grief, too new to loss to know it would not always feel this way, and she was far too young to tell herself she would get over it, feel better later, that she would come through. And so she went in, far into her physical and emotional pain. She let her body feel it all, do the suffering for her.

Somewhere in the dark of that night, Kitty re-formed herself. When she woke up on the third day, it was with a firm resolve never to let another man bring her to that place in her life. She pulled back the curtains, unlocked the door and windows, stripped the sheets and remade the bed.

Kitty told her mother about the miscarriage a week later. She was surprised when her mother cried, had expected her to say it was just as well. She sat silent for a moment, then took Kitty's hand, pulling her down to sit beside her.

'I'm so sorry you went through that alone. I'd have been here with you, I'd have held you.'

Her mother spoke haltingly then, with untried words, a story barely told. She talked about the baby she lost between Geoff and Kitty.

'It was six months, they keep babies alive at that age now, not often, but they do. You see it in the papers, incubators and everything. Not then, though, not this baby.'

Kitty stared at her mother. Her tone was firm, her hand had its no-nonsense grasp, but there were tears for the child she had never had a chance to raise.

'We gave him a name, your dad and I. Your dad wasn't sure, but I was adamant. People said we ought to just try again and get on with it, the best way to get over losing one baby was to have another as soon as you could ...' She broke off and turned to look to the sea behind them as if looking out to a wide horizon might make sense of advice she had never believed. Then she turned back to Kitty. 'And I was glad to fall for you, Kitty, but it was hard.'

She paused, and Kitty wondered if she had ever known this woman in front of her, speaking with a simple openness she had never imagined her mother might possess.

'I did what everyone said,' her mother was saying. 'I got on with it. Spent the whole time I was carrying you terrified, and God forgive me, but when you were born I felt . . . ' She sighed, lifted her hand from Kitty's to ball into a fist, knuckles white with holding. She took a breath and Kitty saw the deliberate act of will that stilled her hands in her lap. 'I wasn't well with you and the birth was hard. It was wicked of me, I know, but I was relieved there were only two of you after all. Wicked and weak.'

Kitty couldn't comprehend the idea of her mother being weak in any way. This was a woman she had never known to give in to a cold, who carried on through the deaths of her father and mother, thought nothing of working five weeks in a row with no time off, welcomed guests at Christmas because they needed the money, no matter that it meant half a dozen extra Christmas dinners and cooking breakfasts as if it was any other day.

'Not you, Mum, you've never been weak.'

Her mother wiped her eyes, blew her nose and then looked up. 'Rationing, worry, the war. It was all hard. All they ever talk about now is Blitz spirit and Churchill and sing-songs in the Anderson shelter, getting on, but it wasn't like that at the time. You were not well the first few months, Kitty, you were a frail little thing, but we had a boy and a girl. We stopped trying because neither of us could take any more. Your father joined up and I looked after you two and counted the days until he came home on leave.'

'Why did you never say?'

Her mother took a deep breath. 'We've told you the things your father saw in the liberation, after the war ended.'

'You told us he was there when they liberated the camps. He didn't tell us more than that, though. I only really know about it from school and from the papers.'

'He was in a terrible state when he came home. Shaking all over from what he'd seen, things he couldn't get out of his head. My home was not bombed, my family not lost, my husband came back. Your father needed me to be strong.'

'So you were.'

Her mother nodded. 'And so are you, Kitty Barker. This has been a difficult time and I'm sure one day we'll look back and see we've learned some lessons and maybe it was worth it. Perhaps. Though if you ask me, I think sometimes we just suffer and that's all there is to it.'

She stood up and smoothed her skirt, folded away her handkerchief.

They walked out onto the deck and Kitty's mother spoke over her shoulder as she stepped down to the path. 'I don't think you need mention anything to your father or brother. We'll keep it between us.'

Then she was gone, stalking along the path to the front, fastening her headscarf as she went, defying the wind.

Twenty-Three

Westmere, June

The summer sun was at an angle Kitty had loved, warm light streaming into the hut from the front door and the big front window. The girls had learned to cook in Kitty's kitchen and had long felt that it was theirs, Kitty welcoming that sense as she grew older and less inclined to cook for herself. Sara pulled pots and pans, crockery and cutlery from drawers and cupboards and they divided them into items that would stay in the hut for now and things that could go to the charity shops that took up most of Westmere's high street.

It took a few hours, but by the time the sun found its way to the side window overlooking the marshlands, they had one useful pile for charity and everything else was back in place, neatly stacked, clean and tidy. The crash of breaking glass made them both jump, immediately followed by another crash and a deep thudding noise, accompanied by the horrible smell of burning lighter fuel.

'What the hell?'

They jumped up and ran towards the sound that came from Kitty's bedroom, both terrified at what they'd see and ready to do battle with whoever had caused it. The bedroom window was smashed and a broken glass bottle lay in shards on the floor, burning fuel flowing around it, smoke rising rapidly as the flames met Kitty's old bedding.

Sara covered her mouth with her T-shirt and ripped the eiderdown and blankets from the bed to throw over the fire. It hadn't had time to spread and, seeing Sara had it contained, Beth ran outside to try to see who had attacked them.

The path itself was empty, but there was someone running away along the overgrown marsh path, impossible to see more than a silhouette against the setting sun. Even so, she found herself chasing as she roared after them, 'Come back, come the fuck back here!'

She was stopped in her tracks by a cry from Sara. She rushed inside to see her sister stumbling from Kitty's bedroom, a smouldering bundle of bedding in her arms.

'What is it?'

'I'm fine. I burnt my hand. I thought it was all out but there was a little pool of burning fuel. I'm taking this lot down to the water to make sure. Go back inside and check. I don't think it had a chance to get any further. Bloody lucky we were here, the bastards.'

'I'll come with you – your hand . . .'

Sara was already past Beth and shouting behind her, 'I'll be fine. Pull out the bed, make sure there's nothing I've missed.'

As Beth walked into the hut, the stink of fire and fuel hit her. For such a small missile, the shattered bottle had done plenty of damage in a very short time. She took in the broken window, the dirty stain of burn marks and lighter fuel on the floorboards, the stink of fire in Kitty's sanctuary. She gasped with shock, taking in their loss all over again. In the anger that superseded her shock, she wrenched the bed away from the wall it was built into. It took three firm tugs to pull it out, the boards bending and surrendering rather than splintering as she'd expected. She pulled it away as far as she could and clambered over it to check. There was no sign of fire, no embers, and it didn't look as if any fuel had made it this far.

She reached her arm into the gap between the inner and outer walls just to make sure she hadn't missed anything. As she groped around, she felt something hard and firm; running her hand over it, she felt a handle, clasps. It took a little levering, but eventually she pulled it out, and in the mess of the room, her heart pounding with grief and anger, she stared down at Kitty's old medical bag. It was the bag she had used after she qualified and all through her first decades as a district nurse. They had played with it as children, playing nurses like Kitty. Beth felt the tears push up from her belly as she ran her finger along the indentations marking out Kitty's initials, the strong lines of the K, the curves of the B, her own letter. B for Beth. She opened the bag. There were several bundles inside and she took them out one by one, laying them on the bare mattress.

When Sara came back to the hut with her armload of wet blankets and sheets, Beth was on her knees on Kitty's bedroom floor, the bag beside her, tears rolling down her cheeks.

'Are you hurt? What is it?'

Beth shook her head and picked up one of the bundles, clattering metal wrapped in a linen square that Sara recognised as the one Kitty used when she taught them how to make a sling. Inside were Kitty's old medical instruments, her first stethoscope and the tongue depressor the girls had played with as children. There were other instruments they had not seen before, although they'd known she must have had them.

'Kitty's work. All her work,' Sara whispered.

Then Beth handed Sara a second bundle, her tears turning to a low wail. 'Sara, look.'

Sara took it carefully from her sister's hands. It was very

light, something small and delicate inside. Her thoughts went to a walk they had once taken through the marsh paths, and a long-dead tern she had found, feathers folded around a weightless body. This was not a bird. She carefully unwrapped the mummified remains of something that was unformed and far too small, but still, it was very much like a baby.

Twenty-Four

Westmere, 1957

Kitty got on with it. There were times, bent backwards and aching beneath an armload of other people's dirty and stained sheets, or carefully wrapping the body of a young mother, gone before her time, when she cast her mind back to the weeks leading up to last Christmas, the glitter and the hope. If she caught herself feeling wistful, she forced herself to remember the nights in hotels or the deep ache that woke her every day. She remembered Danny's boot to her neck and shoulders as she lay on the floor of the hut, and saw how she carried the imprint of him in her physical body as well as her aching heart. With those memories, the weight of the dead was lessened.

What surprised her was how the need to remember also lessened as she found more pleasure in her work, even when she was in pain. Feeding patients who could barely hold food in their mouths, let alone on a spoon, became a challenge and an art, encouraging a smile from a child with a broken leg was her forte, and she discovered a winning way with some of the dourest old ladies she'd ever met.

Kitty became adept at helping the nurses to lift and wash

the patients who could not get out of bed. Her height helped with the lifting and balanced out the awkwardness brought on by pain. Eighteen months earlier she would have laughed in horror at the idea of nursing as a job, now she saw it as a future. The shift work was welcome and it meant she was able to go for weeks at a time without seeing either her parents or Geoff. One month passed, two, and then three months had gone since those awful days and nights in the hut. She was painstakingly making herself a new life.

It was midsummer before Kitty allowed herself to acknowledge she had not had a period for over seven months, her body had not come back to her own, her old life was still within. She closed the curtains and stood naked in front of the dressing-table mirror in the bedroom. She turned sideways. She had tried to assure herself that her bump was simply because she was now doing a hard physical job and eating all the time to make up for it. She had been constantly hungry, helping herself to extra bread and dripping on the few occasions she had visited her parents, her mother shushing her father when he'd suggested she was putting on weight, then taking Kitty aside herself as they washed up to say that she understood the desire to hide her body away after what she had been through, but covering up with a roll of fat was no solution.

Kitty went back for extra helpings of suet pudding and custard in the staff canteen, the cook glowing with pleasure that here was a girl who appreciated her food, not another silly tart starving herself to get a doctor husband. When she was on day shift and the bus rolled in just after seven in the evening, she bought fish and chips from the stall on the pier, made her way through them as she walked home to the hut, fingers warm around the packet, lips stinging with salt and vinegar and the sea breeze. Her arms were chunkier, her thighs meaty. Anyone encountering her for the first time would have seen what the patients and other staff saw at the hospital: a big girl, strong, her body made for carrying and lifting, a great asset to the staff.

Now Kitty stared at herself in the mirror and her hand reached down to where she was carrying. She must have been carrying twins. She had aborted one, another had survived. She shivered and pulled on her old dressing gown. She thought she had made herself an escape from anything to do with Danny, and now she could no longer ignore all that she had done to herself, for nothing or worse. She did not imagine that whatever remained inside her could have survived the blood loss, the twisting spasms and pain, yet it had.

There was a ward in the nursing home, right at the back of the hospital. The people there were malformed, broken from before birth, their minds and bodies matching in their misshapen forms. Kitty saw a life ahead where she cared for a damaged child and adult for the rest of her years, a baby beaten into being by Danny Nelson's anger, a child that had escaped abortion at its own mother's hand, an adult incapable and shunned.

She spent the next few days in shock. Now that she had acknowledged she was still pregnant, it astonished her that no one else had noticed. She couldn't seem to clear her mind, to put aside the likelihood of being found out at any minute. There would be no chance of keeping her job once they knew, no matter how good a worker she had proved herself to be, and there wasn't enough work to hide away in the morgue every day. She stopped eating, she stopped sleeping, every moment she was beyond the thin walls of Lullaby Beach was consumed with thinking about how best to hide herself from others. She was grateful for the summer rain that meant she was allowed to layer her uniform with a big cardigan.

When her day off finally arrived, she took the bus to the largest town with the biggest library in the area, poring through medical books and terrifying herself about what was to come. She went back to work the next day and was sent home within half an hour after she fainted standing at the sluice. She had not tried to make any friends among the staff, had known she was not ready to share confidences, and was glad now that no one wanted her to confide in them. The sideways looks were enough; a fainting girl invariably spelled some kind of trouble.

Sister told her to take some time off, then come and see her before she went back on shift, they needed to have a talk. The talk came the following week, when Sister took Kitty to Matron. The women were kind but firm: she could finish out the month working in the back ward and the morgue, but then she was off. They were sorry, they had no choice. That was the best they could do. She begged them not to mention anything to her mother, and they reluctantly agreed, advising her sternly that she would need a mother's help soon enough.

A fortnight later, Kitty woke feeling strange. Something had shifted. Her belly felt more full lower down, the twinges she had felt for a few days were stronger now, not really twinges at all. She went to the telephone box with her coins and called both the White Lion and the school where Ernestine had finally found a teaching position. She left messages for her friend with the telephone box number and said she would be standing by between four and six that afternoon and the next. She hoped Ernestine would call sooner rather than later, she was scared to be alone.

When the telephone rang at five thirty that afternoon, Kitty wanted to cry with relief. She took a deep breath and began to speak. Ernestine listened with no interruptions. When Kitty had finished her story, there was a long silence, the sound of the crackling telegraph wire between them. Ernestine went to church, Ernestine believed in God. Kitty felt her shame magnified in imagined judgement. She was about to speak again when her friend let out a deep sigh.

'You poor girl. I'll be on the last train tonight. Leave a light out for me.'

After two days in which she barely slept and hardly ate, Kitty woke in the night with a pain low in her belly and warm wet between her legs. She nudged Ernestine awake beside her and turned on the bedside light, thinking perhaps her waters had broken early, and now she must face what she had been running from for weeks. She saw the horror on Ernestine's face before she looked down to see deep red staining her own nightdress and her side of the bed. The pain shifted higher then, taking her by surprise, and she howled in dismay and horror.

The pain did not stop. There were times in the next hours when it seemed to recede for a moment only to come back much more fiercely; times when it slithered away from her belly and reached round to her back, a burning python circling and squeezing her tight. The sound of the sea disappeared, the seagulls were gone, the wind meant nothing. Her life shrank to the hut, to the room, to the damp, bloody bed, time counted in single halting breaths.

An hour later, Kitty woke to Ernestine sitting her up. 'I need you to drink this water, come, one sip, and one more, just one more.'

Ernestine sat on the bed, cradling Kitty, and helped her to drink. She wiped her face of sweat and tears and then, when Kitty's body became a dead weight, she laid her down and stayed alongside. Her whispered prayer was a counterpoint mantra to Kitty's whimpering moans.

Later still, when Kitty had lost all sense of time passing, when her whole world was contracted to sheer pain, it was Ernestine's voice that cut through the blinding light. 'Push now, Kitty. Come on, my dear, you have to push now. It is time. You have to let it go.'

When it finally came away from her, she was surprised to see that the baby had two arms, two legs, little toes and fingers. They were not perfect, but they were there. Then it made a noise. It was more a sound than a cry, emanating from a face that did not have a mouth, gaps where there should have been features, but still a sound came and with it Kitty felt a surging, tingling pain in her breasts.

Ernestine helped her, and carefully Kitty lifted the gaping mouth that was gums, nose, eyes, exposed jaw, and held it to her heart. She cradled and soothed it, she held it as it became still and cold.

An hour later, perhaps much more, the hut was fully dark, the night sky cloudy and without stars.

With Ernestine's help, Kitty took a clean tea towel and carefully wrapped the baby. When it had been inside her body, she had been able to pretend it might yet survive. Once it was born, once it breathed, whimpered, then stopped, stayed stopped, she was torn in more than just flesh.

She set it down in the centre of the bed and leaned over to breathe a kiss where there was no cheek, no lips to kiss. Leaning on Ernestine's arm, she heaved herself up and walked through the hut to stand on the deck, taking in fresh air that did not stink of blood and sweat. Her mind felt clear for the first time in months. They stood in the cool night for a long time, the tide rolling out in the dark.

After a while, they went inside, locking the door behind them. Ernestine helped Kitty wash and put on clean dry clothes. While Kitty sat cradling her baby, Ernestine changed the sheets and scrubbed and cleaned, first the bedroom and then the rest of the hut. They lit a candle, and in the soft light Kitty fully swaddled the baby, this time covering its unmade face, wrapping and mummifying, secrets she had learned in the morgue. They laid it in a dressing-table drawer, the scent of lavender in the room. In the morning they would work out what to do next.

Ernestine helped Kitty back to bed, she closed the curtains and moved the old armchair close by.

'You need to sleep.'

Kitty shook her head, 'If I sleep, then morning will come and this will all be yesterday.'

Ernestine nodded. 'It will have happened.'

'I don't want it to have happened. I want to go back.'

'Yes. And you will bear this too. Kitty, look at me. I will sit here through the night. See how close I am?'

Ernestine held out her hand and Kitty took it, someone warm beside her.

Three days later, Ernestine went back to London. The friends never spoke of what had happened that night, and Kitty kept the baby close to her for the rest of her life.

Twenty-Five

Westmere, June

'Kitty had a baby?' Sara asked.

Beth shook her head. 'It's too small, six months maybe?'

'But why keep it hidden here?'

'Maybe no one knew she was pregnant. She wasn't married. If the father wasn't helpful or kind ...' Beth pointed to the splintered wall in Kitty's bedroom. 'It was in the wall behind her bed. The bag.'

'Did you know about it?' Sara asked.

Beth shook her head, 'No. God, it's just too sad.'

'It's all bloody horrible,' Sara said, reaching out to touch the bundle that lay between them and wincing as she did so. 'Ow.'

They both looked at the deep red welt across the back of her hand.

'I'll get something for that. Kitty's first-aid supplies were always well stocked.' Beth got up. 'Until she took all the painkillers.'

'Selfish. Burn cream will do.'

Beth put the medical instruments back in Kitty's bag and then very carefully lifted the lighter bundle and placed it inside. She shifted the bag safely out of the way before she went to fetch Kitty's first-aid kit from the bathroom.

'Did you ever go to her clinic? In the evening, after the surgery closed?' she asked as she applied ointment and a bandage to the long burn on the back of Sara's hand.

'After Mark Nelson . . . after that.'

'They were good to you?'

'Amazing. The people she worked with were so cool. And all of them volunteers. Looking after these exhausted sole parents and carers, teenage girls needing the pill or abortions or help with STDs. No sign of disapproval or any of the attitude I was expecting.'

'What Kitty called "no side"?'

'Exactly. She was so sweet.'

'Sweet?' Beth asked, smiling in surprise.

'She was. She was soft that evening, careful. Like she was trying to hold in anything too sharp, too brusque. She walked me in, introduced me to the other staff as her niece and then left them to it. Said I needed my privacy.'

'What did they do?'

Sara sighed, remembering. 'Antibiotics for the STD. It was two weeks since it had happened. They got me a session with a counsellor too, and I could have had more, or seen someone when I went back to Newcastle. They said they'd arrange it, but . . . you know . . . ' Her voice petered out.

'I know you,' Beth said. 'Later? Since?'

Sara nodded. 'Yeah, a few times since. I've seen someone when it's all got too much. It helps – well, it helps a bit.'

They sat quietly for a while. Sara added more whisky to their empty tea mugs, then she asked the question they both knew was hanging between them. 'And you? Did you go to her clinic?'

She waited as Beth took a deep breath, both of them glad the light was almost gone.

'Lucy was nineteen months, just becoming her own little person, and I was pregnant again. I'd had a vomiting bug and I must have thrown up my pill or something. It was an accident, but we had no reason not to keep it. Perfect timing according to all the books. But I was terrified. I was feeling like me, real me, for the first time since I'd had Lucy. When I look back, the difference between how I felt then and after I had Etta, it's astonishing.'

'And I wasn't here to help.'

'It wasn't your job to help. Or Dad's. He was still so shaken and alone. And you and I were still grieving.'

'We were very young. Not that we knew it then.'

'So I was just starting to come back to myself, Lucy had a little routine, I thought I might go back to work part-time. Then one day I found myself sitting on the kitchen floor, sobbing, Lucy stroking my hair and saying "There there, Mummy." I'd been on the floor for hours. I was almost three months pregnant. I came down here with Lucy, and Kitty made me tell her all about it. I remember sitting on this sofa babbling on, and when I finished, she picked up a cup and poured it half full of whisky. She said I had two choices. Decide to have an abortion and her clinic would look after me and I could drink the whisky while she made the appointment, or decide to keep the baby and don't drink the whisky and she'd make an appointment to get me some help. Actually, she said she'd make that appointment whatever I chose to do. She said I couldn't keep on the way I was. Not fair on Lucy and not fair on me.'

'You chose the whisky?'

'I chose to go home and talk to Tim about not keeping the baby. We hadn't even thought it was an option, I don't know why, we'd never mentioned it to each other. He said he thought it was up to me to bring it up.'

Sara smiled. 'The only feminist boy at Westmere Grange School.'

'I'll drink to that.'

They clinked their glasses and Beth told Sara how Kitty had talked to them both, made the appointment, looked after Lucy when they went to the clinic; how it felt like Kitty had been looking after the two adults as much as she was looking after their daughter. Afterwards, Beth and Tim had held each other, let themselves feel the sadness and the relief and then got on with the life they had.

'And when you got pregnant with Etta?'

'That was so different. We were the same age as loads of the first-time parents and Lucy was really excited and wanted to help. Even though work had been going to shit with all the austerity stuff and then Brexit and all Tim's work slowing down and we still had no bloody money, we had space for her, you know? And Kitty had retired too. I knew she'd be amazing with the baby.'

'Their special friendship.'

'Yes.'

'And here we are.'

Sara reached out to turn on the light, both sisters blinking as the mess in Kitty's bedroom was illuminated: the exposed mattress where the fire had been, the bed splintered from the wall. She pulled the medical bag closer to them.

'What the hell do we do about this?'

'God knows. But for a start, we're not selling the hut. There's no way we're going to do anything to make Mark bloody Nelson happy, not after what you've told me about him.'

'I'd love that, Beth, but it's stupid. We should sell. You guys need the money and I'm just being sentimental.'

Beth spoke over her before she even finished her sentence.

'Tim's been looking into it. He thinks they must have been hassling Kitty because of the marshlands access. He says there's probably government funding for development if access is part of their programme.'

'Lullaby Beach gets knocked down to make a visitor centre and car park and they get extra cash to do the job?'

'Something like that. So if it all falls apart we can build our own car park and visitor access. I'll give guided tours.'

Sara laughed. 'Beth, I know you love living by the sea, but you've always hated the marshes, and you're not even a tiny bit interested in wildlife. You'd be a bloody awful tour guide.'

'And for all we know this place has still got more of Kitty's secrets to give up. The Nelsons aren't getting their hands on any of it. Besides, Tim is convinced they have something to do with the arson. Every second or third place that's been attacked is somewhere they're interested in buying or developing.'

'They're interested in everywhere, that's no proof.'

'It's different now,' Beth said. 'Someone attacked this place. And if there's even half a chance the Nelsons had something to do with it, that's a bloody good reason to keep them out of it for ever.'

'I always thought she didn't want to sell because she hated the old man. You know they used to go out together? Kitty and Danny Nelson?' Sara asked. 'I wonder if he was the father.'

'If it was more than just a relationship gone wrong, if he left her when he knew she was pregnant, then that's a good reason to hate him, even before she knew what Mark did to you.'

'Should we call the police about the attack?' Sara asked.

Beth frowned. 'We should, yes, but I can't bear the thought of anyone pawing through Kitty's stuff again. Not now we've found this.'

'Me neither,' Sara said, relieved. 'In that case, we should clear up a bit. A messy home ...'

'... shows a messy mind.' Beth finished Kitty's maxim.

Just as she'd had a well-stocked first-aid kit, Kitty had kept a pile of useful DIY items. While Sara used her one good hand to sweep up the splintered wood from around the bed, Beth nailed boards over the window. She and Tim could come back and fix it properly the next day.

They were walking back up the hill to Beth's when Sara asked, 'Why didn't you tell me before, about the abortion?'

'I thought you'd mind.'

'Disapprove?'

'No, just that I knew you wanted kids.'

'Still do.'

'Yes. And then when time went on and I had Etta too and you still didn't ...'

Sara put a hand out to her, 'We're not little any more, Beth. It's not about what's fair, it just is.'

'You sound like Kitty.'

'Cool.'

That night, in the empty middle flat above Beth and Tim's, Sara let herself cry for Kitty, for the life she had lived and for the loss of her. She lay in the room in which she and Beth had argued, laughed, fought over toys, whispered secrets about boys they fancied and dream jobs they might one day do, homes they'd live in, countries they'd visit. In the dark of an early-summer night, she held Kitty's bag close to her, cradling the old cracked leather, crying for Kitty and for herself.

Beth and Tim talked about the arson attack in bed.

'Do you think Lucy could have something to do with it?' Tim asked.

'Why Lucy?'

'Why not? We've said all along it's probably kids, that Nelson's needed someone to do their dirty work for them. Most of the parents we know are worried it's their kids, why not ours?'

Beth turned out the light and turned in to him. 'God knows. She's been so distant and moody, and I know that's just teenagers ...'

'But maybe not? I just don't know for sure.'

'Me neither,' Beth whispered, as if speaking it quietly might make it less likely.

A car pulled up outside, engine idling, and they smiled as they heard their neighbour get out, thank her taxi driver, trip along the pavement in her high-heeled shoes. The first Friday in the month was Heather's party night. She and her mates, the youngest of them seventy-two, went out every Friday to the same club in Eastmere they'd been visiting since they first left school. It had been through half a dozen owners, but Heather and her friends stayed true. Tomorrow or the next day, Tim, who Heather had always had a soft spot for, would get a detailed account of who was there, who was sick or dying, who had a new lover, whose son or daughter was pregnant or divorcing or coming out or all three.

After Heather had let herself in and both houses had recovered from the shock of her front door slamming, they heard distant sirens, a lone seagull screeching into the dark, then quiet.

Twenty-Six

Westmere, June

While Beth was listening to the night, Lucy was waiting on the pier. Like anyone who had grown up in Westmere, she knew how to get past the gates the council locked at midnight, and which parts of the pier to avoid: the corner where the lairy blokes hung out getting drunk on cheap lager, the seat the dealers and users believed was theirs alone, the sheltered section that was the haven of half a dozen homeless people who picked up their bedding in the morning and settled down again every evening.

Since just before last Christmas she had stood in this spot a few times a month, waiting for him to arrive. Tonight was different. Tonight he was going to have to see her, not just bark out orders and walk away. She had received his message just after nine, agreed to meet him on the pier between eleven and midnight. He would never give an exact time, citing his family as the reason he might be early or late. His excuse of walking the dogs worked to some extent, but there were always questions, his wife, his life, he couldn't get away at a certain time, Lucy would just have to wait. Tonight she was going to tell him this had to stop. She had been building up the courage to confront him since the day Kitty died. She was ready.

Mark Nelson was already there when she arrived.

'Oh ...' she said, unnerved.

'Keeping you on your toes.' He looked at his watch. 'Four minutes late.'

'I'm usually waiting for you, and it's always longer than four minutes,' she said.

'Yes, but not tonight. Right then.' He reached into his pocket for his phone, prepared to bring up the map, show her a location.

'No, Mr Nelson.' Lucy stopped him. 'I'm not doing it any more.' Her voice was querulous. She had practised this, promised herself she would get it right, stand up to him. Now that it was time, she was shaking, hating that she sounded young, fearful.

He smiled indulgently. 'Sure you are.'

She tried again. 'I'm not, you've gone too far.'

He frowned. 'I've gone too far? You're a right one to talk. I think it's you lot going too far that started all of this.'

She was on safer ground now, uncertain still but at least she had something to come back with. 'I've found out we didn't start it. All this crap has been going on for years. Long before us.'

'What the hell are you on about? I'm talking about what you owe me. You and your nasty bloody mates.'

'We've done what you said. It's been ages now.'

'I didn't set a time limit,' he said.

'Maybe you should have. We did one dumb thing ...'

His frown turned to a smile. 'Oh, more than one, Lucy. It started with one dumb thing, I grant you, but so far I've counted at least half a dozen fires you have personally started. That's quite a few more dumb things.'

'You said I had to.'

'I gave you a choice. I gave you all a choice.'

'We had no other option, you said—'

'You said, you said,' he mimicked. 'Listen to yourself.'

'But you did, you said that if we did what you told us to, you wouldn't ... I mean, you said that you would ...'

'Can't even bring yourself to say it out loud, can you? Can't admit what you did. No one forced you, no one took your hand and made you do it. Not the crap that started all this, you and your mates being right little bastards, and not the crap since. There is always a choice. You thought you were making a choice tonight, didn't you? A choice to stand up to me, to tell me where to get off. Well?'

Lucy didn't know what to say. Whatever she said he would twist it, he always did. She had tried to talk to him about it when this all first started, but he knew just what to say to shut her up. He made her feel like a child again.

Because she couldn't speak, she pulled a folder out of her bag instead. Inside were two photocopied pages, the writing was Kitty's. The date at the top of the first page was Christmas Day 1956, the second said 12 May 1957. On the first page Kitty had listed the sparse details of the night Danny Nelson made her sleep with Marty Gilbert. On the second were a few lines about Danny Nelson attacking her in Lullaby Beach, kicking her in the back, the neck, the shoulder, creating the damage that Lucy had known all her life and had never asked about. Kitty was disabled, Kitty had a limp, Kitty's head didn't turn properly.

She handed over the pages. 'This is what I mean. It started long before us. Your family has been bullying mine for decades.'

Mark held the pages up. The photocopy was pale, the handwriting unclear, but even in the half-light, certain words on the page stood out. Danny Nelson's name stood out.

'Where did you get this?' His tone was far less hectoring now; he was serious.

'They were with her suicide note, my aunt's.'

'Where's the rest of it?'

'The rest of her diary?'

Lucy waited, she certainly had a choice now. Mark Nelson wasn't to know that only these two ripped-out pages had been in the envelope with Kitty's suicide note, that Lucy had taken them hoping to use them against him. She could tell him the truth and hope that he would think these two pages were bad enough, or she could chance it. What Kitty said on these pages was heartbreaking. And that meant the rest of her diary must have said a lot more. The arson had to stop. She couldn't do it any more, it was too horrible, too hard. If Mr Nelson thought she had Kitty's diary, surely he'd stop blackmailing them.

'I've got the diary,' she said, her voice strong now, calm. She was amazed at herself, she had stopped shaking, she stood straight in front of him. She looked into his eyes and saw that he was worried, and his fear helped a little, gave her some courage to go ahead. 'I've got her diary,' she repeated. 'You keep those pages, show them to your uncle. There are plenty of other things Kitty says too. I expect you can guess what. Or he can. So you're going to stop making us burn things down for you, you're going to stop contacting me and you're going to leave us all alone. If you don't, I'll publish it. Everything Kitty says about your bastard uncle, I'll put it all online.'

Lucy turned and walked away then. Her heart wasn't pounding, her hands weren't shaking any more. She felt strangely clear and light. She felt as if it was over, all the awful stuff that had been going on since before Christmas, finished.

As she put her key in the front door, she had a passing thought, too vague to grasp, more like a remembrance of a dream, there and then gone. It lasted only a second or two, but long enough to shake her sense of calm. She went to bed and slept eventually, uncomfortable and uncertain.

She woke a little after three and sat up in a sweat, terrified. She reached for her phone, and there it was, the possibility she hadn't let herself consider, made plain in a message from Mark Nelson.

You have those old pages, I have the video. Which will work better online?

Twenty-Seven

Westmere, June

Lucy didn't sleep again that night. She texted Sara at seven and told her she needed to talk. Sara agreed. She had felt there was something more than the suicide note that Lucy wasn't telling them, perhaps after a long run she might be ready to share more.

They ran towards Eastmere, a long, straight run along the cliff walk, then down the path to the bay, looping back at the renovated lido, followed up with a strong, fast pace along the beach path that led them back to Westmere, the tide seeping out as they ran, Lullaby Beach waiting at the end.

By the time they stopped at the hut, Lucy was sobbing, her shoulders and chest heaving with the effort of running and crying at the same time. Sara held her niece as she cried, letting her go on until she finally shuddered to a repetitive hiccup of slow, quiet sobs. Then she sat her down, gave her some kitchen paper to blow her nose and wipe her face and a glass of water to follow.

'Drink it all. Running and crying is very dehydrating.'

'What do you ... do ... you ... do when you ... can't stop crying?' Lucy stuttered out her words between sobbing breaths.

'I barely start. I'm crap at crying. Sometimes I cry as I run. A bit. I don't think I'm the person to talk to for tips on crying, Lucy. But that's not why we're here, right?'

Lucy nodded and Sara waited. She had promised herself that she would wait until Lucy told her whatever she needed to, but she was finding it hard to hold back.

'It's hard to talk about,' Lucy said eventually.

'Do you want me to start?'

Lucy looked at her sharply, 'What?'

'I think you know something about who attacked this place. And maybe the other arsons that have been going on around town, or at least some of them.'

'Why? What?'

Lucy's look of guilty horror was enough to confirm her fear. In a small town it was impossible to keep secrets, especially among teenagers. If Lucy didn't know who was responsible for the arson, she was bound to have heard some gossip about it. Sara paused and looked away, watching two seagulls follow each other in swooping circles, and when Lucy didn't respond, she turned back to prompt her. 'Is that what you wanted to talk about?'

'Yes,' Lucy whispered. 'I . . . Yes, I do. But it's not just that. There's stuff . . . It started a while back.'

'OK.'

'I don't know if I can talk about it.'

'I can't help if you don't tell me,' Sara said.

'I want to,' Lucy's voice was a desperate wail, 'but I can't say it. I tried to tell Mum. I know she gets pissed off when I tell you things and not her. I tried to tell her before Kitty died. I couldn't do it. I couldn't even start.'

'How about I just ask? The fire here, was it someone you know?'

Lucy waited a moment and then, stumbling over her words, she whispered, 'It was me.'

Sara was glad that the fierce flash of anger in her stomach overcame her horror, it helped her prod more than she might have done otherwise. 'Christ, Lucy, you have to tell me why. I can't believe you'd do something that stupid without some kind of reason.'

'I didn't, I wouldn't. There's a thing that's been going on. Someone made me, made us . . .'

'Made you set the fires? Others too?'

Lucy nodded and shook her head at the same time. 'Yes. No. There were other times and other people involved, friends. I could have said no, but it didn't feel like we had a choice. And there wasn't anyone I could tell. I even tried to tell Kitty. It's like I know all the words and they're here,' she brought her hand to her forehead, 'but I . . .' she shook her head and slammed her fist into the hard bone of her temple with each word, 'I just – can't – say.'

Sara took Lucy's balled fist and held it. 'I get it, more than you imagine. And much as I know that smacking yourself in the head feels like it helps, it doesn't make any difference to the problem. Not in the long run. What if we talk about talking about it? The thing you can't say, would that be a start?'

Lucy pulled her fist back from Sara's hand and pushed it firmly against her breastbone. 'It makes me feel sick, here. Whenever I think about telling someone what's going on, what happened, I feel sick and hot.'

Sara was increasingly worried that she was out of her depth, wishing she'd demanded Lucy speak to both her and Beth. She turned to fully face her. 'You're embarrassed?'

'Sort of. But worse.'

'Is it shame?'

'Ashamed?' Lucy's voice was small.

Sara frowned. 'We get ashamed of something we think the world disapproves of, but shame's more about something we know in ourselves is wrong. Or maybe it's something that's wrong in others and we feel it because of them, because of how they've been to us.'

'This is inside. Definitely. But everything's got so much bigger than me. Then I tried to fix it, last night, and I've made it even worse.'

It was about the arson and it was not. There had been a party, back before Christmas, before anyone had their decorations up, in the last few weeks of school when it all felt tired and old. They had gone to a mate's house, someone from school, a girl whose parents had a big house with a basement room they used as their own. It wasn't meant to be a party, it was just heading towards the end of the year and the evenings were getting dark earlier and they'd all had a bad week at school and so they decided, fuck it, they'd forget the week by getting pissed. Some kids had brought beer or cheap wine and some were getting stoned, someone had some MDMA, someone else had brought coke. Coming up to midnight, most of them left to go home, the ones with Saturday jobs. Then there were just four of them left.

'I could have gone home then. I wish I had.'

'What happened, Lucy?'

Lucy shook her head and turned away.

'Listen, darling,' Sara said. 'I know there are things that are really hard to say out loud. And sometimes saying them makes it feel like the thing is happening again, but it isn't, it's just you and me here. Whatever you want to tell me, I'll listen, OK? I promise.'

Lucy took a breath and began to tell her story, all the while looking out of the front window and down to the beach so she didn't have to see Sara witnessing her shame.

Twenty-Eight

Westmere, last December

Karl stretched his arms above his head and cleared his throat. 'I've got some fun.'

The space he took up was as much about the way he barely acknowledged the girls as it was about his size. At eighteen, he was already well over six foot and broad with it. He was big and fit and good-looking and had never before done anything but ignore Lucy from the comfort of Ariane's parents' sofa.

Unusually, he had included her in his conversation all night. At first she wondered if she was imagining it. Karl was all about the image, and his image was dark, troubled, interesting. It was not friendly and not chatty. He had a massive old coat that he wore all year round, inside and out, only taking it off at school because their head teacher made a fuss about it. The coat had a heavy collar that Karl wore turned up, his dirty-blond hair was long and messy, he wore old jeans, white shirts, and a pair of massive boots he also refused to take off – and had persuaded school to let him wear them all the time by insisting his parents couldn't afford any others. All the kids knew this wasn't true, but their teachers didn't want to look like they were singling out a poor kid, so Karl sloped around town and the school corridors in his seven league boots looking like he had stepped out of an eighties teen movie, and until tonight Lucy had thought Karl had no idea she existed.

Tonight he had been different. Every now and then he had broken away from his conversation with Wilson to look across at the girls and catch Lucy's eye. Lucy couldn't tell if he was drunk or stoned, or if it was an invitation. She hoped it was an invitation.

It was.

Wilson groaned. 'Mate, you never know when to stop.'

Ariane shook her head. 'I think I'm out. I'm probably too pissed.'

Karl wasn't persuaded. 'Ah, come on, I've been saving them until there weren't so many of us. There wasn't enough to go round before, but now ...' he stood up, reached his hand into his pocket, 'there's enough to share.'

He opened his hand and showed them three small grey pills that looked as if they'd seen better days.

Ariane wasn't impressed with what he had to show. 'You might at least have dusted them off.'

'Nothing wrong with a bit of leftover biscuit,' he said, licking the crumbs from the tips of his fingers.

'How do we know they're not just aspirin?' Ariane asked.

'You don't,' Karl replied to Ariane but he was looking at Lucy. 'You take a chance.' He turned back to Ariane. 'How about I share mine with you? Least I can do after your hospitality tonight.'

He knelt in front of the two girls, hand outstretched, offering.

They were both sitting on the floor, slumped low against the sofa, and Karl was big in front of them, even on his knees.

Lucy wanted to sit up properly, to lift herself to his height, but he was looming over her. She started to get up and he put his free hand on her shoulder, pressed her down without exerting any effort. She could smell a mustiness from the old coat, weed and tobacco on his fingers. Lucy liked the weight of his hand, liked that he left it there, cool on her bare neck where her jumper had pulled to the side. He rubbed her neck with his thumb and she felt a soft scratch from his ragged fingernail.

'Take one for yourself and one for your mate,' he said, nodding to Ariane, who was sitting up now, ready to start again.

Lucy looked up at him, daring him. 'You said you'd share yours with Ariane,' she said.

'And I will,' he answered. Taking his hand from her shoulder, he took a pill, bit it in half with his front teeth, swallowed one half and gave the other to Ariane. 'Here you go.'

From behind him came Wilson's voice, amused and a little irritated. 'Karl, that's our actual friends you're trying to impress with your druggie cool. We all know you, mate. When you've stopped playing your new game, could I have a share too?'

Karl winked at Lucy and spoke over his shoulder to Wilson. 'All gone. Don't worry, I've got some coke you can have.'

He crouched down in front of Ariane, ran his finger along her bottom lip and gently nudged her lips apart, popping the second-to-last pill into her mouth. 'Swallow it down like a good girl.'

Ariane nodded and swallowed and then burst out laughing, but Lucy didn't find it funny, she found it sexy. She wanted Karl to do the same to her. He leaned over her, one hand on the sofa, and offered her the last pill from his hand. There was a scar running along his palm, heavy and red, it must only have been a few months old. She kissed it very quickly before she caught the pill in her teeth and swallowed it. She grinned up at him and they smiled, complicit.

Lucy wasn't used to feeling sexy. She'd always been younger than most in her year, and while it had been an advantage in some ways, she was beginning to feel she'd fallen behind when it came to sex. Her Instagram feed was full of stunning young women of colour and all of them seemed proud of their sexualities and their bodies. Lucy knew she could make herself look like that online too, but it was far from how she felt in real life. A few of their friends had been in serious couples for a while, and even more of them had paired off recently. Lucy was interested, increasingly so, but she was also nervous and scared of getting it wrong, being found out.

Now she looked at Karl and then looked away, astonished by how beautiful he was and that she hadn't seen it before. Ariane turned up the music and the two girls started dancing, swooping around the room, up onto the sofa and low down to the floor, creating an unchoreographed routine that had Wilson and Karl clapping along and then applauding when Lucy collapsed on the sofa and Ariane slid to the floor at her feet. Then Lucy was talking to Karl and Wilson, the boys on either side of her, she was in one of those sitcoms where everyone is sharp and smart and talks twice as fast as real people. She shifted seamlessly from intense and acute obser-vations about other kids at school to climate change and the state of the nation. She felt far outside of herself, away from her constant critical inner monologue. She felt funny and pretty and clever.

Ariane was funny and pretty and clever too. In fact, Ariane was bloody beautiful. Lucy thought they looked like the pic-tures they shared of themselves online, semi-naked photos with perfect lighting and carefully placed emojis in which they were either utterly beautiful or totally bereft, always with an ironic wink or phrase so no one could accuse them of taking themselves too seriously. Images that remained for twenty-four hours or less, there and then not there, showing their lives in an impossible light, open and exalted. Right now, Lucy felt like that girl, the one with the perfect look.

They grasped hands, and Ariane's skin was so soft, and then they were kissing, not the pretend kissing that was really about getting the boys to pay attention to them, but actual kissing. Neither noticed that Karl was filming them.

Eventually Lucy realised Karl had gone quiet and saw what he was doing, and while a faraway part of her was hurt, upset, a much more present part of her found it funny. She began playing up to the camera and Karl egged her on, encouraging them to touch each other, to keep going. Lucy could see herself performing for him, she was both in her moving, touching body and outside of it. When Wilson joined in, Karl kept filming. Lucy looked around then, pulled back into herself by the change in balance, two now three. She saw Karl on the other side of the room, watching the screen on his phone watching them.

At some point they were too hot, clothing was thrown to the floor. Lucy was in her bra and knickers, Ariane had taken off her tights and her jumper and was in a thin little dress. Wilson was holding Lucy close, Ariane dancing wildly behind them both. He reached around her back and Lucy could feel him fumbling with the clasp on her bra. She froze, sober for a sudden moment, looked from Karl's grin to Wilson's eagerness. Then Karl looked at her from behind his phone and nodded towards Ariane. Lucy saw her way out. She directed Wilson towards Ariane instead. Karl kept filming.

Twenty-Nine

Westmere, June

'Oh Luce,' Sara said.

Lucy let herself look up, her voice low and sad, her words stilted. 'It gets worse. Ariane pushed Wilson back to me, she was trying to help him take off my bra. They're mates. They were. I didn't like it, I got angry with her, so I . . . I said they should get Ariane to take her clothes off too. And then Karl and Wilson were chanting and calling for her to strip. I was laughing, we all were, Ariane was laughing as well for a bit. Only it wasn't funny, not really. Then Ariane started crying, like she had only just realised what was going on, only just seen that Karl was still filming it all. She thinks she's not pretty. She is but she thinks she's not and so she hates it when people share her photo without asking, and by then she was doing all this ugly crying and then Wilson got his phone out too and him and Karl were shouting for her to take her clothes off. She was only wearing this little dress over her knickers, no bra, and Karl grabbed it. He ripped it.'

'Her dress?'

Lucy nodded. 'I don't know if he meant it, any of it. It just . . . it went weird. It felt like no time had passed, but later I knew it had, it must have, because all sorts of stuff happened. Ariane's dad came home and he came running down to see what the noise was and he was really angry. He saw Karl and Wilson had their phones out, saw that they were filming. He screamed at Ariane to put on her dress properly, but she couldn't because it was too ripped. She was crying so much, more about her dad seeing her like that, I think. Maybe. Maybe not.' Lucy stopped, frowned, questioning herself, questioning her story. 'He made the guys give him their phones and he went through them, deleted the videos. He was amazing actually, really scary but also kind of incredible. He just stopped everything. He sorted it all out and sent us home. We thought it was over.'

'But it wasn't?'

She shook her head. 'He must have sent Karl's video to his own phone that night. And it's got everything, right from the start. You can see me, I don't stop, not even when . . . '

'When?'

'The other stuff. The guys are touching Ariane. Karl and Wilson. Filming themselves touching her.'

'Hurting her?'

'Yes. No. I mean, they're not attacking her. But she's only wearing her knickers and they're touching her and she's asking them not to. And I'm just laughing, Sara, in the film. I'm laughing.'

Sara nodded, waiting for more. Her heart was racing and her mouth was dry just listening to Lucy's story.

'And I can hear stuff too. Wilson was talking really quietly and I didn't hear him that night, but on the film you can hear him. He's saying all this awful stuff, all this white-girl-on-black-girl crap. It's so horrible. And it looks like I'm laughing about that too. Like I think it's OK. But I didn't, Sara, honest I didn't.'

'Bloody hell, of course not. I know that, Lucy.'

'So then a few days afterwards, Ariane's dad called us all. He said we had to go over to theirs. He made us watch it, Karl's film of us, on this massive TV they've got. He made us sit down and watch it. Ariane wasn't home, she'd gone away with her stepsister, they took her on holiday. We're awful in that video, we're just really fucking horrible. Then Ariane's dad threatened to send the film to our parents and to school. And I couldn't bear Mum and Dad knowing about that, I can't . . . and other kids, at school . . . Everyone knows something happened, of course, but no one has seen the film, not yet. The guys, Karl and Wilson, they played it down afterwards. Like it wasn't such a big deal, just a joke. But it wasn't. And I can't bear the thought of people thinking I'm like that.'

Lucy started crying again and Sara held her until she could speak.

'But I am like that, right? I did it. And that's what I hate the most. I am like that.' She finally ground to a halt.

They sat quietly for a while and Sara knew that Lucy was waiting for her to say something wise and sensible, something that would fix it. The best she could manage was to say that Lucy had done the right thing in telling her what had happened.

'I don't know what to do, Lucy, I'm sorry. Not yet. I need to work it out. But you should never have had to deal with this by yourself, any of you kids. Ariane's dad was wrong to threaten you like that. He should have just deleted the films straight away.'

Lucy frowned. 'Yeah, but I've made it worse since. I did something else.'

'OK,' Sara said slowly. 'What else?'

Now Lucy was sobbing again and Sara found herself torn between wanting to tell her to spit it out and pity for her niece's horrible pain.

'You'll hate me,' Lucy stuttered between sobbing breaths.

'I don't know what I'll feel until you tell me, but even if I do hate you, it won't last. It couldn't. I have to love you, Luce, I can't not. But I can't help either, not unless you tell me what's happened.'

'You're right about the arson. It was Ariane's dad. He made us do it for him.'

Sara started to ask why, but she realised that she already knew. Even before Lucy said his name, she understood who was behind this.

'He owns the big construction company, you know, the one that Dad works for sometimes,' Lucy said.

Sara nodded, and her stomach turned over.

'He said we had to do stuff for him or he'd show the video to our parents, to everyone. So we did. We have. We've been setting fire to places, the huts that burnt on the beach, the old ones along from Kitty's place and those two empty shops in town.'

'But why? When you knew your mum and I were in the hut?'

'I only did it because you were here and I knew you'd put it out.' Lucy's voice was plaintive. 'I didn't think you'd get hurt. I'm so sorry. I had to tell him I'd tried. He told us he'd been down here trying to get Kitty to give the place up.'

'He said that?'

Lucy nodded. 'It's like Dad says, some planning permission stuff about the marshes. Ariane's dad said it's a big deal and that Kitty was just being stubborn. But I don't see the point anyway. They have so much already.'

'If you want it all then almost all is never going to be enough.' Sara's voice was quiet. 'He said you had to set the fires for him or he'd share the video?'

Lucy was very still as she answered. 'Yes. And there's

something else. There was more, on Kitty's bed. Something else I took. They look like pages from a diary or something, only the pages are about old Mr Nelson, Ariane's dad's uncle. Who used to own the company?'

Sara nodded. She couldn't bring herself to answer, she was so angry with her niece.

Lucy went on. 'Kitty wrote on those pages that he made her sleep with another man. And he beat her up. That's why her neck and shoulder didn't work right, he did that.' Lucy took a deep breath and then nodded, as though promising herself she could do this, say the words. 'I didn't want to do it any more, so I showed the pages to Mr Nelson, to Ariane's dad. I photocopied them and told him I had the diary they came from and that I was going to make it public. What his uncle did to Kitty. What he'd made us do. I thought it might stop him.'

'What did he say to that?'

In answer, Lucy got out her phone and showed Sara the text she had received that morning from Mark Nelson.

You have those old pages, I have the video. Which will work better online?

'What am I going to do, Sara?' she asked plaintively.

'I have no idea, but we're going to start by telling your parents.'

Thirty

Westmere, June

Tim and Beth were quiet while Lucy told her story. They had waited until Etta was in bed, and then, with Sara's support, she told them what had happened that night last winter, what had been going on since and what Mark Nelson was now threatening.

Everyone in the family always commented on how similar Lucy and Sara were, right from the time Lucy started to walk. Yes, they had different skin colour, but their height, their strong bodies and long limbs – Sara enjoyed knowing that people sometimes thought she and Lucy were mother and daughter. Now she watched Beth's face as Lucy spoke and she saw a new comparison: the way her sister bit her bottom lip, the slightly crooked line between her brows, her eyes wide and brimming with tears she fought to hold back. Beth looked so much like Lucy had just a few hours earlier when she'd told all of this the first time round.

When Lucy was finished, she curled up against her mother and said, again and again, 'I'm sorry, I'm so sorry.'

Tim stretched out and knelt in front of his daughter. 'We

all screw up. Every one of us. We'll fix this, we'll make it better.'

'But how?' Lucy wailed, and Sara felt like wailing along with her.

Tim's voice and face were grim when he answered. 'I have no idea. But we will, I promise.'

Eventually Lucy was calm enough to go to bed. Beth went up with her and Sara and Tim sat in silence until she came back.

Tim made sure the door was firmly closed before he allowed his hands to form fists. 'Fuck. That. Bastard.'

He was speaking so quietly that both Beth and Sara had to strain to hear him, but neither needed to ask him to repeat the words.

He shook his head. 'What can we do? Nothing, right? And he knows it. If I go over there, and believe me I'd love to, he'll put the film online. If I do nothing, he can keep blackmailing them as long as he wants. I work for that man. I take his fucking money. It pays for the food on our table.' Every word was slow and deliberate, an agony of holding himself back.

Beth reached out, forcing him to take her hand.

She turned to Sara and her words were as careful as her husband's. 'I hate that Lucy took Kitty's note. I hate that she took those pages Kitty left and didn't tell us until now. And you know what, Sara? I'm really bloody pissed off that she came to you with all this.'

Sara reeled back, astonished at the venom in Beth's tone. 'What? Why? I got her to tell you as soon as she told me. What was I supposed to do? Not even listen to her?'

Beth shook her head. 'I don't know, I just wish she'd come to me first.'

'Yeah, well she didn't. And that's hardly the problem right now, is it?'

Tim groaned. 'Seriously? The two of you have been tiptoeing around this bollocks for years and you want to do it now? No way. Get over it or do it later. We have a kid to look after.' He turned to his wife and pointedly added, 'All three of us.'

Sara nodded and sat back in her chair, prepared to let it go for now.

Beth sighed. 'There's something else. Don't worry, it's not about Lucy,' she added quickly, seeing the panic on both of their faces. 'It's about Kitty.'

She went upstairs and came back with three notebooks. 'These are Kitty's diaries.'

Sara looked at the books in Beth's hand. 'Where from?'

'They were in the medical bag.' Beth turned to Tim. 'The bag we found in the fire. With the baby.'

'And you didn't tell me?' Sara asked. 'You didn't tell me there were diaries too?'

'We were ... There was the baby ... and I was all confused, and ... ' Beth ground to a halt. 'No. I didn't tell you. I know you want me to let it go, Tim,' she said to her husband, 'but it's all joined up. I wanted ... I wanted some of Kitty to myself.' She looked at Sara. 'Like you and Lucy. I'm sorry.'

Sara shook her head, furious.

'I have to go out,' Tim said, standing up.

'Tim, please ... ' Beth reached out to him.

'No,' he answered, 'I need to get out. I'm going for a run. I'm not going to do anything stupid. I can't, can I? I just have to put up with it. I can't even look after my own daughter. But if I don't do something with this anger, I think I will probably go over there and kill that man, so I'm going to go for a very long run and hope that no one gets in my way.'

A few minutes later, Sara and Beth heard the front door close, Tim's feet pounding into the night.

'Have you read them?' Sara asked eventually.

Beth nodded. 'It's all in here. Danny Nelson beating her up, abusing her, her running away from him. Some pages are missing, but that makes sense now that Lucy showed us the ones Kitty left for us.'

Sara held out her hand for the notebooks and Beth handed them over.

'There's other stuff too, Sara. About Mum dying, Dad's depression. And the things that happened to us. Her life and ours, in her tiny, tight handwriting. There's not much detail, but it's all there. I think she wanted us to know why she did it, that's why she said "rip it all out". Why she left us the pages about Danny Nelson. I think she wanted us to know. There's a last entry. It's the day she died.'

Sara stroked the cover of the top notebook. 'Poor Kitty,' she whispered.

'She writes about us too,' Beth said.

'You said.'

'No, I mean us. This shit. She writes about our grief, jealousy, our differences. She knew us so well. I miss her knowing us.'

'Me too.'

That night Sara sat up reading Kitty's words until her eyes were sore with crying and wanting sleep. She read until her anger found a plan.

Thirty-One

Westmere, June

When Tim came in, exhausted and sweating from his run, Beth was still wide awake.

'I thought you'd be asleep.'

She shook her head. 'I can't sleep. I want to fix it. I want it never to have happened. I want these last few months to be over and for all the hurting to stop, and I want ... ' She stopped, frowning.

'What?'

She ran her hands over her arms, her shoulders, her belly. 'Apparently I really want to make love.'

'Apparently?'

She shrugged and knelt up on the bed. 'Yeah, my mind is going crazy. My body just wants you.'

Beth wanted to grasp, to pull Tim to her; she wanted to be closer to his skin, flesh, bone. Their child was hurt and the body that had grown that child sought succour in his. The sex was practised and fast and Tim fell asleep soon after. Beth was glad of it. She waited until his breathing was calm and regular and then she carefully got up and dressed again. She went downstairs and quietly gathered her supplies. It was not quite two in the morning. She left the house and made her way down to Lullaby Beach.

Once she got to the hut, her actions were deliberate and careful. She cried as she walked through the few rooms, picking up one item after another and then laying it down again. In the end, she had gathered a small pile of things that were precious, to her and Sara or to the girls. She placed them in a box and took them outside, left them by the path where she hoped she would be able to collect them later.

She slept for a while on the bare mattress of Kitty's bed. Just after six, she sent the text she had written while waiting for Tim to come home from his run. She had waited and she knew it was still what she wanted to do. She checked the text when she got to the hut and then again when everything was ready. She went out to the deck where the reception was better and pressed send.

Then she took up her seat in Kitty's chair on the deck and waited. The summer sun was already warm on her face, the blue of the sea reflecting the clear sky, wave tips rearing up white and then gone. It could have been any summer morning, up early for the best of the day. It was not.

In less than an hour, she heard footsteps on the path, men's voices. She forced herself to breathe slowly, make her face blank.

Mark Nelson wasn't quite as tall as she remembered and his hair was surprisingly grey. He looked healthy, tanned, strong. On second glance, the grey was a carefully managed silver, perfectly toned to his dark blue eyes. He actually looked fitter than when he was going out with Sara, imagining he was so interesting as he shagged her little sister and cheated on his wife. He looked good. She felt sick. Behind him, Danny Nelson stood glaring at her. The same height as Mark, he seemed shorter because he was stockier. He must have been in his late eighties and yet he looked a good decade younger.

Mark smiled. 'If you wanted my attention, you only had to call.' He peered in through the open door. 'Your sister hiding in there, is she? Haven't seen her for a while.' He grinned, and Beth read years of Sara's pain in his smile.

She looked at them both, so sure of their ground, of their right to Kitty's home.

Danny Nelson spoke up from behind Mark. 'You going to invite us in or what? I built this place, you know. I'd be keen to have a look around.'

'Go ahead, the door's open,' she said.

They walked past her into the hut. Mark immediately settled himself on the armchair that had been Kitty's chair indoors and Danny prowled through the two main rooms and the little bathroom, opening doors and cupboards, pulling out drawers, pacing the length and breadth of the space like an old tomcat marking his territory, sniffing out competition.

Beth stood at the door, unsure what to do next. Seeing them here was less disturbing than she'd expected. Mark Nelson was so incredibly ordinary, so typical, in his jeans and freshly ironed shirt, his dyed hair, the tan that set off his fat gold watch.

Mark nodded towards Danny and smiled at Beth confidentially. 'Don't mind him. My uncle's always been very proprietorial about this place, he's been aching to get his hands on it for years. You probably know we asked Kitty to sell it to us ages ago. He's dead pleased you want to talk about it now.' He leaned in. 'I didn't tell him the full content of your message, obviously. The fewer people who know about the mess your kid's in the better, don't you think?'

'I could do with a cup of tea, girl,' Danny said, rubbing his knee as he sat down. 'The lad insisted I come down with him. Bloody early to do a deal, if you ask me. Still, always better over a cup of tea.'

Mark smiled. 'He'll settle down a bit. Old people, eh? Forget their manners. Your aunt Kitty was just the same, ranting and raving and waving her stick at us, never even let us come in. We offered her a good deal on this place. Bad as children once they're in their eighties.'

Beth stared at him. She had promised herself she would take her time, think before she spoke, give nothing away. It was hard, but the longer she waited, the slower she took this, the more likely she was to stay in control. The more likely that he would reveal himself.

She picked up the kettle and held it under the tap, concentrating on the sound of the water hitting the metal, the rising tone as it filled. She focused on the hissing of the gas, the strike of the match, the low roar of the catching flame. All the while the tide rolled in outside and Mark sat smiling, watching her. She knew he was appraising the difference between the woman he saw and her sister, her daughter. She could feel his gaze at the back of her neck, and between her shoulder blades a rising of ancient hackles, an internal rearing-up, spitting-back. She heard Kitty telling her to save her punches. She took another long, slow breath.

Mark started to speak, but his words were drowned out by his uncle's groan. 'Buggeration, got to piss,' Danny said, and struggled out of his chair.

They listened to him bang open the bathroom door. He pushed it shut but didn't close it properly, a dribble of piss slowly and noisily eked its way from him in the otherwise silent hut.

'Sorry,' Mark said, nodding towards the noise. 'The old bastard's impossible to take anywhere. No couth, as my dad would have said.'

Beth carefully poured boiling water on tea bags in mismatching mugs, one for each of the men, nothing for herself. She would not normalise this meeting with the drinking of tea.

'It's going to be a bit sticky if you're not going to talk to me, Beth,' Mark said. 'Hard to work out what to do for the best, you know?'

She turned to him. 'Milk?'

He laughed. 'Yes please. And two sugars for the old fella.'

Danny Nelson stomped back into the front room and sat heavily on the hard chair by the door. 'What happened to the wall by the bed?' he barked.

'Some absolute bastard blackmailed a teenager to burn the place down,' Beth said lightly, placing his mug on a coaster on Kitty's bookshelf. 'We had to rip the bed out to make sure there were no hidden embers.'

Danny snorted. 'Kids will say anything to get out of trouble. You don't want to believe them.'

'Do you have children of your own, Mr Nelson?' Beth asked.

'No I bloody don't,' he said. 'More trouble than they're worth.'

'You'd probably agree with that at the moment, wouldn't you, Beth?' Mark asked.

Now she turned to him and looked at him properly. 'I love my girls. I'd do anything for them.'

'Yes,' Mark said clearly. 'I feel the same. So we know where we stand.'

'We do.'

'Oi, enough flirting, you two,' Danny said with a wink to his nephew. 'We're here to negotiate, let's get on with it.'

'Negotiate?' Beth was still looking at Mark.

'Don't play coy,' Danny answered. 'You're as bad as Kitty,

all butter wouldn't melt and then turning on the sauce when it suited her. I know there's some bollocks going on with you two and your children. You sort that between you and then we'll get on to the real business.'

'Danny, shut up,' Mark said as he stared at Beth, an odd look on his face. 'I've got an idea that Beth thinks there's more going on here than just a land deal. Am I right?'

'Loads more.' Beth nodded. 'I want to see you delete the film the kids made. And so that I can trust you won't ever use it, I want you to make one of your own, confessing to raping my sister.'

'What?' Mark asked, and he was on his feet.

'You heard,' Beth said.

'Bloody hell, you women and your rewriting of history.'

'Really? Is that the best you've got? "Women don't understand us"?'

'We screwed, Sara and I. That's all it was, a fling. She was young but she wasn't underage. And yes, I was married, so what? It's not a crime.'

'You raped her, in Newcastle.'

'I damn well did not. It wasn't anything like that.'

'And you,' Beth turned to Danny, who was looking on in surprise and not a little pleasure, 'you bullied and pimped Kitty. You forced her to sleep with men for a business deal, a bloody business deal. And then you beat her up when she was pregnant with your baby. It's like a hereditary disease, you two.'

Danny spat on the floor, his enjoyment gone. 'I've had enough of this crap. Are we doing a deal or what? Because if not, I'd just as soon burn this place down myself. I'm sick of bloody waiting.'

'Danny, shut up,' Mark said, glaring at his uncle.

'Piss off, lad.' Danny crossed the room to stand in front of Beth, and now his gait was not so feeble, his age less obvious.

Beth took a step away and realised she was backed against the cooker. She reached behind her and felt the heat of the kettle. Mark was muttering angrily at his uncle, telling the old man to calm down, that he had things under control, and Danny was closer, leaning right into Beth. She could smell his breath, sweet and a little rancid, lungs damaged from decades of cigarettes and beer. Mark stepped forward to pull him back, but Danny shoved him away, the younger man tripping over Kitty's old rug in the centre of the room and falling back against the sofa. As Danny stretched out his arm to snatch at Beth, she reached behind her and grabbed the kettle handle, swinging it around in front of her.

'You come any closer and I will burn you. I mean it. I will throw this water in your face. It's only just boiled, it will hurt.'

Danny reared up, and suddenly he seemed far bigger and much younger, puffed up with anger and scorn. 'You stupid little tart,' he snarled in Beth's face, knocking the kettle from her hand and ignoring Mark's howl of rage as he scrambled out of the way of the hot water. 'Your aunt tried that trick on me, you know? I let the kettle burn itself out as I knocked her flat. Stupid bitch didn't have the sense to get out of my way, laid herself down on that self-same rug. Like a dog, she was, waiting to get kicked.

'You're all the same, you Barkers. Prick-teasing bitches the lot of you. You go along with it and then get cold feet and scream and say we got it wrong. Your sister and Mark screwed while she had some dyke girlfriend, so she had to say he raped her. Yes, I know all about it, don't look so surprised. Kitty shagged a couple of blokes I was doing some deals with and suddenly she's all heartbroken that I think she's a tart. Mark's first wife took him to the cleaners after that affair with your sister. I had to bail him out to get her off his back. You open your flamin' great mouths and we're the bastards who have to pay. Let me tell you, I see you. I know you're not as sure of yourself as you'd like to think. You know your daughter screwed up as well as I do. When all this is over and you lie awake wondering what kind of person she's growing into, I want you to remember this moment. I see you, madam, just like I saw Kitty. Even when she was lying on this floor, she'd have got up and taken my hand if I'd offered it.'

Beth's voice was quiet. 'But you didn't offer it.'

'Damn right I didn't.'

'Even though she was pregnant with your baby?'

'Someone's baby. I had no idea if it was mine or not.'

'It was yours. She wrote about it in her diaries. There's a new entry once a year, ever since she first came back to live here, ever since you beat her up and damaged her for life.'

'That's no evidence of anything,' Danny spluttered.

'For Christ's sake, Danny, will you shut your mouth?' Mark was on his feet now, worried about what his uncle would say next, trying to pull the old man back from Beth.

He didn't need to. Beth was moving away herself, twisting from beneath the old man's glare, towards the front door and the fresh air on the deck.

'You're right, you know. I do worry that my daughter is screwed and it's my fault. Like it's all joined up. Kitty and my sister and now my daughter, joined up just like the two of you and your nasty bullying, your brutality. So when you say you see me, you do, I understand that. But I see you too. An old man, scared of dying, scared that this big-deal business he's built doesn't mean anything in the end. You desperately wanted this hut, this little bit of land. Yes, I'm sure the money's part of it, of course it is, but you also wanted it because it was hers. You still wanted a piece of her, even after all this time. Kitty writes about you too, Danny. How frightened

223

you were underneath it all. The scared boy in the big man. You don't know yourself at all.'

Beth was at the door now, and as she reached into her pocket, Mark suddenly realised what she was about to do. He lunged for her, but she was too fast. She flicked the lighter as she lifted it and brought it to the old curtains at Kitty's front window. They went up in flames immediately, as she'd so often told Kitty they would, begging her to stand away from the window if she must smoke, to stand on the deck.

'For Christ's sake, Beth, what are you doing?'

'Delete the video.'

'I already did, you bloody idiot.' Mark was half laughing, half panicked, watching the flames reaching around the room, closer to where Beth stood blocking the door. 'It's got my daughter on it, with your girl and those bastards making her out to be a tart. You think I'd risk anyone seeing that? It's long gone, those kids were just too dense to work it out.'

The flames had taken hold now, and Beth stepped back, onto the deck.

'They're not stupid. It just wouldn't surprise them if you had exposed your own child to get what you want.'

As Mark sprang forward, she took another step back and slammed the door, turning the key in the lock.

From inside the hut she heard a roar of fury, Mark kicking at the door and Danny screaming abuse and then suddenly stopping, choking. She knew they would check the bedroom, try to get out of the back window. She knew that window was boarded up. She had the key and it was the only way out, unless they wanted to smash through the front window and the curtain of fire around it. But the fire was already too big. Beth had laid a line of barbecue firelighters along the old pelmet, it was what Mark had told the kids to do when they set fire to the huts they'd burned down earlier in the year. Lucy had explained it all last night. It made sense, the firelighters burned longer and were harder to put out, more likely to splinter, to make new little pockets of fire if they were smashed.

Danny was moaning and crying out inside. His rancid lungs would find the smoke difficult. Mark was still screaming abuse. Beth stared at the door. She had meant to scare them, she thought. Or maybe she meant to do more. She looked at the key, at the door, at the fire inside the front window, dark with smoke, bright with burning light. Maybe this was what she had meant to do.

'Beth! Beth! Open the door. Let them out.'

She spun around and saw Sara and Lucy on the steps to the hut, Lucy staring in horror, Sara with fear.

'Mum,' Lucy said, 'please.'

'I don't know, maybe this is the only way.' Beth shook her head, holding the key out of Sara's reach. She leaned back against the door and felt it warm behind her.

'You're not like this,' Sara said.

'I am,' Beth said, nodding. 'We all are. We've just held it in. People like the Nelsons, they don't hold it in, but we do. And then they get away with it and we get hurt. This is what they're like.'

'Yes, but you don't need to be like them,' Sara said.

'They hurt Lucy. Kitty. You. All my people. You're all I have, and when our people are threatened, this is what we're all like. Any of us. We hurt back.'

'No, Mum.' Lucy was standing in front of Beth, her face covered in tears, her hand out for the key. 'We can stop this now. Please. It's been going on too long. Please?'

Sara watched them, mother and daughter opposite each other. The moment seemed to go on for hours. And then it shifted. Beth looked at Lucy as if seeing her for the first time, and as she faltered, Lucy grabbed the key from her hand. She unlocked the door and pulled it back, smoke poured out and Sara ran into it.

Mark and Danny were in the bedroom, furthest away from the flames. Mark saw the light behind her and charged forward, dragging Danny with him. He was shouting and swearing as he came, but Danny was silent other than the heaving breaths catching in his throat, causing him to retch. Mark shoved Beth out of his way and slowly, carefully helped Danny down to the patch of grass beneath the hut.

He was smacking the old man's back and reassuring him at the same time, 'Take it slowly, Dan, you'll hurt yourself. Catch your breath. Give yourself a chance.'

Beth watched as if from a long distance. Behind her Lucy and Sara were filling pots and pans with water, throwing it on the fire that burned all around the window, scorching into the ceiling, bubbling the paint on the walls. The Mark Nelson in front of her was a different person, taking gentle care of the old man. Their hands and faces were dirty, their clothes dishevelled, eyes blinking against the pain from the smoke and the bright morning light.

When the fire was out, the hut filled with the stench of acrid smoke, Lucy took the two men cups of water. She stood over them as they drank and then went back into the hut; past her mother, who stood still on the deck, past Sara, who was standing in the centre of the main room, staring in horror at the damage.

She filled the cups again, took them outside. She crouched down in front of Danny, who was still coughing and retching in an effort to catch his breath. 'Drink this more slowly. It will help.'

She stood up and faced Mark. 'It's over now, Mr Nelson. It's too much. We've all screwed up. It's done, OK?'

Mark pushed her aside and she fell forward to where the shingle met the grass. He pulled his uncle to his feet, ignoring Lucy sprawled on the stones, and they staggered off up the path together.

Thirty-Two

Westmere, June

Beth and Sara were sitting on the deck of Lullaby Beach. Beth had taken Lucy home while Sara stayed at the hut in case the Nelsons came down again. When she got back, Sara was in tears on the steps.

'What, what is it?' Beth asked.

Sara indicated the hut behind her. 'In there. The mess. I tried, but ...'

'Is it that bad?'

Sara nodded.

'I'm so sorry,' Beth said, 'I've made it all worse.'

Sara smiled through her tears. 'I'm kind of glad you did. We couldn't just let it go, what they'd done, who they are.'

'Kitty did,' Beth answered quietly.

'Kitty killed herself, Beth. And they carried on. Mark did, blackmailing Lucy and those other kids. He just carried on.'

Beth nodded. 'I know, but the only thing that could really put an end to all of this would be to go to the police. And I can't make Lucy tell the police about it, not with the arson they'd have to admit to, not after what I did this morning.'

'No.'

Beth frowned, 'I don't know what came over me. It just seemed like the only thing left to do.' She shuddered. 'I never want to feel like that again.'

'You scared me.'

'I terrified me.' Beth sat down on the step beside Sara. 'I just wish Kitty had told us they were hassling her. I wish she'd told someone.'

'No one cares about old women,' Sara replied.

'We do.'

'Which is why we can't just let it go.'

'I agree, and I have no idea what to do,' Beth said. 'I've got a teenage daughter who thinks her world has ended, with good reason, and a little girl who I don't want to know about any of this and yet her entire family is in a mess.'

'Exactly. Two girls who need us to step up. Their friends need to see that too, those boys.'

'Sure,' Beth agreed, 'but step up and do what? They've got everything. We could make all this public and join those women who've told their stories about the bastards who were their bosses or the abusers they went out with in their teens or twenties or stayed with for entire marriages, but every single one of those women has been judged. We can't win. And I'm honestly not sure I have the energy for that – or the courage. And you, my baby sister,' she reached out for Sara's hair, pulled on a long strand, 'I don't want you to let it get in and hurt you more.'

Sara spoke quietly. 'It got in a long time ago. And I still want him to be sorry.'

'He'd have to believe he did something wrong to be sorry.'

'Yes. He would.' Sara stood up. 'I'm going for a swim, coming?'

'No. I'll sit here and watch you, like Kitty watched us.'

'I miss her watching us. Witnessing us.'

'Yes.'

Sara walked towards the water, dropping her jeans and T-shirt as she went, stones and pebbles crunching as they smacked against each other beneath her bare feet. She continued her steady pace into the water as it rose against her legs, forward until she couldn't walk any more, until it was lifting her up. She swam out into the darker water beyond the waves that rolled up to the beach. When she stopped, she flipped onto her back to catch her breath. She felt the water trickle up and over her hairline, to her ears, around her chin, and relaxed further. There was no sound, sun in her half-closed eyes. The tide was coming in. She could rest here safe in the knowledge that she'd be brought back to shore as she floated.

It was a while before she realised she was crying. When she did, she also noticed she was shaking, water spilling up and over her mouth, into her eyes, salt water and stinging tears. Sara turned and let herself sink, feet down, she was vertical, treading water. She stopped moving her feet and her arms and allowed herself to drop further, chin under, mouth, nose, eyes were covered and the water closed above her head. Crying for the night that Mark had raped her when her words had been still, quiet, small. Crying for the hurt she had seen in Lucy's bent-over body, her shamed face. Crying for Beth, who had gone to an edge neither of them understood. Crying for an entire life that Kitty had lived at the edge of the water, broken in so many ways.

Her body was cold, she was shivering, her eyes puffy and stinging from the salt that flowed from them and the salt that bathed them. The tide had carried her gently closer to the shore and Beth was standing on the deck. She had a towel in her arms and she was waiting, as Kitty had always watched for them, waited for them. Sara stretched out into the water and began to cut across the waves, swimming in with the tide. She had an idea. Now she needed to persuade Beth to help her.

Thirty-Three

Westmere, July

My name is Sara Barker. When I was eighteen years old I was raped by Mark Nelson. He and I had been having an affair. I was saving money for university and had a holiday job at Nelson Developments. I was flattered when my boss began to pay attention to me. He was the nephew of the man who ran the company, a long-established family firm. I was a teenager, he was twice my age and powerful in the little town I grew up in. At the time, it was the only world I knew.

I chose to have an affair with him. I knew he was married. I knew he had children a decade or so younger than me. I knew it was inappropriate because he was my boss. I was preparing to go to university. Like many young people I thought I was more mature than I was, I thought I was more responsible than I was. I was young, excited to be noticed, delighted to be treated to nice dinners and driven around in what I thought was a posh car. I thought I was an adult. Legally, I was. Emotionally, I was a child.

Mr Nelson was my first proper boyfriend. I first had sex with him in a Portakabin on the Nelson Developments site when they were building the Eastmere hospital extension. We had an affair that summer, and when I left to go to university in Newcastle, we said our goodbyes. I did not expect to see him again and Mr Nelson told me he was relieved that I was going away, that he no longer had to lie to his wife. We began and ended the relationship with both of us knowing that it was a summer fling.

I was starting to find my way at university when Mr Nelson drove up to Newcastle. I was not expecting him, he had not told me he was coming. He accosted me and my girlfriend in the street. I persuaded him to leave us alone and to go home. He came up to Newcastle three more times. One time he grabbed me in the street. I hit him and kicked him to get him off me. Another time I ran from him. On the third occasion I allowed him to come into the house I shared with others to have a coffee. I did so in the mistaken belief that we could converse as adults and I would be able to persuade him to leave me alone. That was when he raped me.

I am sorry that I did not come forward at the time and accuse him of rape. I am sorry that I did not immediately go to the police. I wish I had. But I was eighteen, hurt and profoundly vulnerable. I was also not sure I would be believed. I do not blame myself. I was young and scared. I understand that my younger self – that I – made the best choices in a terrible circumstance.

I am sorry it has taken so long for me to come forward now.

I am sorry I have been part of a conspiracy of silence built on shame – the shame of women forced into sex, of women abused, women raped. A shame that shuts us up and allows perpetrators to get away with it. A conspiracy of shame that names us as victims or survivors and does not name the perpetrator for fear of damaging his good name.

I am no longer silent.

Eighteen years ago, I was raped by Mark Nelson.

*

Beth clicked off the video on Sara's phone, her hand dropped to her side and she lowered herself until she was sitting on the floor. Sara watched the tears rolling down her sister's face.

'Give me the phone.' Sara's hand was outstretched.

Beth shook her head. 'It's going to be horrible. They'll come for you, you know they will.'

'Yes,' Sara said.

'I'm not sure it's worth it.'

'I am. Give me the phone.'

Sara forced herself to watch back what she had said, to be sure she had said it all. She didn't know if she could do it again. It was as short as she could make it, it was very clear, and the whole time her eyes were looking at the camera, at the viewer.

Mark would see this and he would see her looking at him.

She duplicated the video just in case and waited while it saved, sending it to herself as an extra precaution. Then she attached the video to the email they had already written. Lucy had helped. They were sending it to all of the newspapers, to their online sites. She had also set up several new social media accounts and Lucy would post it on those as soon as she got the video and the OK from Sara. She was ready to tag everyone they thought might share it, people in town, people who were known for campaigning about Me Too, as well as people who campaigned against it. Sara knew that their attention would bring them even more notice. They had talked about all of the possible repercussions, what it might be like online, the nastiness, the vitriol, the threats that always came, and still Sara was determined. There was nothing else they could do, nothing else she could do.

She pressed send.

Thirty-Four

Westmere, July

Sara took a fortnight off work and came down to Westmere to stay with Beth and her family so she had immediate support around her when it all kicked off. The backing for her was huge, but the angry backlash, while it took a little while to arrive, was stronger, nastier and much more sustained. Even though Sara knew there was no way of guessing if a story might take off or disappear completely, she was still surprised by the attention; the media seemed to have decided that ordinary people were interesting for once.

The daytime radio and television talk shows loved it. Sara had given them a gift. Neither she nor Mark Nelson was a celebrity, they had made a very ordinary mistake in choosing to have an affair and Sara had decided to make it public after all this time. The women who made their living writing articles and columns about other women's stupidity had a field day. Sara had been complicit, she was jumping on a bandwagon, she was doing women no favours. The men who felt sorry for Mark were quieter in their condemnation but no less damning of her.

The trolls were both worse and far more relentless than

she had expected. Sara worked in this world, she thought she knew it, had advised clients about it, but the anger directed at her was much bigger than she had imagined and the trolling was vile. Every hour she saw there were more abusive responses on all the social media feeds and many nastier comments sent as direct messages. Within two days there was a slew of tabloid articles about the kind of girls who had been asking for it back then and were complaining about it now. More of the articles were written by women than by men. There were memes in which 'going up to Newcastle' became a violent euphemism, and although Sara did her best to stay away from it all, she found herself creeping back late at night, looking at what was said about her. Much of it was exactly as she had expected, she had known what might happen, had chosen to use it. She had not known how much it would hurt, how desperately she would want to respond, to clarify, to argue. She had not anticipated how painful it would feel to be wilfully misinterpreted. Worst of all was being laughed at, her pain ridiculed. She looked, but she did not step in.

Lucy was amazed that she was able to hold back. 'I couldn't. I'd be shouting at them all the time.'

'I so want to, but I know it won't help. I just have to let it pass.'

'Are you surprised it's this bad?'

'To be honest, yes. Surprised and a bit annoyed at myself for not expecting it. Or not realising how horrible it would feel.'

'Do you wish you hadn't done it?'

'No,' Sara answered slowly. 'I knew I needed to do something. I think ... I just wasn't prepared for it being so ...' she paused, trying not to cry, 'so humiliating.'

'I'm sorry, it's all my fault.'

She shook her head. 'Lucy, it really isn't. I did it for me

too. I mean, yes, the crap happening to you was a spur, but I was ready.'

'Really?'

'OK, not ready, but sort of. I just couldn't keep it in any longer, it was hurting me too much. When you told me Mark Nelson was blackmailing you and your mates, it felt like my fault. For not saying something sooner, for not stopping him.'

'It's not, though.'

'I know, but what we know and what we feel aren't always the same thing, right?'

Lucy nodded. 'Do you think it will work?'

Sara frowned. 'Well, even if he did keep the video, I honestly don't think he can make it public now. He needs to seem squeaky clean.'

'Has he been in touch?'

Sara shook her head. 'I've made a formal complaint. I don't think he's allowed to contact me. It's a historical rape case so I doubt anything will come of it, it never does, but at least this way I can hope he won't just turn up out of the blue.'

After a few weeks, the internet found another person to shame and Sara was able to pick up her phone or use her laptop with slightly less fear. The nasty barbs in direct messages still came through for months afterwards, but they felt at a remove, something from a different time.

As she had predicted, there was insufficient evidence to try Mark Nelson for rape. It was too long ago, it was her word against his and so her word did not have enough strength. In a four-page interview with the local paper, Mark Nelson said he must have been confused, in his experience women sometimes gave mixed signals, although of course it was possible he had misread them. He was sincere, thoughtful, and he heartily apologised for any upset he might have caused if anyone considered themselves hurt by his actions so very long ago. It was the perfect non-apology.

More than that, he was a different man now, he said; times had changed and so had he. He considered himself a feminist, he had a young daughter after all, a wonderful, passionate young woman for whom adult life was just beginning. In the end, he said, very reasonably, it was important to pay attention to what we know to be true. For him that meant his life with his wonderful second wife and his beautiful daughter Ariane. Goodness knows there were an awful lot of women coming forward with lurid stories from the dim and distant past, they couldn't all be right, could they?

They really did look a lovely family, standing alongside him in the evening sunlight, perfectly lit for the local paper.

Besides, as the journalist wrote, Mark Nelson was concentrating on his next move, the impressive foreshore redevelopment that would make such a difference for Westmere. It was time to talk about the new stories, not rake over the old.

Sara read the piece and shrugged. She had known justice was not to be expected. She had wanted to protect Lucy and she had succeeded. She had needed to speak her truth and had shone a burning light on her own shame. It hadn't left her and yet she felt curiously relieved. She felt hopeful.

Thirty-Five

Westmere, 1957 to present

Kitty's parents were delighted when she took on nursing as a vocation and not just a job. In some ways her mother was relieved. Kitty would be hard pressed to find a husband after what she'd done, who she'd let herself become in London with that Nelson lad. An unmarried nurse was normal, someone who gave herself to the work, the people she cared for. When Kitty became a district nurse they were even more proud. Their girl on her bicycle, doing her best for the community.

As the years passed, Kitty wondered how proud her mother would really be if she understood the extent of her work. If she knew about the young women who found themselves in trouble, the tired mothers with too many children, the abused wives who came to the hut in the middle of the night, to the only person who dared offer them help. Kitty always hoped for routine visits, but too often the only routine was in handing a handkerchief to a sobbing woman and letting her know that yes, there was another way. Women who walked along the seafront in the dark, looking for three candles in the window, the last hut, the marshes beyond. They came to Lullaby Beach in fear and left relieved or heartbroken or sorrowing. Often all three.

Eventually the daily cycling proved too much and Kitty moved to a practice where she was loved and feared in equal measure. She removed stitches, replaced dislocations, ripped off plasters swiftly and efficiently with no time for malingerers. Later, when the law changed and women and girls made appointments about a headache or a hangnail, whispering about the pregnancy they did not want, she helped them with referrals and clinic appointments. She pushed on with three afternoons a week until a consultant was employed to make the local practices run more efficiently and looked on in horror as Kitty, one shoulder two inches higher than the other, her hip jutting out, walking with a stick and clearly in pain, insisted she was perfectly capable of doing her job, thank you very much. A month later Kitty was called in to the council and thanked for her service, reminded that her disability meant she needed to take care of herself as well as others and made redundant with immediate effect.

Even then, Kitty left her night lights in the window and the path was taken by girls scared to go home because someone was waiting, a young man terrified about HIV, a teenage girl who knew for sure they were a teenage boy. Kitty was not sympathetic; she was direct, useful when she could be and honest when she could not.

For over sixty years she slept with her head just inches from her mummified baby, wrapped tight and laid in her old medical bag. She also kept her diaries in the bag. Ernestine gave her the first notebook, saying that if she could tell no one else what was happening, she could write it down, it was better than holding it inside.

When the abortion laws changed, Kitty wrenched her bed

away from the wall, ripped out the panel behind it and, taking care not to touch the bundle inside, added her instruments to the bag. Then she gently put the bag back into the dark space between the inner and outer walls, covered it with a sheet of thick plywood before screwing back the bed frame. Once a year she went through the whole process again to take out the bag and her memories. She would write new lines in her diary, recount a little more of the lives she loved, and then put it all away again. She covered the work with a new coat of paint, telling Beth that repainting every year, even at her age, was her penance for smoking indoors.

Kitty was not the type to whisper goodnight to the baby that was long dead, had never truly lived, but she was glad to know it was close by in the dark. When she told them to 'rip it all out', she was ready for the girls to know too.

Westmere, 12 May

My dear girls,

If you're reading this, then you found my secrets. I hope that means you ripped it all out. I wanted you to pull everything apart, to bring it all out into the light. It's time to let it go.

I thought long and hard about leaving this for you, writing it here, trusting you would find it. I hope the list of the pills and the whisky means the autopsy and all that fuss didn't take too long. I tried to make it easier for you.

The thing is, I know that grief can make us crazy. It has made me crazy at times. A little mad. A lot mad. So I hoped you would find this a bit later, when your grief has changed, when it's not so much loss. I wanted you to read my diary, see what else is in the bag, when some of

241

the light of hope has begun to come back. I didn't want it to be too hard.

Dear God, I sound arrogant, don't I? Maybe you're not grieving at all, maybe you were just glad to get old Kitty out of the way. Stomping, grumpy, complaining old woman that I've become. I'm laughing at myself now. I'd expect it if you were angry with me. I know a goodbye is always nicer, but it wouldn't have worked, would it? It was better this way – I got to do what I wanted. You know how keen I am on getting what I want.

To tell the truth girls, it's been bloody hard. I have wanted to tell you about the Nelsons, about them badgering me, almost every day now for months. And getting nastier with it too. He's a little sod, that Mark Nelson, far too much like his uncle and with none of the charm Danny had – even now I'll give him that, he was charming once. (And now I'm telling myself off for being a daft old bint.) But I didn't feel I could tell you and I suppose they knew that, the Nelsons. I didn't want to upset Sara by bringing up Mark.

The thing is, what I want to say about what I'm doing is that it really is a choice. You know me, I've pushed for choice as long as I've been able. In your lives and in mine too. And this is my choice.

I'm an old woman, my girls. Eighty-one seems quite old and it's very painful now too. Much more painful than I thought it would be. To be honest, I never expected to get this far. I remember being in my sixties and even then not quite believing I would ever be in my eighties. Thinking that sixty-one still felt so close to forty-one, not that different to twenty-one even, though I knew it wasn't. I knew I was on the downward slope.

And here I am. I don't want them knocking at my door any more. My body hurts so much, every day. I have done my dash.

I made a choice, girls. An honest and calm choice.

You need to make your choices too. Make your lives, keep making them, keep choosing them. And live them fully, right up to the last. I did.

I hope you'll keep a light burning for me.

I love you.

Kitty

Thirty-Six

Westmere, late summer

Over the next year, whenever they had a spare day or weekend, Beth and Sara worked on the renovations to Lullaby Beach. Tim helped a little, but he had less time to spare as he was retraining. Being sacked by Nelson Developments had forced him and Beth to look at their future. Neither could keep working zero-hours contracts. Even if he had had a generous employer, Tim's back couldn't take the heavy physical work for much longer. He enrolled in a conversion course to turn his hard-earned practice into teaching skills for the community college. Money would be tighter than usual during training, but he and Beth knew it was worth it. They had both been deeply moved by Kitty's mention of her life with pain.

Once he was qualified, Beth would do her own course, in interior decorating, and between them they would do up the guest house and finally bring it into the twenty-first century. If Westmere really was going to be the new destination for Londoners running away from the city, they planned to be in a good position to make the most of the tourists' eagerness to spend. Only in the guest house, they were keeping Lullaby Beach for themselves.

The sisters did the bulk of the renovations together. Lucy helped out every now and then, with Etta running in and out of the hut, playing on the beach in all weathers. She reminded Beth and Sara of themselves as Kitty cooked or cleaned, always ready to hold or scold. They thought about her yearly repainting of the hut and how they had never questioned it, it was just what Kitty did. Now, cleaning, sanding and painting the walls themselves, they saw her hands in their own.

One evening they did the final work in the bedroom – replacing and refitting the bedroom wall. Lifting the medical bag and its contents back into the dark space where Beth had found it.

'Are you sure this is the right thing to do?' Beth asked.

'No,' Sara said, 'I'm not sure at all. But it's the only thing I think we can do. We can't bury it anywhere. We can't make sure it stays hidden unless we know where it's hidden.'

Beth nodded, still unsure.

'What?' Sara asked. 'Don't you want it here?'

'I do, very much,' Beth responded quickly. 'But it's Kitty's baby. I want it to have a marker. We're not going to do what she did, get it out every year, acknowledge it, are we?'

'No. It's safer to just leave it.' Sara nodded at the bag. 'Ready?'

Beth picked it up, frowning. She started to open it.

'What are you doing?' Sara asked.

'I don't know. I just think we ought to ...' She picked up the tiny bundle that lay on top of the diaries. She lifted it very gently and held it to her heart. 'So tiny,' she whispered.

'So tiny.' Sara nodded, leaning forward to kiss it.

Then Beth put it back into the bag and together they gently laid it in the gap in the wall. They replaced the panel and repainted the wall.

*

When the renovations were complete, they held a party. All afternoon and evening friends and family were in and out of the hut, in and out of the sea. Beth and Tim looked after the barbecue while Lucy ran the bar with Sara's supervision and Etta's interference.

Late that evening, the summer night thankfully warm, Beth and Sara waved off the last of the guests, then Tim hoisted Etta onto his shoulders and led the way back to the house, with Lucy carrying several bags of leftovers.

Sara and Beth stood on the deck, looking out to the water ahead.

Beth gestured to her right, where the redevelopment was well under way. 'They say the main buildings will go up really quickly.'

'Can't see it if you look straight ahead,' Sara said.

Beth laughed. 'You're planning never to turn your head to the right?'

'Kitty didn't. Now we know why.'

'We know a lot of things. Too many.'

'Do you think you know too many things about me?' Sara turned to her sister.

Beth shook her head. 'You're mine. We know each other. All the things, good and bad.'

'OK,' Sara answered, satisfied. Then she put her glass down and started taking off her clothes.

'Really?' Beth asked.

'Really.'

They swam naked, in cool water, looking back to the three lights they had left burning on the windowsill.